Tori O'Connell

May 2011

Lori,

Thank you for your support!

BLACK GIRL

The Gay @ Channel

Best,

Darlyne

BLACK GIRL

The Gay @ Channel

Darlyne Baugh

Full Court Press
Englewood Cliffs, New Jersey

First Edition

Copyright © 2011 by Darlyne Baugh

Published in the United States of America
by Full Court Press, 601 Palisade Avenue
Englewood Cliffs, NJ 07632

ISBN 978-0-9846113-9-3

Library of Congress Control No. 2011922839

*Editing and Book Design by Barry Sheinkopf
for Bookshapers (www.bookshapers.com)*

*Cover art by Sara Jimenez
(www.sarajimenez.tumblr.com)*

Colophon by Liz Sedlack

To Mark, David, and Catherine

Never doubt that a small group of thoughtful committed people can change the world; indeed, it is the only thing that ever has.

—Margaret Mead

1

The Gay Channel

J ESSE KEPT MOUTHING BACK to the star talent when he
should have shut up ten minutes before and let her
have her way. You could hear a pin drop. It was
deathlike on the stage where Kathleen Pendle—a mean-
faced lesbian with a Betty Rubble haircut—was being pho-
tographed for a billboard campaign that would announce
the launch of the Gay Channel to the world at large.

I liked Jesse a lot. He was a sweet little thing, not more
than twenty-five years old, with blond hair gelled to a point
at the crown of his head. I felt sorry for him because he genuinely seemed confused. Why was Kathleen yelling at him
when he only wanted to improve her image? The Newark,
New Jersey, in me—that's where I grew up—thought, *I'd
love for that bitch to talk to me that way*, but the Brooklyn,
New York, in me—which is where I live now—thought, *Keep
your mouth shut and don't get involved*. I had bills to pay,
children to feed, and a future to secure.

Help was on the way, I knew that, but my boss was running late. I sensed this whole episode would turn around
once she arrived, but in the meanwhile, I stood behind the

camera with the rest of the survivors and watched Kathleen
fire upon Jesse as he continued to melt down. No one
stepped forward to save him. Everyone wanted to keep their
job because, in a bad economy, a person who had a job was
fortunate even if he or she worked for Starbucks. Otherwise
it was unemployment benefits, and who could subsist on
that in New York City? The other option was no money at
all. Living on fumes was not cute. Who had time for it? I
had a job and felt lucky to be the executive assistant to the
general manager of the channel: a position that had fallen
out of the sky when I needed a Godsend the most.

Since the age of nineteen, I had worked on and off and
raised two kids. Not always on my own. I had been married
but most of the time I felt like a single parent because my
ex was a bum. Thank God I'd gotten the job the day after
my divorce was finalized. That was six months ago, and I
was still getting my life together after years of living in true
marital hell. So I kept my head low as Jesse lifted his chin
higher and tried to explain to Ms. Pendle that she needed to
soften her smile so that future viewers would feel compelled
to watch the channel as opposed to being turned off by a
sour face (hers) determined to stick it to the man. This direction from him only creased Kathleen's features into a
hard pucker, a look so stony I believed with all my heart
that a skyscraper could have been erected upon it.

Kathleen was dressed in a silver tunic top and striped
silver-and-white pants. She was perched center stage and
looked like an oversized Hershey Kiss atop the barstool.
Both hands rested in her lap. The only thing moving was
her mouth, a solid "O" that rounded and flattened as she
formulated her words. I could tell she was used to screaming
at people, because she never once moved her hands as she
dressed down Jesse in front of the entire crew. She was as

self-possessed as a moody royal. Her screaming reverberated through our bodies as if we were standing in the path of a jetliner taking off.

Jesse shook but held steady. I was impressed he hadn't passed out cold on the floor from the abuse.

"What does that *mean*? Make a decision I can live with, damn it all to hell," she roared at the top of her lungs.

Jesse hunched his shoulders and dug in. "Just tilt your head a little to the left, into the light." His voice rose from a whisper into a calm command as he tried to keep it together.

"Into the *light*? What the fuck does *that* mean? Into the light. I don't understand what you're *talking* about. But what I do understand is, *your* face won't be out there. Will it? *Mine* will for the channel. Won't it? No one knows who *you* are. Do they? Everyone knows who I am! So don't tell me how to look at the people behind the lens!"

What a set of lungs on her. Reaching the rafters was easy for Kathleen. She could have hollered Stephanie Mills offstage anytime, anywhere. During her twenty years in show business, Kathleen had starred in Broadway shows, movies, one-woman tours, and had hosted a filibuster talk show that had been canceled amid allegations of staff mistreatment and fighting with corporate sponsors. So this scene was cake to her way of handling tension. Her plump white face turned cherry red and then purple with rage as she railed against him. Jesse's eyes were round with fear and terror, but he was determined to hang in there. I assumed he felt that if he could withstand this abuse he'd achieve a career high. Poor Jesse. He was such a clueless tenderoni who didn't understand the concept of Surrender to Win. I adored him to pieces. (And loved his baking. Every Monday morning he arrived at the office with Tupperware containers of cookies, brownies, peanut butter squares, and sugary cakes.) He was such an innocent soul, even the devil passed him by in the dark of night, such an angel to behold with his pale skin and marine blue eyes, but Kathleen Pendle was chewing him up and spitting him out in five-minute intervals. He was so undone his skin trembled.

Jesse was saved from total annihilation by the arrival of Lily Essex, a power lesbian in her own right and possessor of a healthy inventory of taupe pantsuits. Her serene poker face worked wonders in the corporate world of male domination. She was the woman I worked for. I watched as she strolled from the stage door with the satisfied grin she purchased for every occasion. Lily headed straight for our star actress. The concept of a channel for the LGBT community had been such a huge success in itself that in some ways Lily offered herself up as the self-appointed Unknown Soldier charging the front lines and gate-crashing mainstream media. She turned a blind eye to conflicts that might obstruct the ultimate goal: getting the channel on-air by July 1, exactly one month away.

"And who the fuck are you?" the national face of gays everywhere demanded as Lily crossed the stage floor. This was the first time the two women had met, because Lily hadn't come from an entertainment background and, as a result, still hadn't been given full control of the channel. Discovered by a headhunter, she'd been hired based on her track record at re-branding and reorganizing Fortune 500 companies. I had heard a few jealous critics whisper that an added bonus was Lily's neutral yet pleasant face—a figurehead who didn't intimidate straight executives. My boss looked like someone's aunt rather than a butch dyke on a motorcycle barreling down the information highway. Her calm disposition didn't raise questions about her orientation.

She was considered a marketing wiz and a safe-bet mouth-piece. The real power fell to the president of the company, Malcolm Drake, and a few of his minions in the programming department. They decided what shows would go on the air, and they had chosen Kathleen Pendle for the billboard campaign.

Lily never broke her stride as she approached Kathleen. I loved working for the woman. She was so cool and collected. I, a sister who had just been recycled through the wood chipper, could learn a thing or two from a female executive like Lily Essex. As any diligent assistant would have thought to do, I'd warned Lily via Blackberry about the disaster unfolding before me as soon as it started.

Kathleen zeroed in on Lily's advance with sinister eyes; however, Lily's everything-is-fine smile rose up like the morning sun, bright and undeterred by nasty intentions. There was a collective sigh of relief in the room, knowing that the ramped-up mood would dial down a few notches so we could all breathe. Air escaped Jesse like a hissing, deflating balloon.

"Welcome. Welcome," Lily said in her smooth broadcaster's voice. "I'm Lily Essex, general manager of the Gay Channel. Everything's good here? How's it going?" Before Kathleen could answer, Lily leaned over the edge of the stage and reached up for a friendly handshake. "You are one of my favorite entertainers."

But Kathleen's ass had been kissed raw over two decades, and she barely acknowledged the compliment and didn't shake Lily's outstretched hand until it became too awkward to ignore.

"Who's this little prick here? The one just behind you hired to direct the shoot, huh? Whose idea was he? I don't think he knows who I am. *Do* you know who I am?" she asked Jesse as her unhappiness climbed and climaxed into a screwed-up mouth we had all seen countless times in *Star Magazine.* "Have you ever met a lesbian more famous than me?"

I caught Jesse's eye. Both of us thought, *Yes, Ellen,* but we didn't respond. A large tear rolled down Jesse's cheek.

"Oh, please," Kathleen sighed, dismissing the break-down with a wave of her plump hand.

Lily backed up and stood in front of Jesse to save him the humiliation of being publicly branded for another minute. This was a particular talent of Lily's—agreeable and caretaking at the same time—a rare commodity in the dog-eat-dog world of corporate culture. She glanced at me and, on cue, I grabbed Jesse's hand and escorted him out the door. In the hallway, we hugged as he broke out into a sob on my shoulder.

"What did I do, Charlene? She's so cruel! And to think she used to be one of my gay heroes before today. I'm so disappointed. I can't believe how harshly she treated me," he said into my silk blouse. "That smelly c—"

"Shh, honey, let it go. You hear me? There isn't time for trying to fix that. You've got to dodge the poisonous arrows in life," I said, jerking my head at the stage door. "She's probably scared. Sometimes women act that way when they don't know how to act like a lady. You know? Gracious is always more attractive."

"She's not the lady, her wife is. She's the butch," he explained, wagging his head side-to-side, trying to make rhyme or reason out of being reamed out in front of everybody.

"Still, it doesn't excuse bad manners."

"This channel is so important to me. To us." He gestured at the empty hallway.

"I know it is. Now go on back upstairs to the office. I'll let you know how things go, okay?"

He sniffed and wiped his innocent eyes, red from his emotional outburst. His body seemed without bones, his spirit snuffed out. Jesse gathered up what was left of his dignity and lifted his head as if it was a lead ball.

"Okay, thanks Ms. Thing," he said.

I smiled and pulled him in for another hug. He sunk into my bosom. The moment passed, and we both grinned at each other in mutual appreciation.

"I love you, Charlene."

"I love you, too, sugar."

As he walked away, his fairly small butt cheeks twitched to high heaven in Diesel jeans. He had tucked in his t-shirt just so as to accent his tiny waist. The young gay men in the office cracked me up. Each one masterfully chiseled, groomed, and scented. They had been very welcoming when I was hired back in January, likening me to Jennifer Hudson, who had just started on *American Idol* then and who had just been voted off last night. The guys were right. I did look like her. We both had high-hump brick house behinds and glossy full lips. My eyes were a lighter brown, but my skin was as dark. They wanted to nickname me JH but I shut that down. I was a mother of two, not a high school chick hanging around a park bench.

I took a moment before going back inside. Being here was serious business for me. After applying for hundreds of assistant jobs—medical, insurance, automotive, restaurants, and even homeless shelters—during a down market, a Republican president, and a cheating husband, I had gotten this job when I needed it the most. And now that I was at the Gay Channel, my goal was self-sufficiency by any means necessary. Warren, the children's no-good father, was, not only a cheater, but also an unemployed cheater at that. Child support could dry up at any second. I was scared to rely on his checks every month, and I didn't want to log into the vicious cycle of the welfare system. Alone in the hall, I thought about what my mother had said back in the day. I hadn't listened to her when she warned me not to trust Warren. "That man needs to get a job and forget about that rapping career. You're with child. Ain't no baby going to be provided for with that mess he's spitting into a tape recorder. Maybe he should rap about knocking you up while heading straight down to the employment office," she had said. "You're only nineteen years old."

But I was in love and didn't want to heed her advice. At the time my mother's lecturing seemed to drag my dreams down. Plus, the fruit hadn't fallen too far from the tree branch. My mother had hustled two jobs, sometimes three, in order to feed my brothers and me. So it was in my blood not to give up until I had exhausted all possibilities. I had applied online to The Gray Channel on an employment website bloated with graphics and icons. Turned out to be a typo—Gray was Gay—when I turned up for the interview with Lily and said "yes" to opportunity and "shush" to my Baptist upbringing in the same breath. I desperately needed the fifty thousand bucks a year and the full benefits the company offered my kids, Martel and Tinecia. Unpaid bills were still piled up on the kitchen counter, but the basics for my children had been procured. I still needed everything for myself, though—shoes, underwear, bras, work clothes, changed door locks, air conditioner, new sheets, and a dining room set to replace the old one taken by my ex-husband. The last thing my children needed was a poor Momma without sharp claws to provide and look after them. I was a lioness protecting her cubs.

2

Preggers

I WAS PULLED OUT OF my thoughts, hearing Dee Dee's big mouth before I even opened the stage door. When I stepped inside, there she was, a pregnant lesbian the exact height of Mini Me. Out of nowhere she had appeared, taking over directing the photo shoot, already readjusting the lighting just the way Kathleen was telling her to. Dee Dee was a bossy woman who rankled my nerves one hour and cracked me up the next. We had bonded over child-rearing even though I had conflicting thoughts about children being raised by same-sex parents. But of course this was a secret I would never reveal to anyone at the channel. As she darted around the set, making sure Kathleen was comfortable, I reclaimed my spot behind the photographer as he focused through a digital camera.

"You are awesome," Dee Dee said to Kathleen. "Let's have a shot of you looking over one shoulder. . . . Yes, that's right. Turn a little to the left—yes, like that. Strong woman! Yes! Perfect! Gorgeous!"

"Finally, someone who knows what time it is," Kathleen said in her best mock of a black sister.

Click-click of the camera, Kathleen twisting in her silver foil this way and that way, more relaxed and cooperative: I tapped out an e-mail to Lily on my Blackberry, letting her know everything was under control. Kathleen was off the barstool now, throwing her arms out at the camera, a cheesy grin brightening up her doughy face.

A make-up artist rushed to powder her nose, and a hair stylist sprayed her Betty Rubble bob, which hadn't moved in two hours. Dee Dee scurried over to the star actress, who was now in front of a backdrop that read *The Gay Channel, It's Our Time to Shine.* The mood on the set had changed dramatically since Jesse's departure, easing the tension between star and staff. Kathleen entertained us with a few jokes and laughed uproariously. Her mouth exposed a neat row of white teeth. The whole thing was over in less than twenty minutes. Kathleen hugged Dee Dee, twinkled her fingers at us, and left the stage followed by a small army of assistants.

"Bye, motherfuckers," she said as the door closed behind her.

The crew started to pack up slowly. Everyone waited a few minutes before leaving the stage to give the elevator time to whisk Kathleen away. No one wanted to bump into the star in the hallway. The shoot had been awkward enough.

"You really saved the day," I said.

"The whole time I thought I would piss my pants. My bladder is as full as a whiskey flask. I feel so super huge!" Dee Dee caressed her round belly.

"You'll lose most of the weight after giving birth. Are you doing Lamaze?" I said.

"We are, my partner Sandra and I. Down in the Village. Was your husband there during the delivery?"

"Honey child, please. He wasn't even at the hospital.

My best friend Leticia Smith helped me out. We're both from Newark. We grew up together. She's also my neighbor now, in Brooklyn, Prospect Park. We share parenting. She has a little girl named Tonya. Leticia watches my kids after school, and I watch her kid at night. We're both single parents."

"I'm lucky to have Sandy. She's the best partner ever!" Dee Dee blurted out in the elevator as we rode up to the offices. Her booming voice echoed in the elevator car.

"When's the due date again?" I said.

"Labor Day. Funny, huh?"

"Ha! Just what the doctor ordered, girlfriend. Oh, hey, maybe people here will put something together for you at the office?"

"That'll be great. We're registered at a store on Seventh Avenue. If everyone could pitch in for a stroller or a crib, that would be excellent."

Right to the point: Dee Dee never hesitated to tell a person exactly what she wanted, and she'd hound you to death until she got it. The elevator doors opened to the Gay Channel lobby. A couple of chatty interns greeted us as we walked toward our cubicles. Down the hallway I heard "It's Raining Men" by the Weather Girls playing in the press office. Derrick Miller headed up publicity, and he loved his black girls. He had a collection of divas ranging from Donna Summer to Diana Ross to the Weather Girls, and of course the usual Gloria Gaynor, Mary J. Blige, Mariah, and Patti LaBelle. He played a theme song at least once a day to wake everyone up, and it usually summed up the drama in the office. "It's Raining Men" was a comment on the slew of new hires—all men—that had started work in the office that week.

"Do you know the sex yet?" I said.

"A boy. We're going to name him Jethro, after my father."

A big grin broke out on my face and on hers, too. I managed not to laugh out loud. I hadn't heard the name Jethro since watching *The Beverly Hillbillies* on a black-and-white television back in the day. I hadn't yet asked but thought just then was as good as anytime.

"Who's the father?"

"A sperm bank. We just went there, picked out a profile, and voilà, I got preggers on the first try. Awesome, right?" Dee Dee whispered loudly. She didn't have a quiet voice, and being subtle wasn't a trait she possessed.

"Like a catalog order?"

"Exactly! We're so excited. We can't wait to see what he looks like!"

I patted Dee Dee's shoulders as an act of encouragement as the queasiness in my stomach brewed. I got knots at least once a day at the channel when some accepted LGBT notion challenged my straight-girl morals. And I wasn't proud of this reaction either, because I was beginning to care about my co-workers and it felt wrong to have such secret judgments. Still, I had been raised a certain way.

"Let me see what I can do about a baby shower. We're so close to launch, and it's so busy around here, it might be a great distraction. In any case, you saved the day at the photo shoot."

"I love Kathleen Pendle. I know she's got a bad reputation, but she's done a lot for gay rights by coming out, getting married legally in San Francisco, and criticizing that right-wing hag on *The View*."

"That was good T.V."

"Power to the people," she laughed, throwing a small fist in the air.

I didn't respond to that. I waved goodbye to Dee Dee and headed toward Lily's corner office and my cubicle. Up until about a month before, there had only been a handful of employees at the channel, but with launch on the horizon the number of folks had exploded in a fit of hiring. For the most part, things had been going fine, but a few personalities were cracking under pressure. Short tempers and underlying conflicts were coming to the surface. At first I tried not to get involved, but trapped in a cubicle with a handy ledge for people to lean on—my space became known as Boo-Hoo Corner. And boo hoo they did.

3

All A-flutter

LILY WAS UP ON the sixtieth floor meeting with Malcolm Drake. He was the president of the media empire that owned the Gay Channel as well as over a hundred other niche channels. Malcolm scared me to death because he had fired the lead team who did most of the groundwork at the channel the year before Lily had been hired. I was wary of someone who had that much power and could make or break a household by ditching folks on a whim. Plus, I couldn't read his face, and deciphering people's features was something I was good at because, as a black woman living in the subtext of a white world, it was second nature figuring out what was behind tight smiles, bright eyes, and clenched jaws. But Malcolm's surplus of corporate power was beyond analysis. He had so much authority; his face was frozen into a chalky mask with two black eyes resembling cave entrances that dared you to enter. *Just try it*, that face said, *and you'll be dead upon entry*. He spooked me. On occasion when he did visit Lily in her office, he would make eye contact, and my spirit would shrink in fear as my skin retracted in a breakout of goose pimples. I always reminded myself: *This man wiped out a whole group of people. Be cool. You can't afford to lose your job. Be polished and professional, and smile like there's no tomorrow!* I needed the money for too many reasons, and after an exhausting three years ending with my ex moving out, settling the divorce, job hunting, and dealing with my kids losing their daddy to some 'ho, I had barely a breath in me to make another change. I made sure to nod nicely and stare at Malcolm's forehead if I had to interact with him. That way, I wouldn't be sucked into the void of his bottomless stare. Props to Corporate, though: Malcolm was an out gay man, even if he had stolen the channel from another out gay executive before we all got here.

The subdivisions within the LGBT community tripped me up, but only after breaking down the obvious: white, black, Latino, Asian, good looking, nice body, cool haircut, hot lips, pretty eyes, kind of fat, dumpy, gay, lesbian, etc. From this springboard it was easy to segue into economic and educational backgrounds: artists, musicians, white-collar professionals, bartenders, non-profit organizers, hangers on, Ivy-Leaguers, self-made, and GED. But then it just splintered all over the place from there: Lipstick Dyke, Femme, Chelsea Boy, West Hollywood Twinkie, Bear, Transgender, Transsexual, Butch, Bull-dyke, Bisexual, Queer, Queen, Nellie, Homo, Baby-dyke, Baby-butch, Aggressive, Faggot, and Pan-sexual. Added on top were religious backgrounds and geographic upbringings. I knew what it was like to be labeled within a one-dimensional statistic: the black community was as splintered. The difference between a B.A.P.—Black American Princess—and me was like the mile separating the ridge from the river in the Grand Canyon. I was born and raised in Newark, home to gangs, poverty, political corruption, and governmental neglect.

There wasn't a B.A.P. within twenty miles of the projects I grew up in, and for the best, too, as she and her bourgeois crowd wouldn't have survived an afternoon on the rough streets. I was lucky to have gotten out alive. My mother had raised four kids on her own after my father was accidentally shot and killed in a barrage of gunfire. A random crime in the late '70s; that was common enough. My story was a typical one for where I came from.

My Momma had drilled into us the values of education and getting a good job and moving out of Newark. My gift back to her was getting pregnant my second semester at City University, dropping my major, moving in with Warren, having a baby, and turning a shoulder to her advice. That was in 1993. Now, Tinecia was eleven. Martel was eight. After birthing two babies, I was vigilant about not getting pregnant again because it was obvious I was always going to be the primary caretaker. Momma had been downright ashamed of me right up until she died peacefully in her sleep five years before.

At my cubicle, my eyes fell upon pictures of my babies—Martel with his ever-ready smile, and Tinecia with her challenging and wise stare. I hoped to God they didn't break my heart the way I had broken my mother's. I vowed to do the best for my children and leave the past where it was.

On the way to reception to pick up my lunch delivery, I saw Jem lumbering toward the men's room. Jem was a transgender, and it had been explained to me (without asking) that a transgender was a human being who chooses whether they're a male, a female, or neither. Never mind God's hand in assigning gender; that notion had been tossed into the trash like any other discarded assumption, a balled-up piece of paper of someone else's definition. It was a new generation, beyond Angela Davis radical.

I'd always made it a point to wave hello to Jem, not because I wanted to show respect for someone's gender choice but because we were the only brown-skinned employees at the channel.

"Hey, s'up?" I said, squeezing a black power fist.

"Hi." Jem jutted his/her/its/their/both/neutral's chin at me and slipped into the bathroom. The voice was neutral, the clothes were masculine, but the face was gentle and questioning. If I had to guess, Jem was a girl.

"Charlene! Charlene!"

I heard my name and knew it was Barry Trumbull, because he was the only one who chased people up and down the hallways in a flutter of high drama. He advanced like an ostrich running in platform shoes, with a red bandana tied around his slender neck and a pair of glittery sunglasses framing his wild eyes. He was a mobile mess of costumes, shrieks, and fingers splayed as if he were teaching you how to count to ten.

"Barry, what do you have on? Did you get lost in Elton John's closet?"

"You have got to help me!" he said hysterically.

"What?"

"Can you come into the conference room? You've got to, please!"

"Not now, child. I'm about to eat my lunch, because if I don't I'll bite someone's head off," I added, meaning his, shaved bald and gleaming in the fluorescent lighting.

"Oh, Charlene, please come help me out. I'm begging you."

"What's going on?" I asked, giving in with a sigh.

His eyes sparkled like emerald jewels stolen from the *Wizard of Oz*. He grabbed my hand and yanked me in the opposite direction. Jem exited the men's room. Barry practically knocked him/her/it/them/both/neutral down but didn't apologize. The gay guys weren't really feeling the whole transgender vibe, a palpable hostility I had yet to figure out.

"Charlene! Charlene!" I heard my name again exclaimed, this time from the direction of reception where my lunch was. Looking over my shoulder, I saw Jesse shaking a brown paper bag that I knew was food. My whole body reached out for it, but Barry had me secured under one wing and wouldn't let go.

"Can you put it on my desk, Jesse? I'll be right there."

"Aren't we going to eat together?" Jesse said, jealous and hurt. He and Barry hated each other, another undercurrent that threatened to explode any day.

"I'll be there in a second, sweet pea," I said as Barry dragged me down the hallway. I jerked my arm from his. "You better stop messing up my blouse. If you stretch it out, you'd better be prepared to get me a new one. I do need some new clothes, you know, and I'll be right in your face to buy some if you rip up my wardrobe while pulling me up and down hallways."

Barry scanned my outfit and flicked his fingers in a thousand directions. "Girl, I just need you to come with me. Forgive me, honey child. I'm just too excited. By the way, if I were straight. . .you look hot, black girl. I love the spandex leggings and red toenails."

"Yes, darling. Well, what can I say?" I asked, buoyed by compliments.

Derrick Miller had his back to us when we entered the conference room. He was the channel's press guy and the guilty party behind "It's Raining Men," the theme song for the day. He cued up a DVD.

"Hurry up, close the door," he said in a harsh whisper. "I don't want the whole office to know we're watching this."

"Watching what?" I asked innocently.

Derrick waved me over in a hurry. Barry was a flurry of feathers behind me. In contrast, Derrick Miller was a Tom Ford type. He sat cross-legged in a tailored summer suit, black loafers with no socks, and a lavender shirt with cufflinks. Derrick put the *GQ* in our office. I slid into the chair next to him and swiveled toward the black screen. Barry made a lot of noise getting settled into his chair. Once we focused, Derrick started the DVD.

It was a fuzzy image of a black man lying on a giant four-poster bed. Crawling over him were half a dozen white boys, blond nymphs, in various states of caressing his chest, thighs, and arms. The camera was aimed between his long muscular legs; prominent there was his enormous penis— the width of a transatlantic cable. The tip was the size of a squirrel's head. I almost came out of my skin.

"Lord, who is that? Is he who I think he is?" I asked, stunned, intrigued, and glued to the screen. "Where'd y'all get this? Oh, my God!"

"The one and only," Derrick laughed in Barry's direction. "This is about to hit the Internet any minute. Big time!"

"It already has," Barry said, polishing his nails on his shirtsleeve. "Thanks to yours truly."

I knew I should have looked away, but I couldn't. The man in the video was a famous NFL player. My ex-husband could never tear himself away from the television when this man played. In a way I felt redeemed, as if I had something on Warren as I watched his idol being serviced by a bunch of twinkies. The footage was beyond nasty in the most scandalous way. The young men looked like sugar crystals on dark chocolate. When one of them stroked the giant penis—a living thing in its own right—to a climax, I turned away.

"This is so goddamn disgusting," I laughed. "I've got to get out of here."

"Wait, wait, you haven't seen the best part," Barry said, holding my arm so I couldn't get out of my chair. "Check this out."

From the left of the frame, someone's backside entered slowly. The person turned around and lowered a huge palm frond, fanning the sex gang, while stepping more into the picture. Oh, my word! I leaned in closer. I'd have recognized that lavender bodysuit anywhere.

"Don't I look fabulous?" Barry said gleefully. "That's me with the leaf."

"Oh, my God," I said. "Barry Trumball, you should be ashamed of yourself." I couldn't stop laughing. It was so crazy, so ridiculous, and so against all the rules of Human Resources. I had to get out of the room!

"How much?" Derrick asked, his wicked brown eyes slick with knowledge.

"Ten thousand dollars. Can you believe it? All I had to do was wave the leaf up and down while they all had sex."

"Good Lord," I said. "What will Lily say when she sees this on the Internet? I've gotta go."

Derrick dismissed the idea. "Child, please, lesbians don't look at this stuff."

"And don't go telling her either," Barry reprimanded me.

"Why on God's green earth would I do that?" I said. "You have lost your mind."

"For ten grand you can have my mind and my body any day of the week," Barry laughed.

The DVD ended—and not a second too soon. I got up dazed, full of giggles and a growing alarm over what my future might be at the channel. Derrick was hunched forward, ecstatic as a hyena pinning down prey.

"You better hope your mother doesn't see this mess," I said, rushing toward the door.

"That's not why we invited you in here," Barry said, a little embarrassed now but covering it up with attitude. "I actually have a proposition for you."

"For me?" I said, taken aback, wondering how I could get out of any proposal about to come my way. "What do you want from me?"

"Down-low."

"What?"

"Do you know anyone who's on the down-low?" Barry said. "We don't know a soul. Ain't our neighborhood, if you know what I mean."

"You're so stupid, Barry. Why would I know of some-one on the D.L.? I just have to say, you know, the black com-munity doesn't meet at my house every Saturday night."

Barry held my gaze, inspecting my face for cracks. I placed hands on my hips and waited for him to gain ground with me. He raised his eyebrows, guessing correctly that I was full of it.

". . .Yes, I know one person," I admitted.

"Ooh!" Derrick said, clapping his hands once. "See? Didn't I tell you?" he said to Barry. "I knew it, I knew it!"

"Who? Tell us, Char! Give it up, JH."

"Why? Why would I do that? And don't call me Jen-nifer Hudson. I already warned you about that."

"You saw she got kicked off last night," Derrick said off subject, the news a shock to everyone.

"Voice like a goddess, shame, shame," I said.

"Can we stick to the subject? I want to develop a doc-umentary about the down-low for the channel. It's so taboo, but no one I know knows anyone first-hand," Barry said.

"What are you talking about? We just watched a football player being serviced by a bunch of guys, and you were over the bed acting like a ceiling fan," I said, glaring at Barry, not believing he had seriously blanked on what was on the sex tape. "You just met somebody right there," I said, pointing to the screen. "He's married and famous and rich."

"There're a lot of legalities around men like him. We need an ordinary guy. Someone people can relate to. C'mon, Charlene, tell us who it is. Don't hold back."

"I'll think about it. It's a friend's husband—well, ex-husband now. I'll have to check with her." I gripped the doorknob to leave.

"I can make it worth his while," Barry said. "But only if the man agrees to be on camera."

"I don't know, Barry. Can we talk about it later? I'm hungry and not in my right mind. You would've thought I'd lost my appetite after seeing this."

"Really? I thought it was hot," Barry said, a bit puzzled.

"Time is of the essence, as they say," Derrick added, all business. He stood up and smoothed the arms of his suit jacket although there were no wrinkles. "In a month the story idea will go cold."

"Not in the black community it won't," I said, walking out.

As I passed offices along the corridor I saw occupants gathered around computer screens, watching the NFL player orgy. I heard his sex posse lip-smacking and cooing from a chorus of chintzy computer speakers. The halls were strangely empty for a channel about to go on the air in a month. Back at my desk, Jesse was snacking on dumplings, glued to my computer screen. I didn't even have to ask.

"Not at my desk, okay? I really don't need Lily to catch you watching that stuff right here."

Jesse slowly chewed, his mouth screwed up in exaggerated horror. "Can you believe it? It's all over the web."

"Jesse, you better move out my seat and turn that off now," I said, dismayed by a second glimpse of a masculine black man—married, famous, and declared straight—looking like Gulliver tied up during one of his travels.

"Sorry, Charlene."

"Where's my lunch? I'm about to eat my hand, I'm so hungry."

He pushed over my sweet-and-sour chicken. I prepared a plate and listened to Jesse rehash the drama from the photo shoot with Kathleen Pendle and how pissed he was that Dee Dee had finished up the job.

The phone rang. I wiped my mouth and answered. "Lily Essex office, Charlene speaking. How may I help you?"

"Charlene, it's me. Can you come up with the latest creative? It's with Sharon Adamovitz. She's meeting in Roger Ward's office."

"Sure, Lily." I said her name so Jesse knew it was time for him to go.

"I need it as soon as possible," my boss said. "Up on sixty. In Malcolm's office."

I shooed Jesse away from my desk, turned off the computer in case any more curious viewers happened by, and put my lunch in the mini-fridge underneath my desk where I stored Lily's bottled water.

I was off toward the north side of the building where the creative and programming departments worked. Malcolm Drake had hired Sharon Adamovitz away from the Country Channel. She was supposed to be a genius at branding. She was leading our creative effort. Jesse and Dee Dee worked in her department as directors for photo shoots, promotional campaigns, and in-house programming specials. Sharon had the near impossible task of creating graphics and logos that required approval from a lengthy chain of command. Sharon and her team worked their butts off around the clock.

"She looks like Andy Williams," Derrick had said on Sharon's first day. He had played "Moon River" as Sharon walked into his office for a meeting. I'd known it wasn't right, but she did look exactly like the aging crooner—but only because of her Peking duck leather-like tan. Otherwise, she sported the requisite lesbian shag haircut circa 1975. Her personal touch was a cowboy hat from her Country Channel days. She wore it every day, making her an easy target for trendy, fabulous Derrick Miller.

I knocked on Roger's door. Jem, the transgender, was Roger's assistant but he/she/it/they/both/neutral wasn't at his/her/its/their/both/neutral's desk. I knew showing up without being announced wouldn't go over too well with Roger. He was a stickler for protocol and hierarchy, and didn't like subordinates barging into his domain.

"Yes," Roger said from behind the door.

"It's me, Charlene. Lily sent me." Lily was my easy-pass.

I heard a sigh and shuffling of papers. Sharon opened the door; her toothy smile, welcoming me and barring me without specifically being one or the other, made me distrust her on sight. She had a slight Southern accent even though she'd been born in Maine. Her long face gave the impression of an ancient pure-bred horse pedigree. She hadn't done anything to me, yet, but there was always a chance I could get burned. A few people had already been let go because of her backstabbing reports. My human shield was Lily

Essex, so I stood my ground without fear of retaliation.

"Hiya there, darling," she drawled. "What can we do for you?"

"Lily's up on sixty in Malcolm's office. She wants the latest creative. She called you guys to say I was coming over, didn't she?"

Roger Ward, a frosty man who had worked his way up from intern to senior vice president at other channels within the company, had just arrived to the Gay Channel. He was another one of Malcolm's foot soldiers. His personality was as dry as a salty cracker, and he didn't seem to care what anybody thought of him unless they were superior in title. He never spoke to anyone below vice president unless they happened to be in his department. Roger shot me a patronizing glare through heavily lidded brown eyes, and then he shot an accusing glare at Jem's empty desk. He shook his head disapprovingly. Gathering up some large printouts of logo treatments, his spindly arms moving about his body like robotic limbs in an assembly line, he tapped the sheets into a neat pile and handed them to Sharon, who rolled up the layouts and handed them off to me.

"If Malcolm wants the creative mock-ups, I wish he'd ask us to deliver them," Roger said to Sharon, implying I wasn't to be trusted with delivering documents. I wanted to declare that riding an elevator forty-three stories up, and walking down a hallway, weren't a huge challenge for me.

"We could go up there ourselves and update, explain where we're at," Sharon said.

Roger thought about this for a second, held a finger to his lips, cupping his chin in thought.

"Lily said for me to bring them up," I reminded them.

He stole a look at his desk phone. "My assistant isn't here to place the call to make sure we can go up," he said.

Roger knew I was right; Malcolm Drake wasn't the kind of executive people dropped in on. You had to be summoned. Roger gazed over my head, waiting for me to leave, which I was happy to do. I didn't want to be around his stink anymore than he wanted to be around mine.

"If there's a question, have Malcolm and Lily give us a call," Sharon said, ushering me out and closing the door.

The sixtieth floor was like the stairway to heaven—a long white hallway with discreet trickling fountains, an oasis of leafy plants, and assistants who probably earned twice as much as I did. I followed a shiny black woman with a movie star name, Mimi Sable, who had the grace and style of Diahann Carroll and a voice as creamy as whipped hot chocolate. She was Malcolm's assistant on the East Coast.

I remembered the day we met as if it was five minutes ago. Acrylic nails and a cold wet-fish handshake had assaulted my palm. "Oh," she had said as if I were an unappetizing side dish when I introduced myself as Ms. Essex's new assistant. She might as well have had a neon sign flashing over her head: *We're not in the same league. No bonds here, my black sister.* Mimi was a one-woman band, the kind who'd steal your husband without remorse. Every day I imagined she woke up in full-tilt competitive spirit. Females were enemies. She probably figured all women were the same, so she treated me like a threat. "I'll see you backstage during video award season, okay? You know what I mean, right? We'll have a drink," she had said, inviting the enemy in for closer inspection. "That'll give you time to. . ." She had looked me up and down as if I was dressed in rags and weighed four hundred pounds. But I took it in stride because performing high wire circus acts like the Mimi Sables of the world did not top my life list. The fallout was too severe. Everyone knew she had had a baby out of wedlock

with a rap star who had dumped her for a backup singer
touring with Beyoncé. Mimi's reward for raising his child
had been a house in Englewood, New Jersey, and an expense
account for the newborn. She drove a gas-guzzling Escalade
and dressed in designer clothes. Dignity wasn't part of the
plan. At home she probably threw a feather boa over one
shoulder like Zsa Zsa Gabor, poured herself a glass of
Chablis, and gazed out at the Hudson River, cradling her
baby, thinking about which designer dress to wear to work
the next day. On the surface it certainly beat the tiny two-
bedroom I had near Prospect Park in Brooklyn. Still, Mimi
would eventually have to re-cast her fishing line into the rap
ocean—but this time with a baby in tow. I was old fash-
ioned, desiring a less complicated slate. I wanted to be
loved.

Mimi took a right and sashayed down another long hallway, all the while fingering her long hair extensions. She
presented me like Vanna White, waving me inside an office
the size of a Virgin Megastore. In the far corner, Malcolm
and Lily were sitting on a plush sofa, going over creative
printouts spread across an oversized mahogany coffee table.
The office was jaw- dropping, a place where a simple girl like
me would never have imagined herself to be. Never mind
the sweeping views of the Manhattan skyline from that
height and the twenty-five-foot ceilings; there were priceless
marble sculptures and huge canvases of artwork that looked
as if a six-year-old had painted them. The furniture was
out of a museum. It seemed like a fairytale place, except
for Malcolm Drake. I doubted church sisters could lay
hands on that man and cast out his evil, which was so insid-
ious it was like an odorless vapor poisoning those in its vicin-
ity.

"How was Kathleen Pendle?" Malcolm asked, his two

black eyes boring holes into me from thirty feet away.

"The shoot was good," I said.

Mimi took the papers I was holding and walked them across the room. I stood awkwardly in the doorway. Lily looked up and smiled at me.

"Thank you, Charlene," Lily said. "Everything else is okay?"

"Yes, good. Sharon and Roger said to call if you have questions."

But the conversation was over. Mimi showed me out without saying a word to me. I found my breath in the solitude of an elevator car, each floor descending toward normalcy.

Lily still hadn't returned to her office at six o'clock when it was time for me to leave. The office was in full swing, but I had to go home and relieve Leticia of babysitting duties. She had her night job after dinner. I took over parenting the pumpkins: her little girl, Tonya, and mine, Martel and Tinecia.

Cashing In

I OPENED THE DOOR TO my apartment. Martel had chocolate frosting all over his face. His big brown eyes lit up when he saw me, and within seconds he was in my arms. Tinecia was more chilled out. At eleven, she harvested a reserved know-it-all attitude and sharp tongue like her father. She sat on the couch, legs crossed, doing her homework, and waiting for Martel to stop hogging me up. Leticia came out of the kitchen, wiping her hands.

"You got some good kids, Ms. Charlene," she said.

"You're making cupcakes again?" I said, smiling at Martel. "Dinner first, okay?"

"Sugar is no good for you," Tinecia said from the couch. "It's bad for your teeth."

"Momma, last time the frosting melted wrong," Martel said.

"You just got to wait for the cake to cool before spreading, that's all, baby boy."

"I am this time!" Martel said, breaking from my hug and bounding into the kitchen.

"How are you today?" I kissed Tinecia on the forehead.

"Very well, thank you," she said politely. "He got stuff on your blouse."

A thick smudge of chocolate frosting had stained my silk shirt. I rushed to the kitchen and ran my arm under cold water. Leticia dabbed at the spot with a soapy sponge.

"Where's Tonya?" I said.

"She's washing up in the bathroom. I made spaghetti," Leticia said, and whispered, "Tinecia said she'd make the salad."

"Did you set the table?" I asked my daughter.

"Yes, ma'am," Tinecia said. "Daddy called again."

"Did he say what he wanted?"

"Just to call him back." Tinecia joined her brother in the kitchen.

Tonya came out of the bathroom—a frail child with two long braids of good hair like her daddy Otis's, Leticia's ex-husband. "Hi, Ms. Charlene," she said. She was mousy-shy, leaning into her mother, burying her head in Leticia's clothing.

"Hi, Tonya. Tinecia will be making a salad for dinner. You want to help?" I said.

Tinecia pouted. "I can do it myself, Mom."

"Tonya will help. Don't give me any lip, okay? Not tonight."

Tinecia ordered Tonya to take carrots, cucumbers, tomatoes, and lettuce from the refrigerator. Leticia's poor child was as solemn as a soldier under the command of a tyrannical sergeant. Martel, perpetually oblivious, resumed spreading icing on cup cakes.

Leticia sat on the couch and lit a cigarette. It was the only habit of hers I hated; not only did it stink up my house, but it was unhealthy for the children.

"Let's go out on the stoop," I said, waving the smoke

away.

"Yes, please," Tinecia said from the kitchen, annoyed by the pollution.

"I plan on quitting in the fall," Leticia said apologetically, not to Tinecia but to me. "I just can't right now. Too much happening."

"I'm sure it's never a good time," I said truthfully. "Baby girl, make sure to put dinner on the table. I'll be outside. Gotta talk to Tonya's momma."

"Okay, I know!" Tinecia shouted. "I'm not a baby!"

Leticia and I shared a knowing look—we were the same way with our mothers.

It was a beautiful summer evening. The sun hadn't set yet, and Prospect Place was busy with people chilling on stoops, walking dogs, or heading toward Flatbush Avenue and the F train. Leticia looked tired but still very young. She was a light-skinned woman who never wore makeup, too tired to fix herself up after becoming a wife and mother. A colorful scarf pulled her bushy black hair off her delicate face. Leticia's sweet nature always came through no matter what the day-to-day dramas were that we shared as single mothers. Our arrangement worked out pretty well. She lived upstairs in the brownstone. An elderly gentleman lived on the first floor. We all had each other's back and protected our homes with care.

She sat down next to me and tried her best to blow smoke in the opposite direction.

"Girl, did you see Marshall Tucker, the football player, on the Internet today?" I said.

"Oh, my God! No, what happened?"

"Sex scandal with white boys."

"No child, say it ain't so! He's so fine. Ain't he married?" She shook her head, not wanting to believe the fate of yet another woman with a cheating man.

"He *is* married, but I'll bet not for long."

"Girlfriend Charlene, what is happening to our men?" She stubbed out her cigarette, threw it in the gutter—and then it dawned on her. "What were you doing watching a sex tape? You might be the last person in the world I'd think would do something like that."

"You do know me, Leti. I never would have, but two guys at work showed me. I think they got off watching me bug out."

"Oh, my goodness."

"But that's only the half of it."

"What's the other half?" she said.

"The channel wants to do a documentary about men on the down-low."

I watched closely. Leticia's expression hardened as memories came up for her. I reached out for her hand.

"They asked me if I knew of anyone."

"You don't mean *me*, do you?" she said, rightfully alarmed. "Count me out."

"Not you, Otis."

"Charlene, are you seriously talking to me about this right on our front stoop with the kids inside?"

"Hear me out, please, before you jump to conclusions."

"I've already jumped," she said, her bushy ponytail bobbing up and down. "But go on, make your case. The answer is no, doesn't matter what you say."

"Can I ask you a question? How much money does Otis owe you in child support?"

"Well, let's see. It's been two years at two-fifty per month for a grand total not paid of six thousand and counting. But I don't have the heart to take him to court."

Women like Leticia, women with big hearts, had too

much compassion for other people's mistakes, even if it ruined their lives.

"I was thinking about this on the train. What if he agrees to be interviewed and his earnings go to you and Tonya."

Leticia's mouth hung open. "Shut up. Are you serious?"

"I can try."

She stood up and paced about the stoop. I knew how many bills could be paid off, and the new clothes Tonya could have come September when the child went back to school for fourth grade.

"Think about it, okay? It is Tonya's daddy we're talking about," I said.

"Don't take the high road now, Charlene. The cat is out of the bag."

"Let me know, then, and I'll see what I can do at work."

We joined the children inside and had a good meal together. Leticia left for work. I could see the gleam in her eyes. She was definitely going to say yes, but like any good mother she had to weigh the impact it might have on her child. I washed the dishes while Martel and Tonya watched television and Tinecia finished up her homework.

After the kids had all gone to bed, I called back my ex-husband. "Hey, Warren, it's Charlene. Tinecia said you called?"

"I did."

"What do you want, Warren?"

"Why you got to sound all mean to me?" he said.

"I'm not sounding mean. I'm tired, and I want to go to bed. I gotta go to work in the morning."

"That's what I want to speak to you about."

"What about it? You're going to stop sending money for

your kids? I still have to work whether you do or don't."

"The check is always in the mail."

"Okay, uh, what's up?"

"Just want to confirm a rumor."

I was silent. What used to turn me on—this little game of cat-and-mouse—now tired me out and tested my patience. I had prayed to forgive this man for his transgressions, but for the moment, I wasn't feeling much forgiveness. His deep sonorous voice once tickled me in hidden places. Not anymore.

"Are you there?" he said.

"Yes."

"I ran into your brother over on Atlantic Avenue. He told me you're working for gay people. That right?"

"Warren, I'm going to hang up."

"No you're not. I want to know what you're exposing my children to."

"I'm exposing them to paid bills, paid rent, and food on the table. What do you got to say about that?"

He was silent.

"I didn't think you had anything to say about it," I snapped. "I don't know what kind of game you're playing, but whatever you're up to, forget it. You don't have a leg to stand on."

"Are you threatening me?"

"Are you threatening *me*?" I shot back.

"I might go back to the judge and renegotiate my visitation rights. The kids are going to need their daddy if you got faggots all around the house."

I laughed. "What about you and your women, Warren? And don't forget your perpetual unemployment problem."

"I see. It's like that, then."

"That's exactly what it's like."

"Okay, then, but you haven't heard the last of this. I think I have a case."

"Okay, dear. Put your case together and get back to me, because this is the silliest shit I've heard in a long time."

I hung up. *What an idiot*, I thought. The good news was I wasn't in love with Warren anymore. Thank God, because if I had been, that conversation would have been very upsetting. Instead, I brushed my teeth, put a few sponge curlers in my hair, and called it a night while watching *The Bernie Mac Show*. I was safe and sound in *my* home that *I* had paid for. He couldn't hurt me anymore.

5

Getting It

I RAN INTO SHARON ADAMOVITZ at the security desk in
the lobby as we flashed our company IDs to go upstairs.
Even though it was the end of June, she had on a flannel
button-down shirt and her usual True Religion jeans, cowboy hat, and cowboy boots. I was wearing a white linen
sleeveless dress I had found on sale at the Fulton Street Mall
the previous weekend. Next to Sharon I looked like a bride
and she like a groom. Besides the obvious differences—
white, black; straight, gay; dress, pants—Sharon and I were
just two women on their way to work. I was a little self-
conscious about my arms because I had gained a bunch of
weight eating my way through the divorce proceedings the
year before, but it was summer, and the weather was humid
and hot, so I wasn't about to wear a sweater or a shawl to
cover up. Let it all hang out for now. I wasn't one for skinny
anyway.

"Have you heard from our stalker lately?" she asked.

The other people in the elevator turned to look at her.

"Once, earlier this week. I've got security looking into
it."

"What did he say this time?"

"He's accusing the channel of stealing his ideas for a television show about wedding planning. Barry had his home phone tapped because the stalker mentioned his apartment address on the last message."

"Are you serious?" Sharon swept her arm forward like a gentleman, allowing me to exit the elevator first.

"Serious as a heart attack. The guy knew Barry's full name, his title—Vice President of Original Series—and office hours. He was cowering under my desk. We had to send one of the security guards home with him to check the premises. But nothing was out of whack. Still, Barry is looking over his shoulder a lot."

As we entered the reception area, there was Barry as if on cue, in white jeans, white t-shirt, white leather belt, white loafers, and a yellow silk Kangol cap. His bright green eyes widened at the sight of me. He was talking with Nigel Grant from marketing, who checked me out head to toe and grimaced at Sharon's tomboy get-up. Nigel worked as an assistant, but he tried to come off like he was a major player in the New York celebrity and club scene. He was already notorious for RSVP-ing to a movie screening invitation that he had spied on Derrick Miller's desk. It was easy to figure out he had snuck into Derrick's office and stolen the information, because Derrick was the only one who got tons of invitations for private events around town. Nigel had shown up at Sandra Bernhard's apartment, where the exclusive event was taking place, with only twenty-five publicity executives in attendance. Derrick had wasted no time in taking Nigel by the ear and literally throwing him out of the event. The next workday was the only day Derrick hadn't blasted one of his signature songs like "It's Raining Men," because he'd been too busy cursing Nigel's name up and down the halls to anyone who would listen.

"Oh, girl, look at us, we're twins!" Barry said, eyeing my white linen dress. "All you're missing is the hat."

He tipped the Kangol cap at me and wrapped an arm around my waist as if we were a couple. Sharon had already transitioned into work mode and was heading toward the creative department. Nigel glued his oily stare on me. He was the B in LGBT: bi-sexual but leaning more toward men.

"Did you do it with Sharon last night? Is that why you were in the elevator with her?" he asked, insinuating a little smile that begged to be slapped off his face.

"Nigel, shut up," I said.

"You know what they say?" he continued.

"Oh, God."

"Once you've gone black, you don't go back."

"Nigel, please go away, you racist, because I will get ugly up in here. You are the most annoying sight first thing in the morning. Don't you have some papers to file or a marketing campaign to work on? The channel is launching any minute now." I turned my back on him. "And don't forget, you're in a corporate atmosphere. I will report you to Human Resources for making inappropriate remarks."

"Oh, c'mon. I'm just kidding. I just want to know if you've crossed over, because if you have I've got some hot girlfriends who would really be into you."

"Scram now like a good little boy. We've got business to talk," Barry said, ushering me toward my cubicle and away from Nigel. "Did you talk to your friend about the, um, project?"

Nigel didn't budge. I could feel his slimy eyes on my backside. He wouldn't sass Barry, I knew that for sure, because Barry would shred him to pieces and then bend him over to show who was really his daddy.

"I did. Just to sweeten the pot, honey pie, how much would he be paid?"

"Oh. I don't know. I'll have to ask one of the in-house producers to do a budget. Does he want a lot?"

"I talked to his ex-wife. She'll talk to him, but I need a number. Can you find out?"

"Yes, I'll get you a number. Oh, this will be good. A show about the men on the down-low will be a great ratings-grabber." He rubbed his hands together and threw his cap up in the air like Mary Tyler Moore. It hit the ceiling and thudded to the floor. As he was bending over to pick it up, Jesse came around the corner. Barry stood up and came face-to-face with Jesse's t-shirt emblazoned with a pink-and-silver unicorn the size of Texas. Barry didn't hide his disgust.

To Jesse's credit, he just pecked me on both cheeks and kept right on walking like Barry wasn't there.

"I hate him," Barry said.

"Everybody knows that, but I don't know *why*. Jesse's as harmless as a butterfly."

"I just do. I hate him—his cartoon clothes, his hair products, and the fact that he has the cutest boyfriend ever."

"You're jealous he has a boyfriend, so you treat him like shit? That doesn't make no sense to me."

We reached my cubicle. Lily wasn't in yet. I unlocked her office door and placed a fresh bottle of water on her desk while Barry talked. I turned on my computer and noted the red message light flashing on my phone.

"Please, Charlene, don't you know me by now? I slept with Jesse's boyfriend a few months ago."

"You did!"

"At the gym. In the sauna."

"Oh, my God. Does Jesse know?"

"Absolutely not, but the boyfriend does. He was here in the office, and Jesse introduced us. Very awkward introduction, because we had to pretend we didn't know each other."

"So why torture Jesse?"

"Why not?" he cackled, waving as he walked away.

"Get me info about the payment!" I called out after him. "Talk to you later."

The phone rang. I picked up and heard breathing again. The stalker was on the phone.

"Are you going to say anything today, baby doll?" I said. "You know security is monitoring my phone."

The stalker hung up. I called security with the latest update. When I looked up, Jesse had his elbows on the ledge of the Boo-Hoo corner.

"How can you hang around with him? He's such a bitch."

"I'm assuming you're talking about Barry?"

"Icky person—yes, I'm talking about Barry. Did you see that ridiculous outfit? He looks like a West Hollywood hairdresser."

"I hate to break the news, dear, but there's a unicorn on your chest."

We both heard Lily's voice at the same time.

"I'll talk to you later, okay?" I said.

"Lunch?"

I nodded and waved him away. Lily came around the corner, talking on her cell phone. She plopped two manila folders on my desk, smiled good morning, and closed the door of her office. I opened the folders while I checked voicemail and e-mail. One was a multi-platform strategy to be typed up as slides and graphs, the other a plan for the launch party with a sticky note that read: *Please handle.* Just as I was thinking what it was going to be like working between Derrick and Nigel, Derrick rounded the corner with smoke blowing from his ears.

"Is she in there?"

"On the phone."

"You heard?"

"Yes, Lily wrote me a note about it. So you, me, and Nigel will organize the launch party?"

"Is she crazy? I mean, I'm the head of publicity. What I really need is an assistant of my own. Why do I have to work with that little creep? He reminds me of that guy who gunned down Versace in South Beach." He made the sign of the cross.

"Oh, stop it. You're exaggerating."

"I'm not," Derrick said, crossing his heart a second time. "Hope to die if I'm wrong."

"Child, please. Let's just get it done. I'll help keep Nigel out of your hair."

"Somebody better, because I'm going to rip his head off if he says one thing to me. I told you about the invitation, right? How he showed up at Sandra's house?"

"Yes, honey, you've told the world," I said, rolling my eyes at the floor.

"I still can't believe he has the nerve to still be working here. I'm going to get him fired."

"You want to set up a meeting and get started about launch party details, or do you want to talk to Lily and change her mind about Nigel?"

He stared at her door, weighing his options. Lily was the direct connection to Malcolm Drake, and jeopardizing his status with Corporate because of Nigel probably wasn't worth the complaint. Derrick threw his hands up in the air, surrendering to his inner voices. He banged the Boo-Hoo ledge lightly and turned on his heel with a dramatic sigh.

"Jesus! I can't believe what goes on around here. Call me later. I already have a location in mind."

Lily opened the door. An immediate calm came over Derrick. He smiled benevolently and even bowed slightly at the general manager. I stood up.

"I thought I heard your voice. Come in, both of you. I want to talk about the launch party."

Lily had a gorgeous office. Planning and Design had hooked it up in aquamarines, dark browns, and cool silvers. Two walls were floor-to-ceiling windows that looked down over Times Square. Outside I saw the Hudson River gleaming between two office towers in the far distance. On the wall behind me were framed photos of Lily with Al Gore, Hilary Clinton, Aretha Franklin, the head of the Human Rights Campaign, and Pee Wee Herman. Derrick sat on the sofa and crossed his legs. He didn't seem to notice the tranquility in the room. He was a very good-looking man who had thick brown hair and passionate brown eyes. It was clear from the look on his face that he was still considering whether or not to say anything to Lily about working with Nigel on the party.

"I asked Marketing to join us," Lily said, reading his mind. "Until a staff position for an assistant becomes available for you, can you work with Nigel Grant? He's the marketing assistant. Do you know him?"

"I believe so," Derrick said with a straight face. Lily was probably the only person in the office who didn't know about the stolen invitation. "He's quite an inquisitive chap, if I've heard correctly."

Lily grinned in agreement. "I think so, too. He seems to know a lot about the club scene, and I thought he might be a good fit for settling on a venue for the party."

There was a knock at the door. I let Nigel in. He took

a moment at the entrance to check us out and then saun-
tered in as if the whole world was witnessing his red carpet
strut while paparazzi nipped at his heels. Lily's face lit up.

"Thanks for coming over. After our discussion in the
lobby last night, I was just telling Derrick and Charlene that
you'd be a good fit for finding a hip location for the launch
party."

Derrick sat up, all ears. I did, too. *Nigel and Lily had
chatted in the lobby.* He had wormed himself into the plan!
Too bad I hadn't been a fly on the wall for that exchange:
Lily being completely bullshitted by Nigel, master of social
climbing trickery, must have been a sight to behold. A professional snake charmer had mesmerized her.

"No problem, Lily," Nigel said in his greasy voice. "How
can I help you plan this shindig?"

He leaned against a Chinese cabinet. I could already see
the sheen starting to surface on his face. Nigel drank strong
English black tea that he kept in a glass carafe on his desk.
He drank gallons of it all day. The drink produced a glossy
t-zone that, as the day progressed, transformed itself into
an oil slick from his forehead to his chin and across the
bridge of his nose.

"I've already booked a place. Did it this morning, first
thing. We don't need a search," Derrick said to Lily. "The
location I'm talking about had a soft opening last week—
private. The owners agreed having the channel host the first
big party there would be a coup for them and for us."

"Where's that, might I ask?" Nigel said calmly, without
a hint of sarcasm. "Because as you know, Derrick, I have
lots of contacts around the city."

"Let me ask *you* a question first. Where did you obtain
your contacts from? Because I would imagine that most es-
tablishments would rather deal with someone from the

channel who is, um, more senior." Derrick didn't even look in Nigel's direction.

"Well, of course!" Lily said. "Nigel is just going to help you out, Derrick. And Charlene will keep me informed."

"I sure will," I said, expert as I was in booty kissing.

"I just wanted to make sure people are clear about his and her roles during the planning, that's all," Derrick lied.

"Do you mind telling me where? Maybe I know someone there, too," Nigel said, tilting his head to one side like a lamb poised for slaughter.

Derrick searched Nigel's face for any hint of patronization, but there was none. Nigel was neither intimidated nor affected by Derrick's obvious dislike of him. Lily tapped at her Blackberry, clueless to the undercurrent of tension. If she was aware, she didn't care. It was when she looked up during the long pause that Derrick made up his mind.

"Tumbler. Club Tumbler. West Side Highway and Twenty-seventh. Know it?"

"Do I?" Nigel said, excited. "I was trying to get into that party last week! I didn't know you were there. You should have taken me with you!"

I thought Derrick would come out of his Hugo Boss sport shoes. Was he planning Nigel's demise? I couldn't tell, because the look on Derrick's face was as hard as marble.

"Oh, that's wonderful," Lily said, clapping her hands. Nigel's knowledge of the club confirmed for her that this was the place to host the party.

"So how do you want this to work?" I asked Lily.

"Decide with Derrick and Nigel, and e-mail me the details. I have a meeting with Sharon and Roger. If Malcolm calls, tell him I'm on Blackberry."

She smiled at us to leave. We shuffled out the door. Derrick kept right on walking toward his office. Nigel leaned on my computer.

"So that went good," he said.

"Do you really think so? Because Derrick doesn't seem to be too happy coordinating anything with you," I said.

"Really? I like him. We see each other out all the time."

"Like at Sandra Bernhard's?"

"Oh, that was a misunderstanding. Derrick is just intimidated by me."

"How's that?" I laughed. "He's the Vice President of Publicity, and you're an assistant."

"I'm twenty-five, and he's thirty-five. That's why."

"Nigel, please. Go away. That is not a good reason."

"Lily wants me to plan the party."

"Lily wants you to help with marketing materials. Derrick and I will plan the party, okay?"

"That's not what Lily said. I'll check in with her later to confirm."

"No, you will not."

"We're friends, Lily and I. You know that, don't you?"

I turned a shoulder to him and answered the phone. "Lily Essex office, Charlene speaking. How may I help you? . . .oh, hey. . .yes, he is. . . Okay, I'll tell him."

"Derrick?" Nigel said, a bit afraid.

"He wants to see you in his office."

Nigel's face fell about twenty stories at the same time the Talking Heads song "Psycho Killer" started blasting from Derrick's office. Nigel curtsied and acted cute as Lily popped her head out.

"Thanks, kids," she said as she closed her office door and walked away, even though I was probably ten years her junior.

"He's waiting," I said to Nigel as he lingered. "Go get your head chopped off, Marie Antoinette. I have things to do now."

The phone rang again. Nigel stuck his chin in the air, put on a brave face, and headed toward Derrick's office. Flapping down the hall straight for my cubicle was Barry, in a panic. He waved his hands frantically in the air. I picked up the receiver.

"Lily Essex's office, Charlene speaking. How may I help you?

I heard heavy breathing, city noises in the background, and "Psycho Killer" all at once. The stalker was calling from the street. As usual the number was blocked, so caller ID didn't work. Barry practically dove into my cubicle. He scribbled on a Post-It: *The stalker?* I nodded.

"How may I help you?" I repeated, scribbling back: *Get security.*

Barry ran down the hallway. His long legs in those white jeans left a sparkling trail of fairy dust. I cradled the phone, waiting for the breather to say something.

"He's stole my *show!*" he hissed.

"Child, ain't nobody stole nothing from you."

"Where's that Barry Trumball? I know where he *lives!* I'll *strangle* him if he puts my wedding show on the air!"

"The wedding show was produced in Canada. Are you from there?"

Silence ensued as the stalker thought about this.

"Where's that dyke Lily Essex? I'll make *her* fire Barry. He *stole my show!* I'll make her fire *all of you!*"

"Lily's in a meeting. She's not available. Barry is coming now."

Two security guards flanked Barry. The trio power-walked toward me looking like a giant Oreo Cookie: Barry was dressed in white and the guards were handsome in black suits. I waved them forward, urged them to hurry. I didn't want the stalker to hang up.

"I'll get you too, Charlene Thomas!"

"You ain't going to do nothing of the sort. Now, you listen to me. I had a crazy uncle who lived in the basement, so you don't scare me none. I lived and grew up with crazies."

This was true except that my uncle had lived in his own apartment in the projects. The fact that the stalker knew my name was sending a bolt of fear through me. I heard a siren in the background. I also heard the same siren on the street below me! He was in the *area!* I cupped the receiver and whispered, *"He's nearby!"*

One of the guards came around the back of my desk and took the phone from me. He fiddled with the keypad on my phone. A number appeared on the caller identification screen. He jotted it down.

"917-555-2456 is your number. We're calling the police," he said.

The caller hung up. The guard handed the number to his partner. Barry and I breathed a sigh of relief.

"We've got him now," the security guard said to me before addressing his partner. "Go file this with the NYPD."

"I'll do that now," his partner said and left.

"What happens next? I mean, he knows where I *live!*" Barry wailed.

"He knows my name, *too,*" I added. "And I have two little kids."

"Don't worry," the guard said. "This isn't the first time this has happened. A lot of deranged people call our channels believing they have valid claims. The music channels get it the worst. People thinking that Prince stole their song or Madonna took their dance move. Okay, that was years ago, but you know what I mean. The whole conversation was recorded."

"Oh, it was," I said, remembering my uncle-in-the-base-
ment comment.

"Don't worry. Did you curse at him?" the guard asked,
reading my face.

"No, but—um. . ."

"I'll take care of it personally," he said.

I noticed he had a gleam in his eye. Oh, duh, he was hitting on me. He was a rugged brother who had been around
a few blocks in his lifetime. He wasn't superfine, but there
was solidness about him, and it attracted me. Maybe he
could be a strong man to lean on? But Mimi Sable's face
popped into my head, yanking me back to the ground.
Surely, this was not the kind of hook-up at the company
she'd had in mind when she recommended I take advantage
of my position here. On the other hand, it *had* been a long
time since I had a man's arms around me, too.

"Thank you," I said sweetly.

"What about me!" Barry squealed. "Is the company
going to do anything for me? I mean, that psycho's got my
home address! Are you going to walk me home again tonight?
Are you going to protect me in my apartment while I sleep?"

"Go sleep at a friend's house until this blows over," I
said.

"Like whose? Yours? Are you going to let me sleep on
your couch?"

I thought of my ex-husband and his warning that he'd
take the kids away if I had any "faggots" at the apartment.

"Stop being dramatic," I said. "You'd come all the way
to Brooklyn and sleep on my couch. That's silly," I said,
laughing.

"Really? Is it?" Barry said, putting his hands on his
hips. "Can I sleep on your couch or not?"

"Clayton Hicks," the guard said to me, interrupting the theatrics. "I wish I could come with you to Brooklyn."

"Excuse me? We're talking about *my* safety here," Barry said.

Clayton man-pounded Barry on the back. "You'll be all right, man. You're in good hands. I know it when I see it."

Hicks ate me up with chocolate-candy eyes as he handed over his business card. I watched his muscular legs and taut backside amble off. He was taking his time, knowing I was checking him out. When he was out of sight, I turned and met Barry's hysterical stare.

"What about *meeeee?*" he wailed, wagging his egg-shaped head.

"What *about* you?" I shot back. "Momma has needs too, you know?"

6

Launch

LOT OF PEOPLE HAD heard about the Gay Channel
launch party. Rubber-necking party poachers, not
on the guest list, hung around the front of Club
Tumbler. They smoked cigarettes and prayed someone
would sneak them into the hottest event to kick off the summer of 2004. Derrick had outdone himself negotiating the
venue. The club was a warehouse the size of an airplane
hangar. Giant posters had been draped from the rooftop and
secured to the sidewalk. One banner announced: *The Gay
Channel;* the other screamed: *It's Our Time to Shine.*

Shouts went up from the crowd as the mayor of New
York stepped from his limo and waved to onlookers. Guests
in line leaned over the red velvet rope. Reporters crowded
around the mayor hoping for sound bites. Cameramen elbowed each other and angled for best shots. The mayor
showing up was a coup for the LGBT community—not only
for New York City, but nationwide, too. The news feed of
his arrival would be broadcast all over the country. The
whole scene was like a movie of a movie premiere. There
was a red carpet, flashing white lights, and fabulous from

river to river. The few weeks leading up to it had been a pressure cooker of deadlines, budget meetings, logo treatments,
and advertising campaigns. The previous day, the whole
Gay Channel staff had worked until midnight while Lily and
Malcolm made the talk show rounds on local stations.
Everyone was exhausted but ready to party! Gay was the
new black, and our channel promised to be the launch pad
for it all.

I caused a minor stir at the door as gays, mostly men,
tried to figure out who I was as they took an instant liking
to me. They packed the sidewalk in a crush groove of
skinny designer jeans, tight t-shirts, just-so hair, shaggy
vests, waxed brows, and glossy Botox lips. "Hey, girl!" rang
out from somewhere.

"What's going on Ms. Thing?"

"Oh, I like what you're wearing?"

"You're so gay-licious!"

I stood beside Nigel, who was manning the club entrance. He was Lord of the Guest List, and it was obvious
he relished every inch of his square footage of power. I adjusted the strap of my metallic mini dress. Leticia had insisted I wear it to the party, assuring me, "Honey, you know
gay men love their black girls, so you might as well be visible
to share it." I grinned at all the ecstatic faces lined up to
celebrate the launch. The crowd was beautifully groomed,
coifed, and decorated. Several drag queens paraded and
vogued for arriving guests. The costumes were from another
planet. One queen wore a sequined turban and miles of fabric. She was offering to read the fate of partygoers by lick-
ing their palms. Damn, if my Newark childhood friends
could see me now, I thought, gussied up among the crème
de la crème. In the July heat, I spied Gucci by Tom Ford,
crisp Prada short-sleeve shirts, Paul Smith linen jackets, and

of course, plenty of G-Star jeans, pastel canvas belts, and deconstructed Diesel button-down shirts. A few men were bare-chested, literally bare, not a stitch of hair to be found—as smooth and slick as a baby seal. Over the previous seven months I had learned plenty about gay men's fashion sense and how much they valued the gym. And it showed, because there was a stocked supply of tight bubble butts, muscular arms, and six-pack stomachs I guessed had had a little help from steroids and power drinks.

"Hey, Charlene," Sharon drawled, emerging from the club behind me. "Where's Lily? Inside already? I can't find her."

Lesbian fashion, on the other hand, always threw me off a bit. It'd taken me months not to flinch. Of the post-feminists types, I was getting used to the Mom jeans, muted colors, and canvas sneakers. But that night I had to admit that Sharon looked attractive in a black suit with a silver belt buckle announcing the "v" of her private part. She had tipped her signature cowboy hat forward and gotten a haircut, still shaggy and '70s inspired, but it looked good. Wisps of frosted blond hair framed a perpetually tanned face that gleamed with genuine pride at what was taking place for her peeps and for the channel.

"Yes, Lily's in the VIP lounge with Malcolm. You're on the list to go upstairs."

Sharon kissed me on both cheeks and eyed me like a piece of chicken. "That dress is marvelous on you!" I searched her expression for any hint of a come-on, but my imagination had the best of me. There was none. I was still fresh to immersion in a gay world. Business could be blind to office protocol, but when I thought about it, mostly with the guys. There was plenty of grabbing butt cheeks. Jesse regularly exposed washboard abs. Once, Barry squeezed my boob.

The entrance was drenched in klieg lights that shot glowing beams into the night sky. A Bronx cheer went up for Kathleen Pendle, who waved to admirers as she materialized from a black town car. Her wife and partner, a pretty blond with a cropped haircut, was holding her hand. They had been married in San Francisco earlier in the year, and the yelling from the crowd and the flashes from the photographers showed how much of an icon and idol she was in the LGBT community. She may have been a total witch during the photo shoot the month before, but her showing up was a big endorsement for the channel. Other celebrity sightings included Rufus Wainwright, a singer I had never heard of but apparently was quite famous, and Judy Gold, a stand-up comedian I think I had seen on HBO one night. But people in the crowd knew who the "out" celebrities were, and rooting for them as pioneers in media made me feel as if I was a part of a special phenomenon. The only thing missing were black faces.

I went inside to make sure everything was going according to plan. The channel had gone all out—gift bags from Kiehl's for each of the 1500 guests, catering by Jean-Georges, Cristal champagne, a raffle for an all-expense-paid weekend in Paris, and first peek at the channel when it premiered tonight at 9:00 p.m. EST. The decorations were in stark contrast to the scene outside. Derrick had wanted very chic, very French modern, very Philippe Starck, but Nigel had convinced Lily that a theme party would generate more buzz. He had said, "Lily, you don't want the party to look like a hotel lobby. This is the rebirth of gay lifestyle and culture. It's like a renaissance!" Somehow that got translated into Renaissance Faire. I'd had to hire jugglers, and actors to play foot soldiers, jesters, and magicians. Derrick threatened to quit if Nigel got his way to emcee a jousting match with bare-chested knights in armor. As a consolation, the VIP section had been designed by Derrick, plus the Paris raffle thrown in as an incentive so that he wouldn't execute Nigel by firing squad after office hours. "At least let there be a little *haute* style at this event, and not Chelsea boys stabbing and charging each other on papier-mâché horses," Derrick had said. So the launch party was two parties in one: upstairs the famous, the connected, and the executive brass lounged on sleekly designed furniture and drank from stemware purchased at Bergdorf Goodman, while the rank-and-file ducked balls thrown in the air by jugglers and tumblers doing flips, back tucks, and double layouts from springboards strategically placed around the club.

The packed dance floor pulsated to house music. More men took off their shirts, twirling them over their heads like triumphant flags. A tuneless Madonna song blasted from the speakers, and people became a chaotic mass of raised arms and gyrating hips. Within this clutter of body parts, tumblers shot out of the floor and flipped high into the rafters, landing on catwalks that crisscrossed the fifty-foot ceilings. Bodies flew in the air every which way—from an opposite corner of the floor, a tiny human ball sprung toward the ceiling and disappeared! It was a gay circus of high-spirited celebration. I didn't want to be anywhere else in the world, except maybe home with my kids— but I had convinced Leticia to baby-sit after Barry had come through with an eight-thousand-dollar payment for the down-low documentary. Filming was in two days.

Someone pinched my ass, and I whipped around only to fall into the glory of Jesse's love-on-love smile. He led me into the center of the crowded dance floor as Barry looked on resentfully from the bar, downing a shot of booze. Jesse danced around me as if I were a totem pole. He pumped his pelvic rhythm and moved his tiny hips in that butt-swinging, angular way white folks do. And what really delighted me was how he encircled my body like a Hula Hoop. As the song ended, we held onto each other for dear life as gut-wrenching laughter doubled us over.

Out the corner of my eye, a delicious-looking black man who looked just like Clayton—exactly, in fact—caught my eye. He was moving in tandem with a blond man, locked in deep eye contact, their nipples practically welded together. I blinked and shook my head to clear my vision and to get a better look *and* to double-check that my new crush wasn't a player on both sides of the sexual divide, but the Clayton look-alike was gone, swallowed up by the gyrating dance crowd. I was stunned for a second. Could it be? I thought about Clayton and his maleness, but I stopped myself. What a small-minded thing to think, I reminded myself as I was standing in the middle of a testosterone fête. Had to be a mind fuck. I was seeing things. On the spot I decided not to have another drink before leaving the party.

The music stopped, and a spotlight shone on the second level, from which Malcolm Drake waved to the people below. Jesse squeezed my hand as he stared up in reverence at the gay leadership on the balcony level. Barry whispered sharply that Malcolm looked like Evita.

Malcolm spread his arms wide and spoke to us. "The time has arrived for gays everywhere to be a major force in media. First off, I want to thank the mayor for his invaluable support. There are so many people to thank for helping the Gay Channel get on the air. Secondly, I just want to let you know that I love each and every one of you. This is a special time for our company and for gays, lesbians, bisexuals, and transgenders everywhere. There has never been a vessel like this available to the general public, and you can be proud to have had a special hand in its future success." He reached down and pulled Lily up to stand next to him. "I know you all have welcomed the new head of the channel, Lily Essex. We're lucky to have her. She was chosen from a long list of very talented candidates to come in and overhaul the channel, and I think she's done a terrific job. We're excited to see what her team has come up with tonight, as the first images will appear in a few minutes."

Wild cheers and clapping thundered from the audience. I had never heard shouting so enthusiastic except maybe from ardent fans at a baseball game. The mayor, Kathleen Pendle, Lily Essex, and top executives from every channel the company owned all joined in applauding Malcolm Drake and the Gay Channel. I was clapping, too, because I knew what it meant to live outside the mainstream. I knew what it felt like to have prejudices push down on me. I kissed Jesse and Barry, and we all group-hugged. The guys were able to put aside their cattiness and be a part of the huge thing happening before us. It was thrilling.

Then the screens lit up white and pink. Thumping house music deafened the clapping and cheering. A voice said, "Welcome," as suspended monitors around the club transformed into flashing logos: *The Gay Channel. It's Our Time to Shine. The Gay Channel. It's Our Time to Shine. The Gay Channel. It's Our Time to Shine.* We watched clips of upcoming shows: *My Big Fat Fabulous Fantastic Gay Wedding, Sex and the Pretty Black Boys, Lesbian Love Stories, Out of the Closet and into Life, World Gay Travel,* and *Two Dirty Words: Down-low.* Next a series of testimonials from Kathleen Pendle, actor Alan Cumming, fashion icons, an out lesbian CEO from a Fortune 500 company, and man-on-the-street interviews filmed in Chelsea, West Hollywood, San Francisco, Atlanta, Miami, Dallas, and Greenwich Village filled the monitors.

I looked around. People were crying. Others toasted the screens and whooped. I shared their pride and remembered historical moments that had opened doors a little wider—Arthur Ashe at Wimbledon, Vanessa Williams crowned Ms. America, Halle Barry's Oscar win, Michael Jackson's "Beat It" (the first video by a black artist on MTV), the movies *Waiting to Exhale, The Color Purple, Do the Right Thing,* and of course *The Cosby Show* on television. I wanted to imprint the moment in my memory because it was a once-in-a-lifetime occurrence. Other gay channels might launch, but ours was the first.

Upstairs the mood was festive but not overly so. Nigel had been right—the décor did look a lot like a hotel lobby; but the VIPs, stiff and composed, fit right in. Waiters refilled champagne flutes and served finger foods on silver trays. Lily sat next to Malcolm. They whispered to each other and pointed at the television screens still working gay images of the channel.

"Things are winding down. The gifts bags are being handed out," I said to Lily, letting her know I was leaving to be a mother at home with the children.

"Great job tonight." She smiled, her eyes a little wet from crying as well.

Malcolm bore into me with his infinite black pupils. "Did you have fun, Charlene?"

I nodded.

"I like your dress," he said.

"Thank you."

Mimi swayed over in a red sleeveless gown. "Hey."

"You look fabulous, girl," I said.

She pretended to blush. It was apparent she knew exactly how fabulous she came off. Malcolm asked her to get
him water. She did look incredible, but she was fetching just
like any old assistant in any old situation. You would have
thought she'd have taken her expense account and quit
working for Malcolm. I would've. But I guess a high-profile
job did provide access to high-profile prospects for marriage.
Malcolm leaned into Lily to talk privately. That was the signal to go away. I was glad. It was two o'clock in the morning, and I wanted to go home, take my shoes off, sleep in on
Saturday morning, fry pork chops for Sunday dinner, and
return to the channel Monday morning fresh for a busy week
ahead.

I passed Mimi on the way out as she was carrying a tall
glass of sparkling water with fresh lime over to Malcolm.
Willingly, I left the VIP section and its very important airs,
and returned to the true party on the ground level, which
was soaring upon a third wind on the dance floor. It seemed
as if a whole new crowd had pushed past the doormen and
were taking over. There were Chelsea Boys and Baby Dykes
everywhere dancing with same-sex partners. Even the most
jaded person could see that this was one of those events that
slowed down time long enough for a person to realize the potential impact of the Gay Channel. But a sister had responsibilities and wanted to take care of those responsibilities.
Parenting was my #1 priority. The fun that night had come
to an end for me. I headed downstairs to get my purse
locked in a basement storage room.

Nigel, drunk as Janice Joplin or Truman Capote—pick
your favorite—caught me on the staircase. He was a slob-
bering mess. I was trying to wrench my arm out of his grip
when we tumbled a few steps and landed on the floor. I was
doubled over in laughter but alarmed nonetheless because a

sober Nigel was uncensored so a drunk Nigel would be off the hook. I had the worst feeling, and I was cornered.

"You are so stupid!" I laughed, trying to get away from him. "Some kind of hangover *you're* going to have tomorrow. Let go of me, you crazy boy!"

"Kiss me, Charlene." He puckered wet lips and tried to find my mouth as I squirmed and turned my head from side to side.

"Cut it out, Nigel. You're drunk!"

"Drunk for you. I like girls too, just in case you didn't know. See that door there? We can just slip behind it and. . . hmm. C'mon with me," he said, his hot and nasty alcoholic breath encasing my face in fumes.

"Nigel, get off!" I said, standing up, the joke over for me. "You need to get yourself some coffee."

"I need to get myself some of you."

He was sprawled on a couple of stairs in a sexy pose, holding onto my ankle. Partyers stepped over or around his laid-out body on their way to and from the bathroom. His gaze looked as if his brown eyes were dissolving. His skin was extra greasy, as if he'd just come from a facial and the esthetician had forgotten to wipe product off his face. I waved him off, yanked my ankle loose, and had started toward the storage room when he caught the hem of my dress and pulled me backward. Somehow he was able to lift himself up and me along with him. He slammed me against the storage room door. Luckily I had the key and the door was locked, but that didn't stop him from grinding his bony hips into mine.

"You're at the wrong party, girlfriend," a manscaped partygoer observed, exiting the men's room.

"Can you get him off me?" I pleaded.

"Oh, honey, he's not my type," the man said, mounting

the stairs.

Sorry, Nigel, I said to myself before kneeing him in the groin. He doubled over yowling. I shook his scent off me, wiped my bare arms, and ran fingers through my short hair.

"Oh, Charlene, that *hurt*," Nigel said through clenched teeth.

"There's more where that came from if you *ever* come at me like that again. Have you lost your cotton pickin' *mind?*"

Derrick stumbled downstairs. It took him a few long seconds to sum up the scene. He cut his eyes at Nigel bent over at the waist.

"Does he have tears in his eyes?" Derrick asked me.

"I think so," I said.

"Good." Derrick helped me unlock the door. "I'll stand watch while you get your stuff."

I felt guilty about kneeing Nigel in the balls. He propped one hand against the wall to brace himself as fresh waves of shooting pains folded him in two. I grabbed my purse and closed the door. Derrick escorted me upstairs. Over my shoulder I caught Nigel's eye. He winked at me and signaled that this was not the last of our encounters.

7

Money for Nothing

I, CHARLENE, HOW YOU DOING? How're the kids?"
Otis said. Leticia's ex-husband shuffled across the
stage in baggy jeans and an XXXL New York Gi-
ants jersey. He was an average-looking man with a wide
nose and soft curly hair slicked back with ointment as if he
was from the '40s or something. I'd always liked Otis. When
he lived with Leticia and Tonya, he took care of the brownstone, planting wildflowers in spring and carrying our
Christmas trees home in winter as lazy Warren slept on the
couch.

"Hey, Otis. You're cool?" I asked, meaning the filming.
I was back on the same stage where the Kathleen Pendle
photo shoot had taken place.

"You're going to stay during all this, right?" he said
with a sheepish look and a dash of stupid. I knew he had
no idea what he had signed up for. It was just an opportunity to pay his child support in arrears and pocket a few dollars for his on-camera admissions. He was basically a good
man who had done something no black woman could ever
get over: he'd had down-low sex, booty bumping, with an-

other married man.

"Yes, sugar, I'll be right here. You got paid, right?"

"I'm doing it for my wife and kid," he said. "No other reason. I'm just hoping to be forgiven."

Hope all he wanted to, I knew Leticia wasn't feeling that at all. I just smiled kindly at him. He had made a *huge* mistake. Otis was weak for bourbon, and finally liquor had dragged him over the edge into a den of sex addicts willing to get off on whatever, whether it was with each other, women, or sheep! Otis Smith was the saddest of black men—a gentle heart coupled with poor judgment, wrecked with remorse but only after the house of cards had fallen around him. He simply lacked conscientious reasoning.

In my opinion it hadn't been entirely his fault. Otis had done his best having survived the foster-care system. There was a grief deep inside this man that wasn't ever going to be reached. I felt sorry for him, but Leticia was my friend, and it was in my best interest to help her out morally and financially. She had divorced Otis. His sad tale was no excuse for throwing her under the bus of embarrassment.

Barry fluttered in on a wing and a prayer, clearly running away from Dee Dee, who was hard on his heels, asking a million questions about the shoot. Barry had to work with Dee Dee because of his green-eyed dislike of Jesse. Nonetheless, I had to listen to him complain about her. "Does she *ever* shut the fuck up?" he had asked me. I reminded him that *Two Dirty Words: Down-low* had been his idea, and that the show could potentially be a big hit and money earner for the Gay Channel. We had two directors, Jesse or Dee Dee. He had to choose one.

The camera crew loaded equipment, ready to set up for the interview. Barry ran toward Otis, but I knew he was distancing himself from Dee Dee who was bringing up the rear. She worked two short legs to catch Barry, but was unable to keep up. Having a bulbous, pregnant stomach did not help matters either. Otis stuck out his hand to stop Barry from hugging him, believing that down-low behavior was an act straight men did to get off and therefore not making him, or any of his sex pals, gay men. Barry blew off the outstretched hand and embraced Otis anyway, nothing sexual about it. This was business, and if the shoot was a success, Barry's stock at the channel would rise dramatically.

"I'm Barry Trumball, head of original series." He pulled back and then shook Otis's hand, a little too eagerly.

"Otis Smith." Otis looked like he was going to fall over— either from the realization of what he had agreed to do or from Barry's outfit, an aquamarine number beyond description. I couldn't tell which.

"Want some water?" I asked.

"Water would be good. Maybe y'all got something a little bit stronger?" Otis said.

Dee Dee climbed up on stage. She was out of breath. "Oh, don't be concerned, we're going to film you as a silhouette. No one will be able to see your face. And we'll disguise your voice, too." Dee Dee's voice boomed out of her petite body. "Just relax."

Otis looked doubly worried now. Besides the obvious— baby in the oven—Dee Dee had dressed very androgynously that day in jeans, penny loafers, and a white polo shirt. Also, over the weekend she had had her hair cut as short as a twelve-year-old boy's sheared at a country barbershop. She situated Otis in the black wingback chair. The camera crew adjusted the camera and darkened the lights. I set a bottle of water on the table next to Otis, who was pea green with nausea.

Malcolm and Lily were a hundred percent behind the project and lauded its success for the channel. Another "shadowed" interviewee had been recruited as well. After that, down-low men had come out of the woodworks. Buzz was hot. That's when Leticia and Otis had agreed to the project, and to do whatever it took to get the child support he owed. I'd urged them to move fast and not get shut out of the chance to earn.

"Ready?" Dee Dee said, holding a stubby index finger in the air.

"Let's do this," Otis said, pulling together his confidence for Leticia's and Tonya's sake, hoping beyond reality that he'd be forgiven and could come back home.

"Okay, here goes. Mr. Smith, when was the first time you got together with men who were on the down-low?" Dee Dee glared at him.

"Um, I was—well, it didn't happen like that."

"How did it happen, then?"

"I was messing with my daughter's computer, hanging out on the Internet, you know? I stumbled upon a chat room. I guess that's what you call it. I had never seen that before."

"A chat room, okay. And?"

"And I hooked up with this cat named Mosley. He lived right down the street! I thought it was funny you could meet someone on the computer who lived right down the street. We laughed about that later on. Anyway, he invited me over to check out his new game room down in the basement. When I got there, a bunch of brothers were sitting around, drinking and watching the football game."

"Were you attracted to them at first sight?"

"I wasn't even thinking about that. Mosley had a helluva bar. I poured myself a Hennessey. After a few drinks,

I noticed two guys were getting their freak on. I was like—
whoa, what the hell is going on here? But before I knew it,
Mosley was stroking my leg and then my thigh and then my
johnson. You know what I mean?"

"I do," Dee Dee nodded. "Keep going."

"I'll stroke his johnson," Barry snickered in my ear. I
moved away from him.

"Why didn't you stop it? What about your wife and
daughter?" Dee Dee said accusingly. "Were you even thinking about them, about the consequences?"

"I don't know. I just didn't think about what might
happen. Marijuana was passed. I took a few hits. Time just
collapsed, I guess. The lights and television were turned off.
It was blackout dark in that basement. And it felt so good,
what he was doing. Mosley kept saying he just wanted me
to feel good, and that he wasn't, you know, a faggot."

"Do you still see him?"

"No. His wife busted him with another man up in their
bedroom. She kicked him out and divorced him. Sold the
brownstone and moved to Atlanta with her mother."

"How did your wife find out?"

"She found this." Otis dug around in his pockets and
pulled out a mini DV tape. "When Mosley moved off the
block he gave this tape to me as a going-away present.
Something to remember him by, I suppose. I watched it
once when I was drunk."

Barry shot forward. "Can we see it?"

Otis leaned back in the chair. "Cost you extra, man."

Barry looked at me to say something, as if I could per-
suade Otis to hand over the sex tape for free. I didn't even
know about any tape. Leticia hadn't told me either! Wait
until I see *her* tonight, I thought. I shrugged, pretending I
couldn't do anything about getting the tape without the

channel having to pay extra. I wasn't going to take anyone's side. I didn't want to know what was on the tape; the thought of its content had my eyes bugging out. I was a single black woman, and viewing a tape with a bunch of brothers doing it wasn't going to whet my appetite for future dating.

Barry put his hands on his hips. "How much?"

"Can we finish up the interview before compensation negotiations start?" Dee Dee said, annoyed her directing was being interrupted.

"How much?" Barry insisted, ignoring Dee Dee. He was the executive in charge, and she couldn't do anything about the interruption.

"I don't know." Otis shielded his eyes and tried to read my expression. I telepathically thought of a figure and hoped he would hit upon the number, all in the name of my friendship with Leticia. My best friend had better be grateful. Barry instructed the cameraman to turn up the lights. His outfit shimmered like fish scales. Otis appeared lost in the brightness. Dee Dee audibly sighed.

"Can we get on with it? I have another shoot in an hour," she said.

"How much, Mr. Smith?"

"Ten thousand," Otis said.

"Five hundred," Barry said. "And I have to go view the tape right now to determine if it's usable. Deal?"

I nodded at Otis to take the money.

"Yeah, okay, man, that sounds alright."

Otis handed over the tape to Barry. I held my breath, imagining how many people Barry would pull into the conference room to see it. Dee Dee had the camera crew reset the dark lighting.

"Sorry about that," she said to Otis, as if they had both

been inconvenienced by Barry Trumball's rudeness. "So you said your wife found a tape, how did she know it was you?"

"I had my face to the camera, and Mosley was behind me. It wasn't hard to tell. I didn't even know a camera was there. All I can say is, I looked like I was having a good time, drunk and high, hanging with the guys. I don't think my wife ever saw that look of ecstasy on my face before. It really upset her."

Oh, Leticia. She must have had a heart attack. At least my man had been adulterous with another woman. I couldn't fathom what it'd been like for her to find out Otis had let a man fuck him.

"Have you been tested?" Dee Dee asked.

"For what? You mean psychologically? I'm not crazy. It's just something that happened."

"No. For HIV."

"Huh?" Otis squirmed in his chair.

"HIV infection. You know, AIDS?"

"I never thought of that."

"Would you be willing to get a test on camera today?"

"How much do I get paid for that?"

"Mr. Smith, this isn't an á la carte money menu," Dee Dee scoffed.

"What you mean, cart? If it ain't in the writing, then I want extra money for my wife and kid."

I was impressed. Go, Otis. Shake down the man. Maybe that dash of stupid had been suspended just for the day.

"Okay. Charlene, can you go ask Barry how much he's willing to pay Mr. Smith here to take a HIV test on camera?"

No, I thought. "Sure, no problem," I said.

Off to the conference room I went, but was surprised

Barry wasn't in there. I went to his office. Derrick and he were watching the tape in a mini DV recorder. They had their faces pressed into the tiny two-by-two-inch screen.

"This is good, Charlene. You scored the best interview for the show yet. He's looking right at the camera just like Paris Hilton, night vision green. We'll fuzz out his face in the show."

"How many other friends do you have that have husbands on the D.L.?" Derrick snickered. "I'd love it if they agreed to a publicity campaign. A tour of major cable markets, you know?"

"Listen, Dee Dee wants Otis to take a HIV test on camera. He's asking for money," I concluded, wanting to get back to business and back to the stage.

"Jesus!" Barry said, irritated. "Why doesn't he just write a book?"

"I think someone already did. Came out a few months ago. That guy was on *Oprah*," Derrick said matter-of-factly.

"Another five hundred dollars, and tell him that's *it!*" Barry screamed.

Otis took the test and the money—a total of nine grand. He agreed to return the following week to film his reaction to the test results, but he seemed confident there wasn't a chance he'd been infected.

"A couple more questions before you leave. Are you still on the down-low? And if you are, where are your hookups?"

"I don't know if I still am. I'm living with a friend, a man. Sometimes we freak on each other, but I don't look for other men to hook up with. I still visit the chat rooms. After my wife divorced me, I've been kind of floating around Brooklyn. You know? Just trying to figure things out."

"Why don't you just come out and live a gay lifestyle?"

"Because I ain't gay," Otis said with a straight face.

Now it was Dee Dee's turn to be confused. "Okay," she said, but I could see she'd wanted to argue and then thought it better not to.

The lights went up. Otis shrunk into his triple-X clothing. Now that I had heard everything, I couldn't bring myself to be overly friendly toward him. The black community was suffering behind this kind of denial.

"I'll show you out," I said.

"You seen Warren lately?" he said, shell-shocked from his confessions.

"No, have you?" I sounded more defensive then I'd intended to. Suddenly I was concerned that Otis had hooked up with my ex-husband! Please, Lord, Jesus Christ, say it ain't so.

"Nah, Charlene. You ain't got nothing to be bothered 'bout. I was just asking. Making conversation, that's all."

"Sorry, Otis."

"Me, too," he said as I showed him to the elevator.

I called Leticia as soon as I got back to my cube. "Girl, you did not tell me about no tape. You know he brought it with him, don't you?"

"I do, girl. I'm sorry I didn't say anything. Otis thought he could get more money. Did he?"

I had to give it to a sister, chiseling corporate dollars, but there were flames burning in my chest. I didn't appreciate her shaking down my job for cash when I had already put my neck out for her. We had already agreed on the interview. I felt a little betrayed.

"Yup, he got another thousand plus a HIV test. What about you? Have you ever been tested?"

"I have. After I found out. I'm negative. Thank God for that."

"Leticia, don't cheat me again, okay? I was trying to help out."

"I know. I can't tell you how badly I feel. You know we ain't got no money, though. Otis and I thought we'd use the tape to get a little extra for you and your kids."

I considered the backward kindness. "Thank you, honey. But you know it's kind of stealing. I can't steal from my job."

"Well, no one will know where the extra groceries come from, now will they?"

"They will, actually, because my phone is tapped at work," I said, remembering Clayton Hicks had told me the phone conversations were being recorded to help catch the stalker.

"What?"

"The stalker, remember? I told you about the breather? The one who calls for Barry all the time."

"Oh, child, I would have told you this at home," she said, horrified.

I could hear the regret. She really had wanted to do me a favor in return. Clayton Hicks, from security, was still pursuing me for a date. Maybe I could have a word with him? How was this going to work? The whole scam had been blown wide open.

"I might have a solution," I said.

8

They

S O YOU FINALLY LET me take you out," Clayton said over a candlelight dinner up on Lenox Avenue and West 126th Street. I hadn't been to Harlem in years. I shrugged in a precious way and checked out the restaurant, half filled with diners. Guess there weren't that many takers for soul food in the middle of August. Not me. I could chow down on smothered chicken, collard greens, candied yams, black-eyed peas, and corn bread any day of the week, any time of the year. Clayton eyed me hungrily, and it reminded me of my faux pas at the launch party. The man at the club may have resembled Clayton, but the attentive look taking me in right now halted all lingering suspicions. His smile was as wide as 125th was from Harlem to East Harlem. I liked his eyes—kind, happy and deep brown. He enjoyed me without having found out too much of my background. We had chemistry. I hadn't seen that look in Warren's eyes for years before our divorce. It was nice to be admired.

"How could I resist all those e-mails and phone calls?" I said, sipping sweet ice tea. "You wore me out."

"My momma said I would get places being persistent."

"Well, she was right."

"We have a little information on the man who's been calling the channel," he said, wiping barbeque sauce from his luscious lips. We shared the same skin tone, Bernie Mac black (that's what Tinecia liked to call it). After Warren, I wanted the purest black man available without going to the Motherland to get it.

"I can't believe it! Does Lily Essex know? Malcolm Drake?" Paranoia set in. Had security also heard my phone call with Leticia, how corporate monies were being manipulated for the sake of her child's welfare?

"Nah, I wanted to tell you first," he said. "We haven't found him physically, not yet anyway. We don't know where he lives. Apparently his sister caught on to what he was doing. She contacted us, but she wouldn't give us his name or much of anything else. She was concerned for the people at the channel. It was a strange phone call."

"That's a lucky hand to be dealt nonetheless. Barry will be relieved to hear that at least you have a lead. Did you ever think he was in real trouble?" I said.

"I don't know. We've all read the *Post*. A crazy man knows an employee's address. One can never guess what might happen. Security only has so much power. We have to rely on the NYPD for support outside of the company. But they're pretty cool about assisting us in our investigations. The company we work for is pretty powerful, has a long reach, if you know what I mean."

"You said this kind of stuff happens all the time with other channels? You must have an interesting job fielding all kinds of drama," I said.

"All I can say is, it's a big company. Like for your channel, Malcolm Drake thought there'd be Christian Right protests last month when the channel went on the air, but nothing happened. We didn't even get one phone call. In the case of the stalker, we're really lucky a family member came forward."

"I never pictured myself working at a place like the Gay Channel, but I had to get a job quickly and take care of my kids. It hasn't turned out to be that bad."

"You ain't got no man in your life? How is that possible? I can't even imagine a beautiful woman like you on the street without being snatched up by some brother," Clayton said knowingly. My single status was no mystery to anyone I worked with, including security. The whole company was in each other's business from sunup to sundown. He reached across the table and held my hand. I let him for about ten seconds before pulling away, but that was enough time to encourage him. He ordered a bottle of red wine.

"Ever been married?" I said.

"No, never, and believe me that don't sit too well with my Christian mother." He laughed heartily. It was easy to imagine their conversations—him being playful, her quite serious. The waitress poured wine.

"Here's to you, Charlene," he said.

"Thank you, Clayton. I really am having a good time."

"So you have kids? I saw the pictures on your desk," he said.

"Yes. Two. A boy and a girl."

I didn't want to get too personal, so I omitted their names. I also promised myself right there and then I wasn't going to bring up Warren and his Harlem hussy.

"What do you tell them about your job?"

"That I'm an executive assistant, and I work in TV. Why?"

"Oh, I don't know." He thought for a second. "What

about that girl who works over by the pantry. She wears boy's clothes. How come?"

"You mean Jem?"

"Jim?"

"It's spelled J-e-m. A transgender person," I said. I was entering tricky territory.

"What's that mean, 'transgender'? I never heard of such a thing." He screwed his face up in disdain. I understood his point, but at the same time Jem was a person to me, not someone to judge. It caught me by surprise that my attitude had changed. But underneath my righteousness I had to admit my first reaction to "transgender" hadn't been so graceful.

"Transgender is the 'T' in LGBT. You know lesbian, gay, bi-sexual, transgender. Believe it or not, the office is like any other office, Clayton. Sexual orientation isn't a daily topic. Nobody has time for that. We're still busy as hell after going on the air last month."

"But you know what I mean," he said, giving me a calculating look. Not a hint of meanness crossed his expression. He really wanted to understand.

"True. The gay staff had to be educated, too, not just the handful of straight people at the channel. There was a lot of stuff said behind Jem's back, that's for sure. We acted like children after the e-mail Roger Ward sent out. The transgender announcement."

"An announcement about what?"

"How to address Jem. It's complicated, you know? Let me back up to explain. You know what gay and lesbian means, right? Bi-sexual is obvious. I had to look up the other definitions: 'transvestites' are people who dress in the opposite sex's clothing. 'Transsexual' is the sex change. 'Transgender,' 'pangender,' or 'gender queer' is a whole other ball of wax, honey child. They can be whatever they define themselves as being. They just don't want to be associated with any sexual orientation. They express themselves through gender identity."

Clayton stared at me as if I was speaking Greek; I felt the same way, except the concepts weren't that foreign to me anymore. Working at the Gay Channel had educated my small world, too. I finished off the glass of wine in my hand.

"Can you believe I know all this?" I laughed, a little buzzed.

"How the hell does a person express gender identity? You either have a penis or a vagina. I still don't have the faintest idea what you're talking about," Clayton said, his sense of humor getting the best of us. We smiled at each other, actually becoming closer while talking the subject out.

"Transgender people express themselves through dress, behavior, and actions. You can look it up too if you don't believe me. All I know is, if I dress and act like a man— that's my identity."

"That's fucking crazy. Sounds like a prerequisite to a locked ward and years of psychoanalysis. And don't ignore the 'STOP' sign on the way to therapy session," he said comically. "I don't know what to say. How do you all work together and not be ridiculously confused?"

"It's not confusing because mostly it's gay men and lesbian women. There are no transsexuals or transvestites. And the e-mail announcement told everybody how to behave around Jem—our one and only transgender."

"Can you quote it? I'm dying to hear this."

"We're to use the pronoun 'They' for Jem," I said.

"They? They what? They for one person?"

"It's such a long story, but let me back up even further. It started with the handicapped bathroom. Jem uses the

men and ladies' bathrooms, but there were complaints. One
executive, Sharon Adamovitz, suggested 'They' get a key to
the handicapped bathroom and use that. I had to let her
know that the handicapped bathroom is for handicapped
people, and that being transgender is not a mental or phys-
ical problem."

"Oh, I remember that request," said Clayton, putting
two and two together. "Now, she's straight up lesbian,
right? Ms. Adamovitz? Not a transgender, 'cuz she kind of
dresses like a cowboy."

"It's different. You can kind of figure that out for yourself, right?"

"Yes, it's true. There is a difference," he said with a faraway look.

"Yeah, anyway, security, you all, said no to the key.
Then this rumor hit the halls that Jem is a girl. A guy from
the marketing department, this guy Nigel Grant—he's a
pain in the butt, let me tell you—anyway, he said he was at
a urinal and here comes Jem going into a stall. Out of sheer
nervousness he says, 'Hi, They,' in an overly friendly voice
while at the same time zipping up and running out the
door."

"I wouldn't know what to do myself!"

"He complained to Human Resources, so Roger sent an
e-mail that basically said, 'Welcome, Jem Garcia!' Then it
went on to describe Jem's talent of typing over eighty words
a minute, and that Jem would be assisting in the programming department. The e-mail also told us how to spell Jem.
J-E-M. But the punch that put us under the table was how
to reference Jem. It said something like 'Jem is a gender
queer, trans-identified person who doesn't want anyone to
use the gender pronouns 'he' or 'she'. Jem prefers to be
called Jem, or, if a pronoun is to be used, Jem prefers that

you use 'They'."

"How many people did you forward that e-mail to?" Clayton asked with a wild smirk.

"About a hundred."

"It doesn't make grammatical sense," Clayton said. "I'm not the smartest guy, but I do know that."

I felt awful about it, but we laughed for a good ten minutes as we polished off the rest of the wine. Jem's face, as well as the others' at the office, floated through my mind. Something inside me disliked how callous I sounded, because I did care about my co-workers. And I would hate it if people were making fun of me behind my back, though, knowing the crowd at work, I was sure I'd been the butt of many jokes.

"We're not being very nice," I said, wiping away a tear. "Truth is, I believe in what people are trying to do there even if I'm not gay. The channel is already a media sensation."

"I know, but c'mon—the 'They' thing is classic office craziness."

"It is, but now I feel bad laughing about Jem."

"Okay, okay," he said.

We were silent for a spell as the waiter cleared plates and wiped away crumbs. During dessert we talked about his mother and how long he's been working security. Clayton paid the bill, and for a fleeting second I realized that Warren would have asked me for money. I could have been knocked over by a toothpick. Clayton was treating me like a lady, and it felt so good to be out with a good man.

The night air was still muggy even though it was nearly midnight. I thought about Martel and Tinecia and Leticia and Tonya. I still hadn't said anything to Clayton about whether or not security had recorded the phone call I'd had with Leticia about Otis chiseling extra money out of the channel for the down-low shoot.

"I know this badass jazz club down on Malcolm X Boulevard. Nightcap?"

"Yeah, that's sounds good. Then I gotta go home. Okay?"

"You got it. I'm serious about you, so you don't have to worry none."

I wanted to believe him, but my body was in a whole other universe. Clayton locked arms with me and I nestled into his muscular shoulder. Being with this man felt like extra bonus points for being a good mother. Pure heaven. I loved it. Clayton held me tightly as the traffic light changed from red to green. We crossed West 125th.

"Before we go inside, I have to ask you something," I said.

"What's that? Do I have a woman? No, I do not," he offered.

"I am glad to know that!" I paused. "But that's not what I was going to say."

"What, then?"

I took a little breath. "Were you at the launch party last month?"

"For your channel? Nah. Corporate security wasn't on that job."

"Oh, okay," I said, feeling stupid for asking.

"You thought you saw me there?"

"Yeah."

"Charlene, if I was there, you'd have been the first to know."

He hugged me and peered deeply into my eyes. I stood on tiptoes in black flat sandals to embrace him back. Clayton stroked my bare shoulders. His touch resonated throughout my body and sent currents up and down my thighs. I thought I'd have an orgasm right there on the street! I hadn't had any since a one-night fling the previous December to celebrate my divorce going through—that had been more than eight months before.

"What you want to know, sweet Charlene?" he whispered in my ear. "How much I like you? What a pretty lady you are? How good you look in that red tank top and black jean skirt? What do you want to know?"

"I do want to know that, every single detail you want to point out," I said as my tone upended. Romance faded. Pressure was building up inside to be serious for a second. I'd get back to flirting momentarily. "Actually it's a work question."

He stepped back and held me at arms' length. The humidity filled the space between us. I heard a siren wail nearby. All the people around us came alive. The intimacy dissipated like smoke clearing after a wildfire. He had no idea what kind of work question I could have just then, but I had to find out if he thought I was a thief.

"Oh. Did I offend you in the restaurant about 'They'?"

"No, no, no. That's not it. I want to know if my phone at work is still tapped."

"Yes, it is. Any problem with that? I told you we haven't caught the guy. We can discuss it on Monday, back in the office, can't we?" His increasing concern that I might be upset had killed the warmth in his voice.

"You know what, Clayton honey? It's not that deep. I was just concerned that a conversation between my friend Leticia and me had been recorded. That's all."

He chuckled lightly and moved in closer. I was glad he came toward me. I wanted to bury my face in the sweetness of his black skin, and I didn't want to ruin any more hot moments between us.

"I can see why you'd be nervous. No, security isn't recording every call. That would be too much work and a privacy issue. The way it works is, your work phone is programmed to record only when he calls from his cell phone. It's gotta be his number. So far he hasn't thought to use a disposable phone number, but it is registered to a stolen identity."

"Oh, I see. Wow, I didn't know phones could be set up like that," I said, embarrassed to have asked.

"It's okay," he said, reading my thoughts. "Everybody needs a little bit of secrecy when they talk on the phone at work."

"Thank you for understanding. It's hard to find a compassionate man these days."

"Well, here I am," he said, opening his arms wide, looking like an angel sent from God in heaven above.

9

We Do

DEE DEE HAD CAMPAIGNED noisily for a baby shower all summer long. Lily asked me to arrange it because Dee Dee was now a prize possession for the channel. I recruited Jem and Nigel. They were putting the finishing touches on decorating the conference room. Nigel balanced on a stepladder, taping cutouts of puffy white clouds, storks, and baby baskets on the walls. Ever since I kicked him in the balls at Club Tumbler he'd been more interested in me. Neither us had mentioned what had happened, although I was sure if I was cornered again he'd be all over me. Nigel had taken the kick as a sign that I really did want him instead of the warning it'd been meant to be. The grease-ball was hands down delusional. I kept my distance. Maybe he'd been in an alcoholic gray-out when he groped me? Derrick, on the other hand, had let Nigel know in no uncertain terms that it was strike two (crashing Sandra Bernhard's party and humping me), and that, if he did one more thing that pissed him off, he was going to advocate for Nigel's demise at the channel. So Derrick had my back—but only in the interest of getting rid of Nigel Grant.

"Stretch it all the way across," Nigel said to Jem, his unofficial decorating assistant.

Jem secured the banner across the window that announced *Baby Shower* in case anyone had forgotten why we were gathered there. His/her/its/their/both/neutral's frown stretched as widely as the banner. Jem moped to the other side of the conference room to check the banner's evenness. I tried not to stare at the phenomenon that was Jem in motion. The clothes were baggier than ever that day. Were those faint traces of hair over the top lip, a moustache? Maybe They's real name was Jemma?

"Where are you from, They?" I said.

"The Bronx." The voice was neutral, too. Like Lauren Bacall's or Elijah Wood's.

"Like the song 'Jenny from the Block,'" Nigel said. He broke out into the popular Jennifer Lopez song. *"Don't be fooled by the rocks that I got. I'm still, I'm still, Jenny from the block. Used to have a little, now I have a lot. No matter where I go, I know where I came from—South-Side Bronx!"*

Jem winced at Nigel, turning his/her/its/their/both/neutral's back on us. I gave Nigel a dirty look to cut it out. He stopped singing but continued to hum the J. Lo tune.

"You still live there?" I said trying to re-engage his/her/its/their/both/neutral's attention.

"No." Dead air.

I was attempting niceties, but I could see why everyone complained about Jem. It was like talking to a concrete wall or sticking your head inside a deep well. Jem had no personality. You'd think someone standing firm in such a drastic decision about who they were in the world would have a bit more bite to their public persona. But not Jem—this was the longest interaction we'd had so far.

"Hey, Jem, darling, the banner is crooked. Can you see

that? Adjust it, please? A little higher on the left," Nigel
said, pointing a bony finger at They.

Jem did as They was told, literally sinking into folds of
clothing. Okay, so no more dialogue was going to happen
today between the two brown-skinned people at the channel. I arranged wrapped gifts on the banquette, turned up
the volume on "Yeah!" by Usher, and danced a little to the
beat. Nigel did a simulated nasty strip tease dance on the
stepladder, thrusting his pelvis and butt at the conference
room window overlooking Times Square. Jem moved about
like a silent servant. I wanted to shake They out of
his/her/its/their/both/neutral's transgender misery.

The room looked very cute. Candy-colored streamers
draped from the ceiling. The conference room table was
piled with finger foods, cakes, candies, and chocolates. Dee
Dee was due around Labor Day—two weeks away. In the
last month she had become the top choice director for ninety
percent of the projects at the channel. The word-of-mouth
momentum for *Two Dirty Words: Down-low* had catapulted
the channel into new territory. The show had turned into a
major hit, driving viewers to the channel and to the website.
The episode with Otis had been slated for two more re-runs
because so many requests were coming in for it. Dee Dee's
idea of the HIV test on camera had really driven home the
denial down-low sexual behavior perpetrated. Thank God
Otis had tested negative, but that testing had changed the
channel's viewership base. In no time, the Gay Channel
found itself hosting a large African American female audience who wanted to find out more about the down-low online hook-up scene, how to question their men, and what to
do if they tested HIV. It was a crossover explosion, and Dee
Dee was the favorite at the channel because of it. Malcolm
and Lily hailed her as a creative genius even though the con-

cept had been Barry's.

Genius in coordinating outfits, though, she was not. Dee Dee strolled into the conference room wearing a yellow-and-black horizontal striped spandex t-shirt, black knee socks, and a jean miniskirt. Nigel fell off the stepladder he was standing on and ripped down a stork appliqué as he tumbled southward. He rolled over on his side to stifle laughter. I went over and lightly nudged him with my foot.

"Get up," I whispered.

Nigel turned over, his bright red oily face twisted like a locked-up mad man's. Dee Dee barely noticed Nigel as she went about approving of the decorated room. Jem pulled out a chair for the expectant mother.

"Have a seat, Dee Dee," his/her/its/their/both/neutral's indistinct voice murmured. "Take a load off."

"Thanks, Jem," she hollered, planting her pear-shaped body in the chair and placing a manila folder on the table. She gave me a CD. "Here, Charlene, I brought music for the party."

Derrick, Barry, Sharon, Roger, Jesse, and Lily came into the conference room, along with interns, assistants, and other executives hired recently at the channel. I changed Usher to Sara McLachlan. Not exactly get down and celebrate music where I came from, but it wasn't my party.

Seeing everyone together in the conference room brought home how Denver the channel was. My darkness really stuck out. But the all-white Gay Channel was now catering to a newfound African American female audience; hmm—maybe I could cash in on this? My mother had taught me to look for opportunities in every negative, like my divorce from Warren. I made more money now than I ever had in my life!

"Everybody, everybody!" Dee Dee shouted. "I'm getting married! Jethro will have legitimate legal parents!"

She held up her tiny left hand showing off a delicate gold-and-diamond engagement ring. The whole room exploded, clapped, and shouted their congratulations. Dee Dee slid a large picture of her partner, Sandy, from the folder on the table and propped it against a flower vase.

"That's just great," Lily said, beaming.

"And I have the most fantastic idea!" Dee Dee yelled at us.

Derrick rolled his eyes and adjusted the marigold pocketchief accenting his white linen suit. No one had said anything to me yet, but I sensed the gay men were getting pretty sick and tired of Dee Dee's status with senior management. Jesse looked like a seething cauldron of black tar sitting opposite Dee Dee as she jumped to both feet.

"Let's film my wedding!"

The lesbians cheered. Lily gave Dee Dee two thumbs up. Sharon tipped her cowboy hat and kissed the tiny mother-to-be on both cheeks.

"Malcolm will love it," Lily said. "I think this is a terrific idea. When's the date? How will this work, since you're going on maternity leave in two weeks?"

"That's the easy part," Dee Dee said, squirming to get comfortable in her chair. "We're getting married in a few days. We've already gotten the license! It'll be a road trip to Massachusetts where same-sex unions were legalized a few months ago. Let's do it! Let the channel stand up for gay marriage by filming mine!"

"Shouldn't we have a male couple marry, too? That way it represents gays *and* lesbians," Derrick said sarcastically.

Dee Dee's shoulders dropped, obviously not wanting to share the spotlight with another couple, male or female. Lily chewed her lip, thinking about it. Sara McLachlan's somber voice filled the brief silence.

"How about some cake, y'all?" I said. "This is a celebration of new life!"

"Here, here," Nigel said, backing me up. "Booze, anyone? There's champagne."

Most of us crowded around Nigel, who produced a couple bottles of sparkling white wine from a cooler in the corner. Jem uncorked the bottles. I handed out cups. Lily, Sharon, Roger, and Dee Dee huddled to quickly discuss the wedding shoot while we toasted her. Jesse took the moment to change Sara McLachlan to The Black Eyed Peas's "Let's Get It Started." The boys jumped up to the beat. I danced with Jesse, who swung his slight hips from side to side and ran fingers through his blond hair.

"Hey!" Dee Dee boomed, noticing the change in music. "I want to hear the CD I brought."

"Honey, that's for your living room, not a party," Nigel said, throwing his arms up in the air. "Open your presents!"

"We've got it worked out," Lily said over the music, wincing at the steady beat.

Barry crossed his arms and frowned, his delicate fingers tapped impatiently. The show he'd produced, *My Big Fat Fabulous Fantastic Gay Wedding*, wasn't doing so well in the ratings. Bravo's *Queer Eye for the Straight Guy* beat out the time slot every week. He had told me he felt outdone by Dee Dee and her "in" with our lesbian general manager.

"Can I remind everyone that we already have a wedding show on the air?" he said. He crossed one long leg over the other and madly jiggled a foot housed in a giant platform shoe. "I think another wedding show will be bad for ratings."

"But your show is about wedding *planning*, not an actual ceremony. And it's about Canadians, and we're Americans," Dee Dee bit back, her little teeth bared.

"It's the Gay Channel, Dee Dee, not the *American* Gay Channel," Barry sneered. "And cities in Canada passed legalized same-sex unions before Massachusetts did. That's *why* the show is set in another country."

Lily stepped between them. She acknowledged silently that both had valid viewpoints by offering peaceful smiles all around. Barry looked as if he wanted to pummel Dee Dee, but at the same time he backed down. Disrespecting Lily was a big no-no, as she was the one person who had Malcolm Drake's ear.

Barry stopped wagging his foot as an idea came to him. "How about a compromise, Lily?" he said. "We can edit Dee Dee's wedding into channel promotions. That way it's not competing with one of our original series properties. The ceremony can be turned into one-minute vignettes that air over the course of the day."

"Oh, Barry, you're so smart and so creative!" Derrick said, a hint of wickedness in his eye. "You're such a forward thinker, a mighty mind not to be taken for granted."

"I love group decisions," Sharon added, clueless to the irony. "We are family! It's our time to shine!"

Lily nodded approvingly, all her gay chicks in a row. A million emotions crisscrossed Dee Dee's face. Barry, boiling with hatred, dared her with a poisonous stare to disagree with his promo idea. She didn't like being upstaged any more than Barry did; however, she settled ultimately on supporting management's decision.

"Okay," Dee Dee said. "We can do that."

"Barry?" Lily said.

"You bet," he said dryly.

10

Beat Down

HE MINI-VAN CROSSED INTO Massachusetts on a hazy August morning. Lily had appointed me to take the one-day trip as project manager for the shoot. I'd never been to Massachusetts before, but that wasn't why I was excited. Getting out of New York City for a television shoot was a small step up on the corporate ladder. All my life I'd worked as a secretary or had been a stay-at-home mother, so this assignment was a big deal for me.

We arrived in Worcester about noon. It wasn't a small city, but it wasn't New York City, either. We definitely stood out as a motley crew, getting out of the van in front of the town clerk's office: Nigel in tight blue jeans with a purple sash and a white bell-sleeved shirt, Barry in one of his signature rainbow-colored body suits, me in a tight beige number (I had been cast as witness and bridesmaid), Sandy dressed in a black tuxedo, and Dee Dee in a white pantsuit. The couple wore black sneakers and had matching butch haircuts.

Sandy had a super-friendly face with average hazel eyes and flushed white skin. Each time I caught sight of her, she was staring at Dee Dee, pleasantly attentive to whatever Dee Dee was saying or doing. It was the look of love if I'd ever seen one. I tried to imagine explaining the connection between these two women to Leticia, my kids, or one of my brothers. People were people. The emotions were the same. I thought about Clayton and his strong arm around my waist as we walked down the street in Harlem the previous week. I couldn't wait to see him again. Falling in love promised to be a true possibility for me. Being in love was everyone's dream—gay or not.

"Okay, we're here for one hour just to film Dee Dee and Sandy receiving the marriage license, then we're off to the ceremony in Lenox," I said.

"I know, but they already have the license. Why do we have to film them getting a license they already have?" Nigel whined.

"Seriously?" Barry asked, annoyed Nigel was being so ignorant about how television was made. "Are you that dense? There's got to be a story line—get the license, and get married. Can't you wrap your brain around the concept for God's sake!"

"Just asking. Just want to be clear, that's all," Nigel added, satisfied that he'd gotten the best of Barry.

"Nigel, child, c'mon, let's go," I said. "We're wasting valuable time."

"Oh, the project manager has spoken." Nigel used air quotes around my new title.

"Jealousy will get you nowhere, Mr. Marketing Assistant," I said.

"Don't be so sure," he said, strutting the sidewalk like a supermodel.

"He's such a bitch," Barry said to me. "But then again we all are!" He patted me on the behind.

We shuffled into the town clerk's office with a local camera crew in tow and were greeted by friendly locals used to receiving out-of-state same-sex couples by then. They set about making us comfortable, offering instant coffee and store-bought pastries. We set up quickly. Nigel was in charge of hair and make-up. Dee Dee allowed him to powder her face and swipe her lips with a light pink lipstick. Sandy said she didn't want any makeup.

"Just for the cameras, Ms. Thing. At least you won't be all washed out," he said, but Sandy wouldn't let him come near her.

"It's not who I am as a gay woman," she said.

Nigel cut a nasty look at her. There were a thousand comments brewing in his mind. If a ticker tape had scrolled across his forehead it would have read: *A real woman would never leave the house without a little powder and lipstick.* Barry stood in the corner with his adopted crossed-arm stance, nose turned up at the whole thing. Dee Dee stood on an apple box next to Sandy for the shot of a town official handing them the marriage license.

"Action!" the cameraman called out.

A town official handed the couple their license. The women hugged and smiled into the camera lens. We filmed it a few more times for safety. Once we got the shot, there were kisses all around as we piled back into the van, waving goodbye to the locals and hitting the road.

"That was awesome!" Dee Dee bellowed, her voice ricocheting throughout the van's interior. "I know we already had the license, but doing it in front of people and with cameras rolling made it feel so *real*. Like this is really going to happen. We're going to be married!"

Sandy gazed at Dee Dee through Cupid's eyes, shot through with love. Barry navigated the vehicle onto a two-

lane highway. He shifted in the driver's seat, his eyes soft-
ening as he spoke up.

"Can I say something?" he said, his perfectly toned body
erect in the driver's seat.

"You've been so quiet today. We love loud Barry," I
said. "What's up, darling?"

"I know I've been close-mouthed to those of you who
know me and love me." He patted my hand. "It's because
I've been thinking about something," he said.

"Do tell," Nigel said. "We all want to know what the il-
lustrious Barry Trumball has on his mind."

"I want to apologize to Dee Dee and Sandy. I'm realizing now how important this shoot is, not just for you two,
but also for gays everywhere. This is history we're making
today. Two people of the same sex, in love, obtaining a marriage license—this is happening in our lifetime. Think about
that for a second."

It hit us. First off, a gay channel owned by a major company. Second off, we had just filmed two women entering a
municipal building to get a marriage license. A poetic silence
connected us. The van sailed down a country road, and for
a little while we let the impact of what we'd done sink in.
Nigel broke the spell. He tuned the radio and turned up the
volume on the Peter Frampton song, "Do You Feel Like We
Do." We loosened up our serious mood and sang together
as loud and as out of tune as any group of friends on a road
trip would. At a 7-Eleven we celebrated our part in history
by taking pictures in the parking lot, drinking bad coffee
and eating corn muffins.

We headed west toward the Berkshires—a rolling land-
scape of hills, farms, green pastures, and cows. I had re-
searched and found on the Internet an 18th-century
farmhouse that was willing to let us film the ceremony there.

The property turned out to be breathtakingly serene, and as we walked the grounds I thought about Warren, our modest wedding in my mother's living room, and how he had broken my heart by cheating and leaving me for another woman. The last time we spoke he'd threatened to take the children without considering how they'd live without their mother. Never mind how I, in turn, would live without them. Warren didn't think of my welfare at all. In stark contrast, Sandy didn't seem as if she would ever leave Dee Dee. I wanted to find a man who would love me to my very core. Clayton Hicks, and his Billy Dee Williams' smile, popped into my head and a warm rush of calm settled my mind.

The farmstead where the ceremony would take place was nestled in a small valley with a working mill in the distance. A few of us walked the grounds and discussed the logistics for filming the wedding. The afternoon was blessed with blue skies and majestic white clouds. Sunshine reflected off green grass, and a slight breeze was cooling the late August heat. There would be no family or friends, just Dee Dee and Sandy, a justice of the peace, staff from the channel, and the film crew to witness the ceremony.

"My parents don't approve," Dee Dee had said during the drive.

"Mine do, but they're in Nebraska," Sandy had added cheerily.

As I called Lily to report our progress, I thought about my wedding day. We'd both grown up in New Jersey, and no one from our families had ever left the area, so it was indeed a family affair. I couldn't imagine getting married without loved ones around. *But my wedding wasn't a political and social statement, either,* I reminded myself as my boss answered the phone.

"We're at the wedding location," I said. "Everything is going fine."

"Terrific job," Lily said. "I trust you're handling details perfectly. How's Barry?"

"Doing okay," I said honestly. "He has come to terms with the idea. We get how important this is."

"Excellent. I like hearing that. Very good." Lily wanted to move on.

"If anything else goes down, I'll e-mail you. Otherwise, I'll see you in the morning. Oh, and Lily, thanks for trusting me."

"Yes, yes, very good. Call if anything else happens. Have footage in my office first thing, okay?" she said, hanging up before I could say goodbye.

Loud voices were coming from upstairs. I found Dee Dee and Sandy in the bathroom, arguing with Nigel. He had Sandy blocked by the bathtub, wielding a makeup brush near her face. Dee Dee, half the size of Nigel, was tearing at his backside with her tiny hands.

"You fucking *jerk!*" she screamed. "Get off her. Get *off* her! Leave my Sandy *alone!*"

"No, no, no," Sandy whimpered, turning her head from side to side.

"Honey, it's not like I want to make you look like a drag queen who's beat her face into a *Mildred Pierce* molded mask. I just want to add a little powder, that's all," Nigel said.

"*Nigel!*" I shrieked. "What are you *doing?*"

My thunderous voice snapped him back into reality. Sandy's cheeks were flushed blood red. She was as confused as a mouse stuck in a glue trap. Dee Dee was still pounding Nigel's back.

"You *asshole!* You hurt my Sandy. You *hurt* her!" Dee

Dee cried. The volume of her voice almost brought down the walls.

"It's okay," Sandy said, suddenly composed and concerned for Dee Dee's welfare. She placed a gentle hand on her partner's shoulder.

"No, it's not, baby," Dee Dee said, punching Nigel in the arm, but feeling Sandy's touch she was calmed instantly.

"Stop it, you hostile dyke!" Nigel said to Dee Dee. "Any woman worth her salt would want a little blush on her wedding day. What's wrong with you guys? Right, Charlene? Am I right?"

"Did she say she wanted blush, Nigel?" I asked, the voice of reason penetrating the madness. "If she asked for blush, put it on her, but if she's in the corner of the bathroom with both hands up, I would guess she doesn't want any. What do you think? How do you see it?"

He thought about this for a second as he realized he did have Sandy cornered. Dee Dee burst out crying. Sandy pushed past Nigel and cradled her future wife by the shoulders.

"It's okay, honey. We're okay," Sandy said. "He was just trying to help."

"He's ruining the day. He's *ruined* it," Dee Dee sobbed.

"I guess I got out of hand," Nigel admitted, coming out of a deluded state.

"Are you on drugs?" I asked him seriously. "Because you're acting like a crack whore."

"You'd think!" Dee Dee yelled at him.

"Okay, okay, it's over, let's go downstairs," I said, grabbing Nigel by the arm. "I'll send the justice up to talk to you two. You're getting married in less than an hour. This is a dream come true. Let's not forget that."

I manhandled Nigel. "What's wrong with you?"

"I just don't understand why Sandy won't get a little makeup, that's all. It's not normal."

"She wants to go *au naturale*, okay? Just leave it be. Why are you always forcing yourself on people, Nigel?"

"I'm not forcing! I'm just trying to help, Sandy said so herself. I just don't understand why she doesn't want to look pretty. Is that a crime?" he pleaded.

"Nigel, she looks fine," I said, adjusting my hair and dress in a window's reflection.

"You, on the other hand, look great. And I don't mean it in a derogatory way, either," he said, a veiled apology for attacking me at the launch party. It was a moment of intimacy I immediately wanted out of. Thank goodness Barry was walking toward us, because I didn't have any more patience for Nigel.

Was I ignorant to think that there were unspoken rules in the gay world? For myself, I had broken it down in the most basic terms: some gay men were groomed to the point of heyday Hollywood, and some gay women believed adorning themselves contradicted their inner selves. Why was he being so crazy about it?

"Everything is ready," Barry said.

Nigel waited for me to acknowledge his apology, but I couldn't be bothered. Barry locked his arm through mine, and the three of us entered a quaint living room with mint green walls, a carved walnut fireplace, and white crown molding. A gorgeous view of gentle hills, wildflowers, and a creek were visible through four large picture windows. Classical music was playing quietly, and white lilies had been placed on the mantle and windowsills. The film crew was checking angles and lighting. By the time the justice of the peace, a short white woman with tawny brown hair and wire-rimmed glasses, escorted Dee Dee and Sandy into the room, whatever tensions lingering from the makeup fight had disappeared. An aura of true love surrounded the couple. I stood across from Barry, who was the substitute best man, a last-minute decision made in the van. We held the wedding bands. The justice began the ceremony.

The women had written vows for each other. Sandy spoke first. "Nothing will ever get between me and my feelings for you. Never a soaring mountain, a vast blue sea, nor petty laws can change my commitment to love you for the rest of my days. I will honor you always."

While Sandy recited her vows, large tears rolled down Barry's cheeks. Nigel looked bored as the single guest sitting behind the camera crew. As the newlyweds hugged, the sun lowered in the sky, and orange rays of light filled the windows.

11

The Gay Channel

RETURNED TO BROOKLYN. Martel and Tinecia, my
sleeping angels, had made a mess of the apartment,
which looked like a fort built with kitchen chairs and
bed sheets. Leticia and Tonya were curled up on the couch.
The television was tuned to paid programming. I leafed
through unopened mail left for me on the kitchen table—a
bunch of catalogs and supermarket fliers.

One envelope stood out and spiked fear in me. It was a
certified letter from New York Family Court. Tearing it
open, I read a "Modification in Order of Custody" petition
filed by Warren's lawyer. I sat down heavily and re-read the
petition. Warren was filing for full custody of our children
with limited visitation rights for me. The reason? Poor parenting. He really was pursuing that course of action.

The walls of the apartment contracted and expanded
as I felt fear quickly change into a furious rage. He was
often late with child support payments, *and* we had divorced
because of his adulterous behavior and his lifelong commitment as an unemployed lay-about. This was also going to
cost a lot of money, and I was just getting on top of my bills.

Warren was lucky it was late at night, the kids were sleeping, and Leticia and Tonya were across the room, because I wanted to call and lay him out on the floor like the lazy dog he was. The nerve! It took everything not to call him up and curse his lazy-ass ways. I couldn't believe he had the audacity to do this to us! It must be that no-good husband stealer he left us for that put him up to this. No matter— he had gone along with bad advice without a conscience. There was no consideration for the children and their emotional welfare. I could just strangle him for being so selfish. As I ranted in my head about this change in events, my cell phone beeped an incoming text message from Clayton.

"Hope you got home safely. I look forward to seeing you in the office tomorrow. Good night! xx Clayton."

How sweet! Just a little something, something from him made me feel less alone in the world. I couldn't wait to see him either. Kicking off my shoes, I stretched my legs, cramped from the long drive back from Massachusetts and the town car ride from Times Square to Brooklyn. I checked the court date. The hearing in family court wouldn't be for six weeks—first week in October—so I had time to come up with a response to Warren's petition or talk some sense into his bonehead. I savored Clayton's text and put Warren out of my mind for the time being. I had faith that my good intentions as a single parent would prevail over this wickedness Warren was sending our way. Forget him! He wasn't worth another wasted moment. I washed my face, said a prayer, and crawled into a troubled sleep.

In the morning, the children jumped on the bed, welcoming me home. I kissed and hugged them tightly before getting dressed for work. Leticia and Tonya had slipped out earlier that morning. Leticia had left a note saying she was sorry about the petition. I folded up the notice from family court and slipped it into a drawer. Who had time to agonize about such nonsense when I had two kids to get out the door to school?

At the office, tapes of the wedding shoot were on my desk. Lily had yet to arrive. I set about my morning routine—restocking the mini-fridge with bottled water, checking my messages (one from the stalker—just breathing, though), and going through unread e-mails. Lily arrived about 10:30 a.m. She took the tapes and closed the door to her office to view the footage. I heard her oohing and aahing. She liked what she saw. I wanted to ask her if I could manage some future projects as well. I daydreamed about being promoted to a full-time project manager. Derrick, Barry, and a new face—a medium-built brown-skinned man with arched eyebrows—disturbed my trance. The threesome leaned over my desk.

"Girlfriend, we finally have a boyfriend to introduce you to. Meet Troy 'delicious' Dalton. He's the new head of finance for the channel," Derrick said as if presenting me with a gift-wrapped box, his charismatic smile as bright as Mr. Clean's.

Troy had soft, perfectly aligned features like Terrance Trent D'arby's. If he and Halle Berry had had a baby boy, that's what Troy looked like. Fine and as fem as all be.

"Troy, meet Charlene Thomas. She's our resident Jennifer Hudson. Doesn't she look exactly like her? We wanted to call her JH, but the nickname didn't stick. So we just call her girlfriend, honey child, Ms. Thing—the old standbys."

"Hey, girl," Troy said, lengthening the greeting, already bored with the black-people connection. "Nice to meet you."

"You too, Troy."

"Well, we'll leave you two so you guys can get acquainted," Barry said flourishing his fingers and walking off with Derrick. They both had shit eating grins on their faces.

"You want a bottle of water?" I asked, reaching toward the fridge.

"Sure," Troy said as he eyed Lily's door. "How long has she been here?"

"Not too long, about a half hour. She's checking out some footage we shot yesterday. Why?"

"I met her with a friend of mine once, and I want to re-introduce myself. You know my husband? He created *Sex and the Pretty Black Boys*. You know, the new show?"

"Oh yes! Premiering next month. Is that how you got the job here? Through your friend?"

"He's my husband, not just a boyfriend, and no, that is not how I got the job," Troy said, already adopting a condescending tone with me.

"Oh, really. Were—"

"You can't have a problem with that, girlfriend. Not in an office atmosphere like *this*." His lip curled in disdain, totally misreading my response. He was already a handful, and I'd known him for two seconds.

"I was going to ask if you were married in Massachusetts," I said. "We just got back last night from filming a lesbian ceremony there."

His light brown eyes brightened. He had chilled out on his first assessment of what kind of black woman I might be. When he smiled, there were two distinct dimples. I understood. Our community, black people, wasn't very gay-friendly. I had had my doubts about working at the Gay Channel, too. But a job was a job, and now I couldn't be happier.

"No, he's just my husband. We aren't legally married.

Not yet," Troy said.

Lily opened the door, hugged him, and welcomed him to the channel. While they chatted, I left to deliver the marriage tapes to Dee Dee, who would work with an editor to transform the footage into programming vignettes.

Troy was gone when I got back. I popped my head into Lily's office. She waved me inside. "I'm very pleased with how yesterday went, Charlene," she said. "How would you like to help me manage another project?"

"I *loved* working on the shoot yesterday. Yes, what's up?"

"This one will be more challenging," she said, inspecting me for any kind of chink in my armor. I held her gaze steadily, ready to move forward and to make more money in case I had huge bills from family court.

"Lay it on me," I said.

"Kathleen Pendle—you know, from our billboard campaign— well, she's doing a holiday special for the channel. It'll require you to spend a lot of time with her and her staff, preparing the shoot. She's a very powerful and public advocate in the LGBT community, and I need someone levelheaded who can deal with unforeseen problems. Since Dee Dee will be out on maternity leave and another director will have to be called in, I can't think of anyone else to handle this internally. I need someone I can absolutely trust to make this as smooth as possible. Know what I mean?" Lily's worry never surfaced in her expression, but her strong delivery made the point that the project was going to be difficult.

"When do I start?" I said, composed, ignoring the lump in my throat, choosing instead to believe in Providence.

"Not until next month. But there will be some preparations. Malcolm and I are meeting Kathleen today in his

office, and I want to introduce you as the point person for
the project."

"Gladly," I said as a light rain started outside. Strands
of water pearls had soon streaked the windows. The sky
over Times Square changed from overcast to dark gray. I
prayed this wasn't Mother Nature warning me to back out
now.

Lily read my thoughts. "You've worked very hard for
us, so I'm going to raise your salary by five thousand, to
fifty-five grand a year, because there will be extra hours and
a little bit of travel involved. I know you have children. Are
you okay with this? With the pay increase?"

She was like a dignitary, incredibly poised. Her hair was
a spray-starched blunt cut that matched her pressed light
wool suit. There wasn't a hint of sexiness about her, but I
admired her business savvy and her bottomless control. I
felt a sense of possibility in making something out of myself
that I had never felt before. I was first in line for Team Lily.

"Yes. Yes, I am. Thank you, Lily. I'm very thankful
for the raise," I said. And I was—for being knocked down
and getting back up and for my kids. In less than a year I
had had two financial blessings: getting a well-paid job, and
getting a raise at the well-paid job plus a second title of project manager. "I'll call Mimi and tell her to include me on
Malcolm's calendar."

"Good," Lily said, already on to the next thing. She
shuffled some papers and tuned me out. I left, leaving her
door slightly ajar.

A few minutes later, Troy sashayed-parlayed toward my
cubicle with a man built like a bean stock. His midnight-
black skin absorbed all the light in the hallway. It was rich
and dark and flawless. He fastened two black-cat eyes on
me. Quick on the black men's heels were Sharon, Roger, and

Jesse. I dialed Mimi, already feeling the responsibility of two jobs.

"Uh-hum, I'll add you." Mimi warned me in a silky voice not to be late for the four o'clock meeting. When I hung up, everyone was standing around my desk.

"I need to talk to you, Charlene," Jesse pleaded as he draped himself dramatically across the Boo-Hoo ledge.

"Is she in?" Sharon drawled. She had hooked her thumbs into the silver belt buckle. "We need to talk."

"This is my husband, Jerome," Troy butted in. I shook the tall man's hand. He had to be, at a minimum, six foot four inches. "Jerome, baby, this is Charlene Thomas. She works for Lily."

"Jerry, is that you?" Lily called out.

"Yes, Ms. Lily. I'm out here. What're you up to in there? Working hard?" Jerome said with a flick of the wrist, as if I was a gnat. Troy followed him into Lily's office. Sharon and Roger were not happy with second billing. They shared a dissatisfied look.

"Can you put us on her call list?" Roger said, staring into the middle distance because, if he looked at a subordinate, it might devalue his senior management job title.

I smiled at Sharon, who conveyed to Roger that I'd gotten the directive. They walked off talking under their breath about Jerome. "He thinks he's so great."

"Charlene." Jesse stretched an arm out toward me. "Everything's the matter. Help me please."

"Like what, child? What is wrong in your world now?"

"Like *him*," Jesse said, pointing at Lily's closed door. "Of course you've heard about the Kathleen Pendle holiday special?"

"Yes, of course I have," I said, glancing at my computer screen of unread e-mails.

"Guess who's directing?"

"Jesse, get to the point, darling child. I'm pretty busy here."

"Jerome Hammond, that's who. The creator of *Sex and the Pretty Black Boys*. Can you believe I'm being pushed out? First by Dee Dee taking over Kathleen's photo shoot last June, and now by an outsider who doesn't even work in the office! I'm beginning to hate this job! I'm always being overlooked. My ideas get stolen. No one likes my work!"

Music was blasting from Derrick's office down the hall. He had recently switched to Gloria Gaynor's "I Will Survive."

"I'm going to quit," he declared, crossing his thin arms but staring toward the party music and picturing Derrick's movie-star looks.

"Already? The channel has only been on the air for two months—July and August. Give yourself a chance. You know the channel is a huge hit? Lily's on the cover of *She Magazine* next month and has a blurb in *Time*. All my girl-friends can't stop talking about the down-low show. Just chill."

"Well, that's just it," he grimaced. "Nothing is being said about the gays in *my* world."

He had a point, but I couldn't let him spoil the success I was enjoying from getting more money and an added title. Jesse tossed his golden hair and waited for me to comfort him. I didn't have anything to say. All the differences at the channel, diversions really, were already mind-boggling, and none of them seemed to get resolved out in the open. Jesse would just have to go behind the scenes and scare up support for his own agendas.

"Child, please, I can't right now."

"Oh, you too," he said accusingly. "I thought we were

friends, Charlene. We barely have lunch anymore."

"I had lunch with you last week!"

"What about today?"

"I can't, Jesse. I'm still catching up from being out of the office."

"See what I mean? What about your four o'clock coffee break? Let's go to Starbucks together."

"I have a meeting."

Jesse planted hands on his hips, turned on his heel, and said over his shoulder, "I see what kind of person you are now."

I wanted to say, *Jesse, stop being so childish, get off the cross, we need the wood,* but I let him go. Clayton e-mailed, saying he'd visit later in the afternoon, and I still had to decide whether or not to call Warren and ask him what his problem was.

"Charlene, I want to formally introduce you to Jerome Hammond," Lily said, opening the door to her office.

I shook Jerome's hand—a bony oversized mitt that would probably be found on an anorexic grizzly bear, if there ever were such a creature. He sized me up as I smiled up at him, a bit undone by his height. Jerome's legs came up to my shoulders and his Eartha Kitt eyes cast a spine-chilling spell. But the brother could dress. I had to give him major props for wardrobe. The solid dark blue double-breasted suit jacket, accented with brass buttons, was a check plus. His striped shirt was tucked into pencil-thin jeans. What shocked me were his eighteen-inch-long feet, encased in Donald Pliner mandals, leather slip-on sandals for men. I tried hard not to get stuck on his giant toes. They were like hammerheads! Troy snuck out from behind Lily and Jerome, begging our pardons, as he had to get back to work. I noticed for the first time that a bejeweled headband was pulling the curly hair from his striking face. They were quite the fashionable pair.

"Lily said you're going to head up the Kathleen Pendle shoot?" Jerome said.

"Yes, that's right."

"Well, maybe I'll see you at her house this weekend?"

"Oh, I don't know if she'll be there," Lily said nervously. "Malcolm and I are introducing her this afternoon, just to get started. . . Oh, you should come up to sixty, too."

"Oh," he said reevaluating my importance, "maybe not this weekend then. Okay, Ms. Lily, I'll see you upstairs. I'll give Ms. Mimi a call. That's my girl, you know?"

"Nice to meet you," I said, turning toward my ringing phone. I was left alone as I picked up the receiver and recited my standard greeting, all the while hoping I could move into project managing full time and leave assisting people behind.

"Kathleen Pendle called. She won't be coming in to meet Malcolm, but he still wants to see you and Lily. The meeting has moved from four to two. Please let Lily know," Mimi said.

"Will do. Hey, girl, Jerome Hammond might join us," I said.

"Oh!" Mimi declared in a rare moment of exhilaration. "I love that motherfucker."

I STROLLED THE SNOW-WHITE corridor toward Malcolm's office. Lily had sent me ahead while she finished up a conference call with Sharon and Roger. Mimi wasn't at her desk, and, it being 1:59 p.m., I didn't want to be one second late for my first big meeting. Maybe a few minutes alone with Malcolm would be to my advantage or at the very least help me to get over my phobia of him. His door was slightly open. I was about to knock lightly when I heard noises. I peeked through the opening and saw Jerome sitting upright behind the desk, regal as an African king. His head was thrown back, and his eyes were closed. It didn't take a genius to put the smacking noises together with the pleasured expression on his face. Plus, if I wanted to plead ignorant, I couldn't, because Malcolm's feet were sticking out from the left side of the desk. The president of the company was on his knees.

"Yeah, like that, a littler harder," Jerome ordered. "You should get some Botox, Malcolm, it'd be better for you and for me."

I was glued to the door, horrified and intrigued. This was beyond juicy, beyond scandalous—my goodness, beyond anything I had ever witnessed in my whole goddamn life! And I couldn't stop watching!

"C'mon now, turn around. Let me get some of that white ass," Jerome directed.

Malcolm's head appeared where his feet used to be. Jerome tossed one mandal out into the middle of the floor and rose to his full height. Balancing his body on the desk, he raised his knee like he was about to kick Malcolm in the behind. But that's not what happened.

"Hmm, Jerry, stick it in a little harder," Malcolm pleaded. "Wiggle it, yes, like that. Oh, that feels so good."

Jerome's knee bent and straightened, bent and straightened, and bent and straightened. What the hell was he doing? *Oh my God*, I thought, as it dawned on me. He was toe-fucking Malcolm.

"How many of my shows are you going to produce for season two?" Jerome growled.

"You can't make me tell," Malcolm moaned.

"Yes, I can, little man. You want me to put the other

one in there? Keep it up. How many, goddamn it?"

And then a little yelp as Jerome penetrated the little man deeper with his big toe. My mouth was open from New York to Miami just as a manicured hand reached under my arm and closed the door. I turned to meet Mimi's questioning look.

"What are you doing, Charlene?"

"Nothing," I said like a child in trouble.

"Couldn't you have waited by my desk?" she demanded.

"Ah, no, I couldn't, if I wanted to be on time for the meeting," I said, disliking her tone, realizing I had the upper hand because she had left her boss exposed, literally, with a foot up his ass. "If you wanted me to wait in reception, you should have left a note on your desk."

"Do you mind?" She meant for me to follow her back to reception.

I checked my watch. "It's past two," I said. "You said not to be late."

"I know what time it is," she hissed over her shoulder.

"Do you?" I snapped back.

Mimi twirled around in her black designer dress, one spiked heel at an angle. I pointed to Malcolm's closed door and raised an eyebrow. She stamped her foot.

"C'mon, Charlene. You're going to get me in trouble," she said, eyes as big as silver dollars. "You can't tell anyone, please, okay?"

I pursed my lips maybe and followed her as she stomped back to her desk. She pointed to a guest chair for me to sit on. I leaned forward, because I was definitely going to find out what I had just witnessed.

"Does he do that all the time?" I asked.

"Do what?"

"Mimi, don't play. You've got to know what Malcolm is

up to in there."

"He's meeting with Jerome Hammond."

"Meeting is not exactly the word I would use to describe what's happening in his office right now. In his *corporate* office."

"Oh, don't be so fucking naïve, Charlene. Take that good-girl shit back to da hood and get a life."

Oh, I got it: Mimi thought she was better than me because she had gambled on a rich rapper, won a little cash and a big house for her and her baby. Covering up for sexcapades in her boss's office probably had its rewards, too.

"Listen Ms. Sable, don't get fresh with me, okay? I will get ugly up in here. You know I have the goods on you and Malcolm. I'm sure Human Resources would love to hear about what I just saw in there."

Mimi switched gears. She grinned knowingly at me, adjusted her long black fake Indian hair, the volume enhanced by add-on extensions, and replaced the strain in her face with a plastic smile. She reached across the desk as if we were best friends.

"I'm sorry, girl. I'm just stressed. You don't even know how nasty that man is," she whispered.

I knew she was full of shit, but I played along by lightly touching her extended hand to let her know I understood her stress. She thought I hadn't registered—*da* hood—as she resumed a professional disposition. The phone rang a few times. She lied, said Malcolm was out of the office, and kept her back to me as she checked e-mails. All the while I couldn't for the life of me get the image of Jerome with his head thrown back in ecstasy receiving fellatio, a.k.a. *blowjob*, from the top executive who oversaw the channel I worked for. And to beat the band, getting plowed by his big toe—it was too much. I had to stifle the urge not to bust out in

laughter. I couldn't believe how okay I was with the ridicu-
lousness of the situation, though. Now I had the big gossip,
ha, and it felt damn good.

Lily finally appeared a few minutes later. Mimi escorted
us to Malcolm's office. The door was now open. He and
Jerome were sitting on the sofa, having tea and French pastries, dressed impeccably, as if they'd just been discussing
financial reports. I nearly died when Jerome shook my hand
and Malcolm kissed me on both cheeks. I yearned for a hand
sanitizer and a long hot shower knowing where their hands
and feet had been in the last half-hour. The office was sur-
prisingly fresh smelling, a little too fresh, the scent clearly
artificial room freshener. It took all my control not to look
at Jerome's foot, prominently displayed as he had his mile-
long legs crossed and the foot stuck out for all to see.

"Charlene will manage the shoot with Kathleen," Lily
said, settling into the couch cushions.

Malcolm bore his hollow black eyes at me and said to the
space over my head, "That's impressive."

"Thank you," I managed to get out of my mouth,
sounding as normal as any employee grateful for an opportunity.

"Have you done this before?" Jerome asked, looking
down his short, wide nose at me. "I like things very chop-
chop-chop."

"She just did an excellent job on the wedding shoot,"
Lily said calmly, dropping a hint that Jerome shouldn't
question her decisions in front of Malcolm.

"I'll work with you hand in—" I stopped myself. "I'll
work hard to keep everything on schedule."

Jerome nodded, not convinced but careful about offend-
ing Lily. I was sure he was going to be a pain in the ass, but
I didn't want to give up the extra money from my raise or

the better title as project manager. I was a fighter, and if I had to fight this lanky queen, I'd do it. No one was going to hold me back from advancing. I had spent all of my twenties being held back by Warren and his time-wasting bullshit.

"Jerome, you don't have to worry about me," I dared to say.

Lily grinned at me to be quiet. Malcolm wiggled in his seat, from recent exertions or because I'd overstepped some unknown boundary, I couldn't tell. A flash of Malcolm on his knees had impaired my judgment. I'd seen his eyes squeezed together, his head thrusting to and fro like a chicken, as Jerome lorded over him. Back in the moment, I noticed Jerome was giving me the who-do-you-think-you-are throw-down stare that my grandmother used to give my brothers and me when we got smart with her.

"I better not have to worry about you," Jerome said under his breath.

"Okay," Lily said brightly, shifting the mood, "it's all set then. Charlene, I'll see you back downstairs. I'm going to go over some details here, okay?"

"Thanks, everyone," I said in my best white girl voice.

Getting out of there was like being released from a crammed bus in the middle of Calcutta. I took a few deep breaths of lobby air and hauled ass toward the elevator. I ignored Mimi like the fake bitch she was and rode back down to the seventeenth floor.

12

Community Art

SO WE HEARD YOU were invited to Kathleen Pendle's party this weekend," Barry said, leaning over my desk in a black spandex t-shirt, his nipples prominent and taunt through the fabric. His emerald green eyes sparkled with goodwill at my advancement at the Gay Channel. Barry knew my story. He was happy for me. "You've got to tell us all the dish: what the house looks like, what closeted celebrities are there, and oh, whatever else you think of!"

Bringing up the rear and always ready to pick a fight, Nigel pushed his Crisco oil face at me. "She may be married to a blond, but I heard she likes the black girls, so you're a perfect meal for that sloppy 'ho!" Nigel jeered.

"I'm going with my husband, Jerome. We're invited, too," Troy bragged, standing next to Nigel. They were the same height and build, except Troy was adorable and Nigel was not.

"So all the black people get to go, but none of us," Derrick said, adding his two cents. He didn't really care, but why not join in?

"Lily's going and, of course, Malcolm, you haters," I shot back.

"But she's a lesbian, it doesn't count," the gay boys said in unison.

"Who's going to help me dress?" I said.

"I'll do your makeup. I've been dying to bring out your dark brown eyes," Nigel said. "Seductive smoky-gray eye shadow will look good on you."

"You should wear red," Barry said. "Let's go shopping after work."

"I've got to go home to the kids," I said. "But at lunch tomorrow?"

"Okay, lunch time. Saks," Barry said.

"I'll go, too," Derrick said. "You can't show up at that cunt's house wearing *trousers*. You'll blend in with all the other dykes!"

Everyone laughed, including me, even though the joke was cruel.

"Who're you bringing?" Troy said.

"A date. It's a secret."

"Girl or boy?" Nigel winked.

"Boy!"

"Or you could bring Jem. That would fuck everyone up," Nigel laughed. "But don't forget to get his, her, whatever's moustache waxed off."

"Okay, time to get away from my desk, y'all. Playtime is over!"

"Jem should go. Maybe you could get THEY an invitation," Derrick said. "That would confuse those bitches like nothing else." He adjusted a gold cufflink.

"Except if she took a militant black dyke as an escort," Barry said, thinking, then, "Where are all the feminists?"

"Well, there ain't any around here," I said full of attitude.

"You got that straight," Troy said, rolling his eyes at the heavens. "Nary a one."

KATHLEEN PENDLE'S FIVE-BEDROOM duplex had a bi-level living room and wrap around terraces with views of Central Park and midtown Manhattan. It occupied the top two floors of an East 68th Street apartment tower between Park and Madison Avenues. I had only seen these kinds of New York apartments in throwback Hollywood movies. Clayton, my date, held my hand while we sipped champagne. He was as nervous as I was, even though he radiated male confidence, maybe too much, compensating for being the only straight man in the place. He certainly was the finest black man at the party, his only competition being Jerome Hammond and tiny Troy whose junior-size butt cheeks were stuffed inside tight white leather jeans topped off by a furry mohair sweater and riding boots with spurs. Jerome towered over partygoers. He was hard to miss in head-to-toe feathers—boa, cuffs, and pant hems. If Carmine Miranda were alive, she'd thought he'd stolen her outfit. To complete the picture, all Jerome and Troy needed was Barry fanning a palm frond from the side, just like in the down-low video. They purposely stayed across the room from us, thank God. I had had enough attitudes from Jerome for one week.

It certainly was an A-list crowd. Eighty-five percent of the guests were women, some of them very well-known but not out—an actress who had starred as a suburban mom in an '80s sitcom, a black comedian who had acted in a Chris Rock movie years before, an Academy Award actress famous for her low-cut Armani jackets, and a local news anchor. Malcolm and Lily stood with Kathleen Pendle and her wife, receiving guests near a working fireplace. Clayton and I made our way over. The closer we got, the tighter his grasp.

"Don't worry, Clayton, nobody's going to hit on you," I said teasingly under my breath.

"It's not me I'm worried about," he said, leaning against a wall so I could talk to Lily alone.

Kathleen Pendle held my handshake a little longer than I was comfortable with. I managed to slip my fingers out and clasp her wife's hand. My jaw hurt from smiling so hard. I didn't know what else to do: I was nervous.

"Beautiful dress, Charlene," Lily said. "You look very nice tonight."

"The boys in the office helped me."

"Beautiful red."

"God, I haven't worn a dress in a hundred years," Kathleen exclaimed in her Broadway voice. "I'm not sure I could get my fat ass into something so revealing anyway!" She laughed like Santa Claus, holding her belly and throwing her head back, exposing two rows of white teeth. Everyone in the room turned toward her as if she were a magnet. She slapped me on the back. "I hear you're helping with the holiday special."

"Yes. I'll be working with Jerome Hammond on details."

"He's very talented," Malcolm said to no one. He was too busy checking out Clayton standing off to the side, waiting for me. I think Malcolm recognized him from the office, but I couldn't exactly be sure because my observations of Malcolm were clouded by yelps, toe-fucks, and demands for Botox lips. Now the tables were turned. I felt as if I had to save Clayton from Malcolm instead of Clayton saving me.

"Good to have you on board," Kathleen said. "Because Dee Dee's not available, I'll need someone who can stay on top of the director. Sometimes they think the project is about them instead of about me."

Kathleen was in a good mood, but there was a simmering fire in her personality that could erupt at any time. Even though she seemed filled with merriment, hardness prevailed, and it couldn't be suppressed. She had bitched out so many people during her career that, as she got older, it was impossible to mask the meanness. It oozed out of her pores.

"Looking forward to it," I begged off, holding up my empty champagne flute.

"Is that your date?" Lily asked before I could get away.

"Yes. Clayton Hicks."

"From security," Lily said in a low, disapproving way.

"Yes. That's right."

For this, I had to stand my ground. I wasn't going to be thrown off my dating game because of present company. Not only was I a single mother; I was also a single black woman, and Clayton so far had been a gentleman—an interested gentleman who had gladly escorted me to an event full of gay people. I had to give him major extra credits for not being an ignorant homophobe. If not for the future, then for something I very much needed: sex. I joined him with a pleasant backward glance at Lily. I hoped to convey that my private life was none of her business and please don't punish me for it at work. I couldn't read her face; she blended into her tan pantsuit and turned to answer a question Malcolm had asked.

Clayton and I took our refilled champagne glasses up to the top floor. On the last stair he put an arm around my waist and held me close. I smelled his cologne, a woody scent with a hint of Neroli, sensuous and alluring. A gallery of original art led to the wrap-around balconies. We passed display cases of porcelain figurines. Clayton caressed the small of my back. To either side of us were large pink floral oil paintings.

"Your dress is silk, your skin is silk, your voice is silk, and your personality is pure satin," he cooed, the bass in his voice echoed the promise of hot sex. I thought I'd break out into a sweat because his lips were so close to my ear.

"You're sweet, Clayton. You're really sweet for escorting me to this party. I know it can't be easy."

"It don't mean nothing," he said. "Just a work event for you, right. So no big deal for me. Just want to be here, have your back." He tightened his grip.

We took a few steps in silence. A couple of gay men were hunched over a glass display case, pointing at figurines. One of them laughed, grabbed his friend's shoulder, and buried his face in his friend's chest. He wore a silk scarf tied ostentatiously in a frilly bow. The friend was the Clayton lookalike I'd seen at the launch party, and I hadn't been mistaken—the brother looked exactly like my date. My gaze traveled quickly from Clayton to the man down the wide hallway. The resemblance was uncanny.

My mouth was open. "Clayton," slipped from my lips. He was still engrossed in his love-lust stare. He broke eye contact and followed my stunned expression.

"Steven! I'll be goddamned, this is something!" Clayton said excitedly, grabbing my wrist as he progressed toward the man. "Bro, what the hell are you doing here?"

Bro? The man, Steven, flickered between obstinacy and cautiousness before a small smile surfaced on *his* Clayton face. The two men had the same hard body build, except bro had obviously spent more time at the gym; his muscles were lean but very masculine. A pair of slender jeans, and a form-fitting gray dress shirt, easily revealed the outline of six-pack abs and hard, sexy thighs. He also had short dreads that, from a distance, gave the appearance of a groomed haircut just like Clayton's. They were mirror images of one another, except that Steven had a tasteful vanity moustache as well. Clayton didn't waste a moment embracing his brother and holding him at arm's length, clearly moved and joyous.

"I should ask you what you're doing here," Steven said, a bit more relaxed.

Frilly Bow threw his hands up to heaven. "What the hell is going on here?" When neither man answered because of their focus on each other, he looked to me for an answer.

I shrugged. "I have no idea either."

Clayton hugged Steven a second time. "I haven't seen you in a dog's age."

"Steven?" Frilly Bow said. "I thought it was Stefan." He pronounced it stef-*fahn.*

I stood there awkwardly with Frilly Bow asking questions but getting no answers. We were both shocked onlookers, but it wasn't a hard guess that the twins hadn't seen each other in a long time and there was family history overloading the moment between them. Clayton was the first to realize I was still standing next to him. He positioned me in front of his body, placing his hands on my shoulders.

"Steven, this is Charlene Thomas, a very special lady. She works at the Gay Channel. We're here together."

Steven, a.k.a. Stefan, shook my hand politely but then saw something in my face and kissed my hand lightly. He was about an inch shorter than Clayton; however, his disposition was as composed and confident.

"Charlene, this is my baby brother by four minutes," Clayton laughed, amused to reveal an old joke.

Steven chuckled. "Okay, okay, let's not go there."

Frilly Bow had had enough. He stomped the carpeted floor with hands on hips, a poked-out mouth demanding an explanation. "You didn't tell me you had a brother! There're two of you—hottie number one, and hottie number two?" He fanned himself dramatically. "My word."

"Ditto," I said, smiling, relieved to know I wasn't crazy. "So you were at the launch party? I saw you on the dance floor. I thought it was Clayton!"

"You went to the Gay Channel party and didn't invite me?" Frilly Bow asked Steven, who burst out laughing.

"Not in a million years would you see Clayton at a party like that!" He turned to his friend and said, "Child, please, get over it."

"Don't go underestimating me, you hear? I told you about making assumptions back in the day," Clayton said, half-serious.

There were a few beats of silence as the mood shifted.

"How's Momma? The same," Steven said answering his own question.

Clayton lovingly gripped his brother's shoulder. "She's fine. You don't mind if I tell her I saw you."

"Up to you, Clay, up to you." A painful thought flushed Steven's face, but he recovered quickly. "Fucking crazy, right? Did you see this stuff?"

"She has got to be kidding!" Frilly Bow chuckled and snorted, holding his stomach as laughter bubbled in his belly. The bow flopped up and down as his head bobbed with amusement.

"What?" I said, following his pointed finger.

"This," FB insisted, meaning inside the case.

We looked inside. I didn't see anything out of the ordinary, just miniature statuettes and replicas of the paintings on the walls.

"Like I said, fucking crazy, right?" Steven asked.

I looked closer. Those weren't flower porcelains. They were vagina lips, pink labia figurines decorating the inside of the case! I covered my mouth as Clayton and I scanned the images on the walls. Those weren't paintings of flowers; they were paintings of vagina lips, as well as Kathleen's portrait in the style of. . .

"Oh shit, that's Xena the Princess Warrior," Clayton said. "But as—"

"Kathleen Pendle," Frilly Bow declared. "Check it out. Every other painting is of Kathleen as pussy conqueror."

The guy was right. Alternating paintings represented Kathleen Pendle in *Xena: Warrior Princess* motifs. Action paintings—Kathleen as Xena wielding a sword, Kathleen as Xena riding a horse, Kathleen as Xena comforting a wounded and dying warrior—had been hung from ceiling to floor. There had to be fifty paintings of her in that gallery and about fifty more of giant flapping vagina lips. What made the Xena images so funny was the painter's decision not to slim Kathleen down. Buckled and bound in leather warrior garb, Kathleen's fat thighs and sausage-like arms were depicted realistically, without any creative license to beef up or tone the body shape. As outrageous as it was, I had to give it to the big-boned sister—let it all hang out, just as in real life.

"Is she serious?" Frilly Bow said. "Any woman choosing to put her head between Pendle's legs has chosen an abyss!"

"I can't take it. I've got to get out of here," Steven said. "Let's go."

The brothers had a moment between them. Frilly Bow kissed me on both cheeks and headed toward the staircase.

"You know I love you, brother," Clayton said.

"I know, Clay. I love you, too."

"Can we get together sometime? I don't like the silence. Water under the bridge?"

"I think I can do that," Steven said. "I'm sure I can."

They embraced again. Clayton rested his head on Steven's shoulder. When they released each other, Steven had misty eyes. I was very moved. He hugged me lightly and said goodbye.

A couple more people were coming up the stairs as the two guys left. Frilly Bow spread the news of the paintings and porcelain figurines to the unsuspecting guests. A cool breeze blew through open glass doors. Kathleen had so much money she didn't know what to do with it. I wondered what it was like to be so financially loaded. This on my mind, Clayton suggested we get some air. He guided me toward the open doors, the encounter with his twin brother occupying his mind—there were memories creating a distant look in his eyes. I held his arm tightly, so that he knew he wasn't alone. We stepped out onto the balcony.

Central Park was a silhouette of black treetops. Clayton draped his jacket over my shoulders, pulling at the lapels to make sure it fit securely. Even though it was a warm evening and I didn't need a coat, I liked having his scent all around me. We kissed a little and were silly about the grandiosity of the apartment, how on our salaries a place like this was only a fantasy.

"Wow, I can't believe I ran into him," Clayton said, finally ready to talk about Steven.

"That was intense," I said.

"It was. It's been over a year since I've seen him."

"I'm taking a guess here, but your mother doesn't approve of Steven being an out gay man?"

"That's just the tip of the iceberg. Family. A reflecting pond of floating daises or a swimming hole full of sharks."

"What's with the Steven–Stefan name change?"

"Oh, he took off to Amsterdam after two years in college. He lived there most of his twenties. When he got back to New York, it was as if the Atlantic Ocean was still between us," Clayton said gazing out at the view.

"But he lives in town?"

"Yes, in Chelsea. I love him, but we're not close."

"But that can change," I said, seizing his chin and making him look at me. "You don't have to have the relationship on his terms. You can make your own rules."

"I never thought of that," Clayton said, and an intuitive thought lit up his smile. "I can call him and make it happen."

"That's right."

"You." Clayton shook his head, pleased with my company and my advice. "You are a sweet woman."

"Well, you are a sight to behold, and now that I know it's times two, my stars, I barely could keep my eyes off you two stunning black men."

"Think you can sneak out?" he said. "Let me phrase it another way. Think you can pass through that hallway again?"

"Yeah," I said drowsily, ready to strip off my red dress. "Keep your eyes down, though. Kathleen is watching us from all those paintings. The other ones I can't even. . .just don't get seduced."

Outside Kathleen's apartment, we hailed one of the black sedans waiting to drive guests home. The car door hadn't closed before we were lip-locked in the backseat. I was so wet by time we got to his place—a modest apartment building in the Bronx—I was sure moisture had soaked through my clothing. We kicked off our shoes and fell to the floor. Clayton groped at my thighs and breasts. He hiked the dress over my hips. I heard him unzip his pants, and before I could count to ten he had climaxed.

Clayton rolled over on his back, breathing heavily as if he'd just run a marathon. I thought to myself, *Are you fucking kidding?* I was fuming.

"Listen Charlene, that ain't it," he said. "I gotta have a quick release before I can get with you all night."

"What makes you think I want to be with *you* all night long?" I said, pissed and ready to leave.

"Don't be like that. Just give me a minute. I'm going to take care of you."

"You jump me like a teenager and expect me to wait for you to catch your breath? You have got another thing coming, Clayton. I did not come all the way up here to the Bronx to be fucked like a schoolgirl."

"I'm sorry, Charlene. It's an old habit. Let me make it up to you." He stroked my hair.

I pushed his hand away. "Don't be touching my hair! Are you crazy?"

"You ain't got no weave. I like a natural sister," he said, missing the point entirely.

"It's not about that, Clayton. I just don't want you touching me right now, that's all."

He took off all his clothes. I saw his muscular outline in the darkness. He unzipped my dress, draped it over the couch, and led me to his bedroom. Clayton was hard again. I could see his erection against the light of the bedroom window. Wanting to forgive him, I slipped between the sheets. Clayton kissed me tenderly on the lips, the neck, my shoulders and both breasts. He tasted my sex until I convulsed with multiple orgasms. When I thought I'd pass out from the climaxes, he fucked me missionary, doggie style, and twisted sideways until I couldn't see straight. Into the early hours we kissed, talked, laughed, watched television, and fucked again and again. I think we went through a whole box of condoms.

"It's four in the morning. I've got to go home to my kids," I said as I lay in his sturdy black arms. "My neighbor, Leticia, was kind enough to take another night off from her job to watch my kids, so I could go to Kathleen's party. Now I've got to get home. Don't want to take advantage of her, plus I promised I'd take Martel and Tinecia to Prospect Park tomorrow."

"I could hold you all day," he said. "But I understand. I know you've got business to take care of."

"You did take care of me, Clayton," I said by way of apologizing.

"I'm glad you stayed so you could get to know me better."

"I can't wait to get to know you a little more," I said.

I felt Clayton grow hard again, but unfortunately the faces of my children were calling me home. I turned over and kissed him.

"You save that for me later, you hear?" I said.

"I hear you loud and clear."

LETICIA HAD SMOKED ABOUT a pack of cigarettes sitting at the new dining room table set—a purchase that had been part of the plan to refresh my life. The whole apartment stank, and a haze of blue smoke hovered in the air. Her sweet daughter Tonya was sleeping on the couch. Leticia was in my bed. I checked in on my own kids in their bedroom, kissing them on the foreheads and pulling their blankets up a little bit.

"Did you fuck him?" Leticia asked with a wicked glint of curiosity as I undressed in my bedroom. "You've got to tell me all about it."

I told her about the premature ejaculation and how he'd made it up by fucking me within an inch of insanity. We had to cover our mouths so we didn't wake up the children, we were laughing so hard. I emptied full ashtrays and opened a couple of windows.

"So I can't tell you, girl, how appreciative I am that you watched my kids tonight."

"How was the party?"

"Mad-ass apartment off Park Avenue. Two floors, three-sixty balconies, a big fucking fireplace, waiters in black jackets, and town cars for all the guests to get home in. Some crazy artwork, though."

"What! Is she that fucking rich?" Leticia asked.

"She is that fucking rich. Richer than anything I've ever seen in person. You could smell money everywhere." I told her about the closeted celebrity lesbians at the party.

"Shut up," she said. "The six o'clock news lady. I can't believe it!"

"You don't even know. It's a whole other world. And you won't believe who else was there."

"Who, child? Don't tell me Wesley Snipes?"

"No," I said laughing. "Clayton's twin brother!"

"*What?*"

"His twin brother, girl. And he's as fine as Clayton."

"And straight! Let's double date!"

"No, honey, he's gay, but straight up all maleness."

"I've seen some of those honeys in the neighborhood. I just want to grab them and say—just one night. Just give me one night of pure heterosexual lovemaking!"

"Wouldn't you be the lucky one," I said jokingly.

"You know I would."

"All in all, it was a good work event and a great personal

step toward having a steady boyfriend. Praise the Lord."

"Well, you're getting paid and laid, that's all I care about. But you know what's funnier? Otis is acting like a local celebrity. He's telling everyone he's the silhouetted guy from the down-low documentary. He can't stop talking about his fifteen minutes of fame."

"You'd think he'd have some shame."

"You'd think, but he's too stupid to know that, plus he's all paid up on child support. He even had the nerve to ask me on a date."

"After his bottom-feeding whoring? Honey, please."

Leticia was silent.

"No! You didn't!"

"I did," she said.

"When?"

"Two days ago. He came over one morning. I had just gotten home from work. Girl, it had just been too goddamn long. I had to have me some, and he's as good as any."

"Leticia, you can do better than Otis," I said. "He cheated on you, and, might I remind you, it was with another man. . . Not man. *Men.*"

"You're right," she said. "But he is Tonya's daddy, and I did love him when we got married."

I didn't know how to talk any sense into her. I needed a steady man too, but I wouldn't go back to Warren if you paid me all the money in the world. She not only looked guilty, she looked sad. Her light brown skin had a sallow dullness to it. I didn't want to lecture a sad woman.

"Well, try, okay, for me? And if not for me, then for Tonya?"

The door to the kids' room opened. Martel shuffled out in his Spider Man pajamas, rubbing his eyes and yawning. I scooped him up and hugged him tightly.

"You look real pretty, Momma," he said sleepily.

"Thank you, baby, you're my number-one man. I'm glad to be home."

13

Whac-a-Mole

ELL, THE DAY HAD COME. I took the morning off to go before the Honorable Judge Tilton in family court. God was on my side, because she was the same judge from our uncontested custody case the previous year, when Warren and I were finalizing the details of our divorce. The judge was a black woman with a no-nonsense personality who brought the gavel down on the side of common sense. On a side bench sat tired-ass Warren, wearing the same old dark blue track pants and Mets baseball cap. His lawyer sat next to him, a stocky man in a gray suit. I was in a conservative dark gray dress and low-practical heels, and I carried my papers in a neat leather folder. Leticia had lent me a string of pearls. I wasn't going to be outdone; no one was going to take my kids away from me. Not if I could help it. I'd fight to my last breath.

"Hi, Charlene. Ready for this?" My lawyer greeted me with a handshake.

"Yes, I am. Do you think Warren has a chance?" I said, wanting to ease my mind by getting to the point.

"I just got here and found this out: the only difference

is his marital status. He's remarried as of a few days ago."

"Remarried?" The news kicked me in the gut.

"Yes, and so he's using his marital status to leverage the state, saying your children would be better off in a stable two-parent household."

"He's lucky we're in a court of law! I could just go over there and—"

"Well, don't, because we've got to go over some details, okay? Let's take a moment to do that."

We went over questions and answers. I was burning up with anger, but I managed to concentrate on what she was saying. The bailiff called the session to order, and the two attorneys went before Judge Tilton.

Warren Thomas: Seeing him across the room, he sure had changed from the aspiring rapper I had met in 1992. I had just graduated high school a year younger than anyone in my class because of skipping sixth grade. The whole neighborhood had had high hopes for me. "Look at Charlene—always got them books, girl. You go." I never got into any trouble, was always studying, and was always doing the right thing. I enjoyed my A-student reputation and believed my destiny was to get the hell out of Newark and make something of myself.

I had seen him around, mostly near the corner store, hanging out rapping, coming up with beats and rhymes. But one day, early summer, we locked eyes, and I never saw him the same again. All us kids knew one another. We'd grown up together. My mother knew Warren's mother. She managed the laundromat. I lived in 14H, and he lived in 8F. We would meet on the stairway or in the utility room. Warren was the best kisser. Better than Clayton, if I had to be honest with myself.

That first summer passed in a blink as we made out behind bushes, in hallways, and leaning against cars. "I love you, Charlene."

"I love you, too."

We wanted to be together for the rest of our lives. I wanted to be a radio announcer, but my mother insisted I get a nursing degree. "The world will always need nurses," she said. I went to City University and daydreamed in biology classes about Warren. "I've got what it takes, Charlene. Listen to this," he said, breaking into a rap about poverty, abuse, and survival. Being more responsible, younger, and plain stupid, I supported his dreams and aspirations by working nightshifts as a cashier at CVS and on the weekends as a secretary in Newark Hospital. My mother said, "Get your degree, Charlene. That boy ain't no road out of here." I tried but was so in love and so convinced Warren was the one.

My pregnancy coincided with rap changing course from Public Enemy to Vanilla Ice. Warren saw more of the couch then he did the inside of a recording studio. Once Tinecia was born in late 1993, Warren had lost interest in his career and just stayed home. We moved to Brooklyn, where his grandmother had a spare room. He gained weight and could barely get his heavy depressed self from the bedroom to the living room. Then he announced he had gotten a job as a security guard and would be working nights.

Leticia was the one who told me about the affair he was having. She'd been coming home after the night shift and seen Warren on Flatbush Avenue with his hands down the shirt of another woman. I had had enough, and filed for divorce after years of hoping he would recapture his youthful dreams. It was my turn. Next year I'd be thirty years old. My time had finally arrived.

Judge Tilton set a date in January 2005 for us to return

and present our cases. She wanted time to think through
the petition modification and ordered more evidence from
Warren's lawyer of my poor parenting. Warren and I ignored each other waiting for the elevator. The sight of him
made me sick. I would need a healthy dose of church that
weekend to get his poisonous accusations out of my soul, or
I could just strangle him right now, I told myself. I weighed
my options carefully.

Back at the office, the hallways buzzed. Televisions suspended from corner ceilings blared with the news that the
Gay Channel was the most talked about cable network of
the year after only four months on the air. Malcolm walked
the halls and congratulated everyone from interns to assistants, creative directors to vice presidents. Lily had organized an impromptu meeting for the entire staff. To our
surprise, famous faces came to pay tribute to how fabulous
the channel was and how it represented the changing face
of American media.

RuPaul was the emcee. An English actor from the *Lord
of the Rings* films was there with a twinkie—a very young
gentleman with the face of an angel. A well-known financial
adviser told us to "put people first" because that was the secret to true success. It was such a festive atmosphere after
the coldness of the courtroom and the hateful thoughts I
had had of Warren. I ate pastries Jesse had baked over the
weekend.

To celebrate the Gay Channel busting out on the media
scene, the guys invited everyone to an after-work party at
the Gaiety Theatre, across the street from our offices in
Times Square. The notorious male burlesque club had been
slated for demolition, so the gays had thought it significant
to send out the trashy venue with a high salute and a big
bash. It'd been Derrick's idea, which won out again after

Lily paired him with Nigel, to figure out where to continue the celebration after work. Nigel had suggested a defunct bathhouse, but no one had wanted to party in an old toilet. Lily had reluctantly approved Derrick's choice because the location was easy to get to. In the end the two most prominent lesbians at the channel, Lily and Sharon, didn't show up. And once I sat down for the show, I knew exactly why they didn't. Dee Dee was on maternity leave, so that left Jem and me to represent the "other" genders among screaming hallelujahs from horny gay men.

The lights went down, and a spotlight glowed on metallic curtains. In the bull's-eye of the spot, an erect penis poked through the streamers. The place went wild. Guys sweated the short distance to the stage. What a gorgeous piece of human anatomy! My goodness, the young man behind the curtain was blessed beyond Greek God statuesque. Barry jumped up and down like a cheerleader, his shirt twirling overhead and his naked chest muscles working overtime. Most of the spectators had taken off their shirts except older men busy committing the whole show to memory for later fantasy use. Nigel tried to act indifferent, but I could see he wanted the penis owner. Jem was the only person who looked bored. As if in a game of Whac-a-Mole, five more erect penises poked in and out of the silver streamers. Altogether, half a dozen appeared and disappeared to Michael Jackson's "Beat It." I thought everyone would pass out from overexposure.

"Give it up for the sextuplets!" an announcer said.

The curtains parted. Six men in crotch-less leather underwear jumped off platforms and did a supermodel's walk down a small runway that jutted out into the frenzied audience. Money showered the stage. The dancers bent over, butt cheeks to the audience, picking up coins, bills, and phone numbers scrawled on cocktail napkins. Men screeched out for solicitous dance moves.

"Shake it harder!"

"Sit on my face!"

"Love me!"

"Crawl, baby!"

Barry thrashed next to me. At any other time or place, I would have thought he was having epilepsy convulsions. He wrapped his gold lamé jacket around his head like a turban and waved his arms overhead and side to side as if leading an aerobics class. Once the show really got started, the performers on stage, hard bodies with "members" healthy in width and length, delivered the most raunchy sex show ever. It was so outrageous, I nearly forgot about my court appearance earlier in the day. During intermission, we did tequila shots and ate chips in the Snack Room—a tiny reception area where the dancers mingled with audience members who couldn't get enough of the good-looking performers. In my lifetime I'd never imagined myself in that kind of environment. I realized how much I had changed, never mind my assessment of Warren earlier in the day. I was living in the moment and not in the fear of feeling I would be alone for the rest of my life. I now had a little change in the bank, my kids were provided for, we had health insurance, and I had a new man interested in holding my hand *and* pleasuring me beyond my wildest dreams. Barry had insisted I come over to the club for a little while. "Shake off that ex-husband, honey! It's your time to shine!" he had said. I knew it wasn't wise to attend a male burlesque performance after being accused of poor parenting in family court, but, somehow, rebelling against Warren's petition gave me limitless nerve and strength to fight.

The lights dimmed and the announcer came on again to

introduce a solo act, Sultry Sue, to screams of joy from the
audience. Barry whispered, "Sue's been here for twenty-five
years. Can you believe she survived the days of AIDS? All
her friends are dead." From opposite sides of the stage two
dancers swung out on jungle vines, met in the middle, gave
each other a peck on the lips, and swung back as the curtain
parted, revealing a busty transsexual in a butter yellow sequined gown with white feathers sprouting from her head
like a fountain centerpiece in a Busby Berkeley film. Sultry
Sue put a finger to her lips and the audience whispered,
"Shh," in unison. She bumped and grinded to a slow jazz
trumpet as the announcer led the audience in a call and response ritual: "Shh." Bump. "Shh." Grind.

The announcer breathed heavily into the mike, and the
audience breathed heavily, too. Sultry Sue put her finger to
her mouth and the audience went, "Shh," in unison. Barry
elbowed me. His face had lost color, had turned ghost white
as the announcer breathed heavily into the mike. We stiff-
ened at the same time, realizing that the breathing was the
same as the stalker's breathing voicemails on our phones!

Barry leapt over my head and sprinted backstage. Derrick caught my arm as I followed, "What's going on?" but I
couldn't stop because, if Barry reached the stalker first, I'd
no doubt be testifying at a murder trial. I raced behind
stage and found myself in the middle of naked buffed bodies
slick with oil and sweat.

"Hey, missy, you can't be back here," one of them said,
his penis swinging around.

"Where's the announcer? He's about to get his ass
kicked," I said.

"Jesse? Who would hurt that cute thing? He's harmless."

Jesse Nolan! Our Jesse! Sweet Jesse, whom I had gone

out to lunch with a million times! *He* was the stalker? It could be true. He wasn't in the audience, and he hadn't been at the office party, either. This was very bad. Barry was going to pulverize that little shit. I ran after Barry, a glint of his gold turban rounding the corner up ahead. The jazz number continued on the other side of the curtain with the audience going "Shh" and breathing prompts from Jesse off-stage. Then I heard a crash, a thump, a bang, and a scream. The mike fell to the floor. The audience didn't know what to do so they tried to imitate the sound. A collective "!@#$%^&*."

"You fucking asshole! You fucking *asshole*," Barry shrieked.

In a tiny sound booth, I saw Barry choking Jesse. Two naked men tried to drag Barry out by the ankles, but he held onto Jesse's scrawny neck as if he was a starving dinner guest going for the last piece of turkey meat at Thanksgiving.

"I'll fucking *kill* you! How could you *do* this to me?" he screamed.

Jesse's face was blood red. His tongue was protruding from his mouth, but his gelled blond hair remained intact. He kicked and bucked and attempted to push Barry off. Finally the two nude dancers were able to wrench Barry away and pin him down on the floor—any other day, it would have been a dream come true for him—as he screamed bloody murder. I approached Jesse. The disappointment on my face made him ashamed.

"Sorry, Charlene," he said weakly, stroking his neck. "The only way to make it legitimate was to leave messages for Lily, too."

"Why did you *do* it, Jesse? Why would you risk your job?" I asked.

He pointed an accusing index finger at Barry. "He slept with my boyfriend!"

"News flash! Your boyfriend *sucks* in bed!" Barry cried as he was being held down by the wrists and ankles.

"And you *did* steal the idea for the wedding planning show," Jesse said.

"I did not!"

"Yes, you did!"

"How the hell did I steal the idea, asshole?" Barry said.

"I told Derrick, and he told you," Jesse said.

Derrick had told Barry he should develop a show about gay wedding planning. I knew that was true.

Barry stopped writhing on the floor. "*I* didn't know you told Derrick," he said, making the connection. "Why didn't you just come out with it? Why not leave scary freak-a-zoid noises and threats on *his* voicemail?"

"Because," Derrick said, appearing at the scene like a prophesying detective. "You guys can let him go. I'll explain."

"You better!" Barry said.

"Don't let him go! He's crazy!" Jesse said to the naked guys restraining Barry.

"You're crazy!" Barry said. "I'll have you committed."

"Oh, who cares?" Derrick said. "This is so 'T' for tired."

"What, Derrick? What's the explanation?" I demanded.

"My little disco during the day—you know, when I play a song to get everyone pumped up?" Derrick said.

Jesse covered his face. Derrick jutted his chin at Jesse and stuck the tip of his tongue in his cheek. My mouth fell open. Barry stopped writhing on the floor. The music blasting from Derrick's office had been a cover-up all along.

"You all are some nasty boys," I said.

"There go cookies and brownies on Monday morning,"

Barry said. "Your fucking baking days are *over*. I'm going right to H.R. tomorrow."

I threw my hands up in surrender. "Y'all, I have got to go."

On the subway back to my apartment, I made some hard and fast decisions. The first thing I did when I got home was ban Leticia from smoking in the house. The second thing I did was shower. The third thing I did was reach out to Lily Essex and Clayton Hicks to let them know that the stalker had been discovered.

"That's funny," Clayton said. "We had just confirmed it was Jesse Nolan late this afternoon, but he was nowhere to be found in the office."

"I would never have guessed Jesse was responsible for the calls," I said.

"You never know people," Clayton said.

"Aint' that the truth."

"How are you doing after this morning?" he said, switching subjects.

"Confused but ready for the fight."

"You think hanging out in male strip clubs is going to help your case?"

"Probably not, but it's part of the job," I said. "But believe me, if I'm invited again, I'll think twice."

"You ever think about getting a new one?" he said.

"What are you trying to say, Clay? Get a new job?"

"I mean, you are a single mother in a custody battle."

"Ain't no battle yet, just a second court date. My ex doesn't have the best record, you know. Sloth. Adulterer. Cheap ass."

"Don't be defensive. I just wanted to ask you. It seems like working somewhere else might look better to the judge."

"Until you can pay my bills, Mr. Hicks, I wouldn't suggest too much if I were you," I said, irked.

"Okay, okay, you're right. I just thought I'd bring it up."

"Well, you thought wrong."

We were silent for a minute. I was seriously mad. Clayton emitted a little laugh.

"What are you laughing at?" I said. "My situation isn't a laughing matter."

"That's not why I'm laughing."

"Then why?"

"Because you are one independent sister, that's why, and I like that. I like that you have a solid point of view. It's attractive."

I didn't say anything in response, still not in the mood to be sweet-talked by a man who wasn't contributing to my household.

"Clayton, I'm tired. I've had a long day."

"Don't hang up angry," he said kindly. "I don't want us to get off the phone like that."

"I'm not angry, just tired."

"I wish I was there. I'd rub your feet, kiss your hands, and maybe even run you a bubble bath."

"Maybe?"

"Definitely," he said.

"Okay."

"Let me take you out this weekend," he said. "Somewhere special."

"I'd like that, but I think I'm going to stay home with my kids."

"I can take all of you out," he said.

"Really? I have to think that over. It might be too soon for them."

"You let me know," he said. "Whatever you decide is

fine."

"I'll see you in the office tomorrow. I'm not looking forward to what's going to happen to Jesse."

"That young man is in a lot of trouble," Clayton said. "The channel will have to decide how to proceed. Corporate will have a say, too."

"Goodnight, Clayton. I'm sorry I was so. . ."

"You don't have to apologize to me, Charlene Thomas. Just let me know what you want to do, and that's what we'll do."

I thought about Clayton's offer and imagined his smooth brown body next to mine as I drifted off to sleep and put the close on a long day.

14

High Notes

ROUNDING THE CORNER, HEADING toward my desk, I saw clusters of employees surrounding my cubicle. Sharon had her ear to Lily's door, listening to what was going on inside. Nigel met me halfway down the hall. He gently took my hand and looked at me compassionately.

"Nigel, stop it," I said, yanking my hand away.

"I had no idea it was Jess," he said, concern creasing his brow.

"No one did," I said. "What are all these people doing around my desk?"

"Everyone's inside. Jesse, Human Resources, Security, Lily, Malcolm, Barry, and Derrick."

Sharon leaned over the Boo-Hoo bar. "This is awful. What if this gets out to the press?" she said, only concerned with the public image of the channel.

"I'm sure nothing will leak," I said. What a strange question, I thought. Jesse was in her department. Didn't she feel any responsibility?

"I don't know about that. Straight media is always

looking for a way to keep us down," she said, expecting me
to chime in from the black point of view.

"I hear you, Ms. Sharon," Troy said, taking up her position. "That's all they need is news of a deranged gay man
stalking his own place of work."

More employees arrived. Roger Ward cut through subordinates and leaned on the partition between my desk and
the little reception area. He had his back turned so that his
full attention was on Sharon.

"After 9-11, I thought Corporate did background checks
on all employees," he said.

Was his question for me, or an observation concerning
the hiring practices of Gay Channel staff? His personality
was so vague. Come to think of it, he hadn't been at the
burlesque show the night before either.

"Can you believe Malcolm has to be involved in such
trivia?" Sharon said, disgusted. "Like he's got the time to
be dealing with this nonsense."

"Jesse is so inconsiderate and not very bright," Roger
said. "This is the end of his career. No one will ever hire
him again."

"Well, he wasn't doing so well anyway. Dee Dee had to
take over all of his projects because he was so incompetent,"
Sharon said, suddenly Southern-accent free.

"And don't forget Jerome was assigned to direct the
Kathleen Pendle holiday project," Roger said, "because of
how he debauched the photo shoot earlier in the summer.
I'm sure that didn't go over too good. I mean, Jesse is obviously unstable."

"The channel needs an overhaul," Troy said. Ha! He'd
only started the previous month! "Obviously there are some
hiring problems."

I took note. Everyone was glad to throw Jesse right

under the bus without a care. What mattered was Malcolm's schedule and sanitizing the staff. They weren't the ones who'd received the threats!

"We don't want to be seen out here," Roger said, cautioning Sharon. "Charlene, can you let Lily know, if she needs anything, we'll be in our offices?" His back was still to me, so I didn't answer. The brief silence made him turn around. "Can you?"

"Oh, of course," I said. "No problem. I'll e-mail you when the meeting is finished."

The two executives left. Troy and Nigel took their place at the Boo-Hoo ledge. I waved my arms around at the little gathering.

"Can you all go back to your workstations? Security is handling this situation, okay?" There was a collective moan of disappointment, but slowly people made their way down the hallway. Troy and Nigel didn't move. "Y'all can go, too," I said.

"Come on, Charlene," Nigel said.

"Don't you have some marketing initiatives to work on, Nigel? And you, Troy, don't you have some bills to pay in accounting? Y'all need to go back to your departments. This isn't a zoo."

Troy harrumphed at me.

"You're no fun," Nigel squealed. "My other black girlfriends are much more fantabulous than you are."

"Younger, too," Troy said, bitch that he was.

"I could pretend to be your teenage mother and slap you from here to Chelsea. Want to play that game?" I scowled.

Troy understood immediately the tone I was speaking in. I was sure he had heard it many times growing up. All black children had—don't mess, you are about to get a beat down. Troy pursed his lips, flipped his hand at me, and stalked off.

"Don't be afraid to follow your little friend," I said, fed up. Nigel departed reluctantly.

With everyone gone, I heard a muffled voice. The door opened. I stood up as Clayton exited the office and closed the door behind him.

"What's going on?" I whispered.

"Jesse's been fired. The channel and Corporate won't be pressing charges. He's just a disgruntled employee." Clayton looked cool and collected, as if he was used to catching bad guys all day long. "He's making sexual harassment accusations about the head of publicity."

"Derrick Miller," I said.

"Yes, Mr. Miller. That's usually the first thing an employee does when they've been dismissed and want to fight back."

"What happens next?" I said, feeling guilty, knowing that Jesse was telling the truth.

"I'll be escorting Mr. Nolan from the premises."

A washed-out Jesse emerged from Lily's office. He had worn his cutie-pie unicorn shirt over what appeared to be a pajama top. His eyes were glued to the ground as he did the walk of shame down the corridor toward the exit. Clayton held him by the elbow. My lunch buddy looked over his shoulder at me before slipping out the glass doors. A little depressed, I tried to switch gears, thinking it was a good idea to get my game face on before anyone else emerged from Lily's office. The intercom on my phone signaled.

"Yes, Lily, I'll be right in."

The last thing I wanted to do was go into that office, but I smoothed my black pullover sweater and opened the door with a bright morning smile. I almost said, *Hello, everyone,* but instantly caught the mood in the room. A rep-

resentative from Human Resources had the look of an exe-
cutioner. She was wearing a chain-mail-colored skirt suit
and had a molded coif of helmet hair. She cast me a doubt-
ful glance, even though we were both blue-black. This
stopped me short, so I wiped the pleasant grin off my face
and sat down next to Lily on the couch.

"Charlene, we called you in here because we need con-
firmation or denial of charges against Derrick Miller," the
H.R. lady said without taking a moment to introduce herself.

Derrick's drunken tongue-in-cheek confession sprang to
mind. Evidently, Jesse had provided enough detail for his
claim to be substantiated. Barry and I had both been at the
club, and we had both seen and heard Derrick's admission.
Jesse had put his face in his hands. That was as good as saying, "It's true! I did do it every afternoon."

Lily and Malcolm were furious the channel had to jus-
tify clean behavior to Human Resources, although Malcolm
certainly had no just cause for his sourpuss face. He had
"entertained" Jerome in his office not too long before. Lily,
on the other hand, was a straightforward, shoot-from-the-
hip businesswoman and an excellent employee when it came
to office protocol, corporate politics, and the success of the
channel. She nodded in total agreement with the H.R. representative—whatever insight or truth I could provide was
needed just then.

"I joined channel staff at the Gaiety Theatre last
night," I said.

"A strip club, is that right?" the H.R. representative
asked.

"It's a burlesque club."

"But naked men are there, right?"

"What does that have to do with the charges against

Derrick?" Malcolm asked, coming to the rescue. I was surprised he was pulling rank. Usually top executives sided with the personnel office. But he was speaking out as a gay man against a judgmental straight person. Barry and Derrick were impressed by the outburst. I could see gay pride written on their faces. Lily was the only one who was towing the party line. It was every man and woman for himself or herself in this meeting. I would thank God later that I was a quick study.

"You're right, Mr. Drake," the woman said. "I was just trying to establish atmosphere, that's all."

"This isn't a court of law," he said nastily. He spoke to her as if she were a field slave. And she heard it exactly the way I did. She straightened the hem of her skirt to gather her thoughts and returned to questioning me in a more neutral tone of voice.

"Tell us what you know."

"We were celebrating the channel being recognized for its number-one status. Everyone was in a good mood," I said. "We heard Jesse over the PA system. That's how we knew he'd been making the phone calls."

"Was there anything else?"

Collectively, I felt everyone's eyes on me. How had I gotten in that position? I knew my employment record had to be clean, especially if the custody petition turned into anything drawn out. What if my personnel records were subpoenaed? Could Warren's lawyer even do that? I had no idea. Playing it safe was my only option. Along with Sharon, Roger, and everyone else, I made a decision to throw Jesse into the fire. It had to be done.

"Nothing else. We were upset he turned out to be the stalker. Jesse admitted to the calls because of *My Big Fat Fabulous Fantastic Gay Wedding*—a show he said he'd told

Derrick about."

Malcolm stood up and opened the door. "Okay, we're done here—if there's nothing else?"

"Thank you all for your time," the H.R. lady said, frustrated to be derailed but not in a position to challenge the president of the company. She picked up her papers. "Charlene, please call if you remember anything else." She handed me a business card.

"I'll walk out with you," Malcolm said, ensuring that she was leaving the premises and not snooping around for more salacious information. "Lily, we'll talk later."

Derrick and Barry got up to leave, but Lily said, "Stay here. Charlene, can you get the door?"

I desperately wanted to return to my desk. I hadn't performed any sexual acts—why did I have to stay in the room? The phone rang. I jumped to answer it at Lily's desk across the room.

"Lily Essex's office, Charlene speaking. How may I help you?"

"It's Jerome."

"Hi, Jerome," I said, checking if Lily wanted to talk to him.

"Tell him we'll meet at Kathleen's apartment this afternoon," Lily said.

"I heard her," he said, hanging up. No love from Jerome. Working with him on the holiday project was already proving very challenging.

Lily was in the middle of making a point when I joined them in the seating area.

"When were you born, Derrick?"

"1970."

"So you weren't alive for Stonewall, and you weren't old enough to understand Women's Lib, am I right?"

"Yep, I guess so," he said, ready for a lecture.

"But you understand what we have here?" she asked opening her arms, meaning the channel. He nodded. "Good, because if I hear one more thing, whether it's true or not, I will take action. This channel means the world to me and to the LGBT community. We're not a sex shop. The Gay Channel has been given the chance to shine."

"It's our time to shine," Barry said in agreement.

"I'm not dimming anyone's light," Derrick said.

"One more accusation, and you're out. No more music blasting from the office," she said. "Tone it down."

"Jesse's gone, so I won't have to," Derrick mumbled.

"What did you just say?" Lily snapped in a rare moment of losing her cool.

"Nothing. Nothing at all," Derrick said, challenging the lesbian with a twisted little smile.

"Charlene," she said, turning to me. "If the channel has any more celebrations, it'll be your responsibility to find a place that isn't controversial to Corporate. Okay?"

"Okay," I said.

I was so glad to close the door on that episode of drama. Barry slunk back to his office. Derrick waited until we were alone. He leaned on the Boo-Hoo counter.

"Thanks for in there," he said.

"I don't know anything about anything," I said, not looking at him. *Please go away.*

"Oh, I see how it is," he said, storming off.

I put my head on the desk, exhausted. It wasn't even noon yet. I half expected Jesse to come around the corner, but by early afternoon, it was apparent he was gone forever. I ate lunch alone at my desk, thankful for quiet phones and Lily's closed door.

A few hours later, we were in a taxi, going up to Kath-

leen Pendle's duplex apartment to discuss the holiday project. Jerome, overly tall, was waiting for us outside the building as a nervous doorman kept his eye on him.

Kathleen opened the apartment door already shouting
at us in her powerful voice, "I heard about the blowjobs!
Can't you people keep it together down there?"

"I don't know what you're talking about," Lily said innocently.

"It's all over the Internet, honey. Don't front," Jerome
said, breezing into the oversize living room as if it was his
own. "Oh, Ms. Kathleen, the place looks divine. It's so
huge. At the party I saw how spacious it was but without
all those people in here, it's just like a football field. I love
it!"

"Thank you," Kathleen said. "We're getting a giant
Christmas tree tomorrow, even though we're Jewish. It just
makes the place feel festive."

"Oh, and you can do some cinnamon pinecones over here
and bowls of candy canes there," Jerome said, sweeping
around the room. "I just *love* how you live, girl."

"Well, I worked my ass off. Girl from the Bronx," she
said.

"Like Jenny," I joked.

No one laughed.

"From the block," I added for clarification.

Jerome rolled his eyes at me. Lily hadn't moved, she was
obviously still reeling from the news of the Jesse–Derrick
"insider" blowjob being all over the Internet. Jerome continued to rant and rave and kiss Kathleen's ass.

"Has your show launched?" Kathleen said to Jerome.
"With the blowjob blowup, pun intended, it's a perfect com-
panion piece—" she hit Lily on the arm— "to what's really
going on inside the Gay Channel. Hahahahaha."

"Oh, it has launched, honey. *Sex and the Pretty Black Boys* is on after primetime in a terrible timeslot." He had no problem giving Lily a dirty look. "The head of programming, this no-name motherfucker named Roger Ward, put *my* show on at eleven o'clock Friday nights. Can you believe that shit?"

"Who's home on a Friday night at that time?" Kathleen said.

"Not a fucking soul," Jerome complained. "The Gay Channel needs to step up its commitment to good shows!"

Lily wasn't amused. In fact she was totally poker-faced as Kathleen and Jerome bonded over trashing the programming schedule. Kathleen's wife came down the stairs. She had vacant blue eyes like the women in the '70s movie *The Stepford Wives*.

"You all have met my wife," Kathleen said.

"Yes," we said.

"Are you married?" the wife asked Lily.

"No." Lily blushed. The wife asked Jerome if he was married, which gave the director permission to brag about how fabulous Troy was. "He irons my shirts. Can't find a man like that anymore."

"And what about you?" she asked me.

"Divorced."

"Oh. Do you have children?"

"Yes, two. Tinecia's eleven, and Martel is eight."

"Barry told Troy, who told me, about the custody battle," Jerome announced to the room.

"It was just a court appearance. I had to answer a petition. My ex and I share custody right now." Fucking Barry. He was on my get-back list.

"Are you looking to foster them?" Kathleen asked. "Because, if you are, my wife and I might take a gander. We're thinking about being foster parents and maybe adopting."

"What?" I said, sounding just like my mother when I told her I was dropping out of college and marrying Warren at the age of nineteen. Lily put a hand on my shoulder. I shook it off. "No one is going to take *my* kids anywhere, you hear me, Ms. Pendle? No one!"

"Ooh, girl, no, you did not," Jerome said.

Kathleen's face went from an open smile to beet red, as it had when she yelled at Jesse months before. Now Lily was the one suddenly animated. She took Kathleen by the shoulder and led her toward the couch. The wife smiled pleasantly at me, as if she was about to offer tea or coffee.

"Let's talk about the project," Lily said to the star.

Kathleen wasn't about to be appeased in her own home. She turned right around and came within inches of my face. I was surprised when she wrapped her arms around me for a tight bear hug.

"I am so sorry. That was totally insensitive of me," she said in my ear. I said nothing and didn't hug her back. "I want to hear all about what happened in court, if you want to tell me."

"I just want to get on with the project," I said. Lily visibly relaxed. "Forget it, okay?"

"Girl, you are fierce! I wouldn't mess with you if I were your husband. You're going to pee all over that unsuspecting dumb fucker."

"Ex-husband," I reminded Jerome.

"Yes, ma'am," he said.

THE FIRST DAY OF THE HOLIDAY shoot was the first freezing day of the holiday season. We stood outside Radio City Music Hall while Kathleen talked into the camera about holiday cheer and queer events around New York City. No one was happy to be outside. A frigid wind whipped up Sixth Avenue, and an ogling public disrupted several shots by shouting at Kathleen, quoting lines from her feature films and comedy specials. The Gay Channel had rented a double pop-out RV, thirty-six feet long, custom wrapped with the channel's logo and tag line *It's Our Time to Shine!* I huddled inside on the phone, reporting the progress of the shoot to Lily.

"Is she happy?" she asked anxiously.

"For the most part, yes. There's a little tension between her and Jerome."

"Make sure he doesn't out-diva her."

"I'll do my best, Lily. You know how he is."

"Yes, I do. But it's your job to keep the project on track. I have faith in you."

"Oh, but I'm not the problem, so you don't have to be troubled about me," I said.

"Good. Call once you get to your next location."

Our next stop was Lincoln Center. Kathleen would serenade crowds from the plaza where a giant Christmas tree had been assembled the night before. But in the meanwhile, I had ten minutes to get this location wrapped up if we were to maintain our schedule. I looked outside at the grayness of the winter day.

Jerome was wearing a brown mink stole around his neck. The noses of the dead animals lay motionless on his back. To top off this furry extravaganza, he had thought it wise to wear more fur—a Russian hat of silver fox, with earflaps. The hat looked like a giant gray Afro. With his slanted almond eyes and Vaseline lips, he could have been a model gone AWOL from a fashion shoot. I zipped up my parka and slipped on gloves. I had to go outside to see what was going on.

Kathleen was bundled in black wool. She stood by with a curdled look on her face, sipping coffee with a laser-sharp eye on the director. Jerome was adjusting the lens with the cameraman. A hair and makeup person came by to powder Kathleen's forehead. We had roped off a small section of sidewalk adjacent to Radio City Music Hall, a busy corner we could hardly keep clear because of the foot traffic and curious onlookers.

"Kathleen, can we get you anything else?" I asked, rubbing my gloved hands together for warmth.

"You can get me the fuck out of here," she said. "What's taking him so goddamn long? Don't we have the shot? How much bullshit can I talk about the Rockettes?"

Jerome must have heard this. Everyone working the shoot—a total of six people—were within a few feet of one another. But he just kept right on fiddling with the lens and looking through the viewfinder, making sure what he wanted visually was perfect.

"How much longer?" I asked him quietly, coming over to tug on an Ugg.

"As long as it takes, Ms. Thing," he said without looking at me. "Put her in the trailer if she's cold. I don't want to get back to the office and not have exactly what I want in the picture."

"But it's goddamn Radio City Music Hall!" Kathleen yelled theatrically. "How many times do you think every filmmaker and news outfit has shot this goddamn place? You're not Spike Lee! Let's go!"

"You have your art, I have mine," he said calmly, not to be outdone or derailed by her. "I will have want I envision and I will *not* be rushed."

"Jerome, honey," I said as nicely as I could, "we've got to move locations. Lincoln Center expects us in a few minutes. We have a short window of time to shoot the Christmas tree there. We have to move, okay?"

"Nobody's rushing me, okay? Not you. Not Missy over there. Not Lily. No one. I have a vision, and I'm going to work hard to get it."

I took a deep breath. There was nothing I could say to Kathleen to make this better. I concentrated on convincing Jerome it was time to wrap it up and get in the RV. A cop had been inspecting our permit to park on West 49th Street for about an hour. The vehicle not only took up a lot of space, it was a magnet for people. There was a crowd continually circling it, admiring the custom wrap job and peeking into the windows.

"Let me see," I said, about to step up on an apple box to peek through the lens.

To my surprise, Jerome lifted me up. I saw his problem right away. Kathleen was so short that only half the building in the background could be filmed. It did look bad. Jerome was right. He put me down.

"Can you fix it?" I said.

"With a walking shot, yes," he said. "But I'm in no mood to fight with her. If you want to convince Kathleen to walk from half way down the block back to this corner, then we can pan up and get the whole building in one shot."

I approached Kathleen with neutral body language. She was the type of woman who smelled fear a million miles away, and any hint you were scared of her only made things worse. I didn't want her to scream at me because I knew I wouldn't be able to take it.

"Good news," I said to her.

"Better be," she said snidely.

"Jerome is going to put some movement into the shot. The camera will come off the tripod. He'll reposition you about half way down the block. The shot will be a walk-and-talk. You'll come back to this spot here, right where you are now. Then the cameraman will pan up the length of the building and up to the sky. That way it's a clean cut in edit. At Lincoln Center, they'll pan down from the sky like you were magically transported to another location. Sounds good, right?"

"I'm not rehearsing. I'll do it one time. Then I'm leaving. I'm not bending over backwards to get fucked by that faggot."

Jerome mumbled loudly as the camera came off the tripod, "This is the closest I will *ever* come to you."

"I'll eat you alive," she said loudly.

"Come near me, and I'll have you arrested for assault." He walked down the street with the cameraman.

She chased after him, criticizing his lack of potential in bed. "You couldn't fuck your way out a paper bag! You'd be lucky to be with someone like me instead of that mosquito-size boyfriend back at the office."

"Don't be talking about my husband, okay? What about that block of ice you have to cuddle with at home? I don't care how big your house is, at least there's not a North Pole wind every time my husband comes into a room like there is when your wife does."

"How *dare* you insult my wife?" She blew up, her face crimson in the harsh wind as she stood in her new spot, ready to walk and talk about Radio City Music Hall.

"How dare you insult me and my husband?" he whined. "I mean, the nerve! I don't know who you think you are. I don't care how many shows, films, billboards, radio interviews, Broadway stages, or television specials you've been on. No one insults my Troy. I love him. He's my *life*." Jerome was on the verge of tears.

"Well, I love my wife. If it wasn't for her, I wouldn't be where I am today," Kathleen said, equally emotional.

"Then what are we fighting for?" Jerome asked, having lost the thread of the conflict.

Kathleen searched the ground. "I don't know."

They stopped what they were doing. Looking at one another, Kathleen and Jerome busted out laughing, realizing the stress of the holiday season. Jerome flattened the flaps of his fur hat against his cold ears.

"This is so silly," he said. "We're here for one reason and one reason only." He pointed at the RV blaring the Gay Channel tagline. "It's our time to shine."

"For gays and lesbians everywhere!" Kathleen sang out like Ethel Merman.

We got the shot in one take, thank God. And we were on our way.

15

Jockeying for Position

HOLIDAYS AT THE GAY CHANNEL seemed like extra
work on an overblown Hollywood musical, with a
lot of dramatic entrances, song-and-dance numbers, and scandalous side stories. Camps had finally divided.
People lunged at each other's throat, or they benefited from
acquiescing to corporate standards. Roger and Sharon, expert brown-nosers, couldn't be trusted at all. Nigel had felt
their corporate wrath after Jem told Roger how uncomfort-
able it had been helping to decorate the conference room for
Dee Dee's baby shower back in August. Nigel had been
taken out of the loop for attending photo shoots even
though he was the point person for marketing at the channel. I don't know what the vice presidents had said, but his
ship was sinking pretty fast. On the other hand, Derrick
and Barry had their own love fest going on. They were
joined at the hip and as wicked as ever. After Jesse was fired,
they had taken credit for getting rid of "the stalker," repeat-
ing the story with flair about tackling Jesse at the Gaiety
Theatre. Unsuspecting new hires were taken aside and told
the tale of breathing voice mails and incriminating threats.

Derrick even twisted the daily blowjobs received from Jesse into "the stalker" pleading, begging not to be found out. "I told him to pucker up, you little turd, or I'll tell everyone what he'd been up to." Derrick obviously wasn't heeding Lily's warning about gossiping. Malcolm and Lily presented a unified front to the LGBT community and reported great ratings to the corporate board of directors. It became hard to keep track of the lies and the truths.

In the office our figureheads rarely communicated or acknowledged personnel who weren't executives. They even hosted a private holiday party for vice presidents and above at Malcolm's Tribeca loft. I wasn't even invited. This caused a rift among the rank-and-file, who complained about not receiving the coveted holiday gift—an expensive scented candle—from the channel's top bosses. We were gifted key chains and generic holiday cards. Several assistants gave notice and quit, saying the Gay Channel was like working at any old corporate job. The revolving door spun a little harder.

Being the only straight woman at the channel and one of two blacks (Troy and I) in the office, I hadn't picked a camp. In fact, I knew I had special privileges because of my close proximity to Lily and the added responsibility of overseeing high-profile projects. The shoot with Kathleen Pendle had been considered a huge success for the channel. The ratings were good, the press was excellent, and Kathleen had seemed very happy when she had dinner with Lily and Malcolm to talk about future projects. She especially gave me high praise, and I was grateful to her for that.

Work aside, it went without saying that my personal life was definitely divided into camps: mother of two, girlfriend to Clayton, and an ex-wife embroiled in a custody battle. The date to reappear in family court had been set for the

second week in January. Because that was only weeks away,
it was hard not to feel a lot of pressure during the holidays.
Major relief came to me knowing I provided for my kids—
they were going to be spoiled with a lot of gifts this year, all
from my earnings—and falling in love with Clayton Hicks.
He still hadn't met my children, and I had made the decision
that I wouldn't bring a new man into the apartment until I
was sure there was a future between us. Still, it was challenging, because he was so sweet, so caring, so available, and
so patient. My resolve was slowly wearing thin. Luckily, I
hadn't seen Warren since the last court date. His visitation
rights entitled him to every other weekend, and Leticia, my
darling sister girl, dear neighbor, and friend, offered to hand
off Tinecia and Martel, so I wouldn't have to discuss anything, or even pretend there was anything to discuss, with
my ex-husband. My resentment toward him renewed itself
daily. I just wanted to crack his skull open for doing this to
us. A little sigh escaped, and I was immediately sorry, because Nigel pounced, picking up immediately on the anxiety
my thoughts were creating.

"Don't be so tense, Charlene," he said, taking the sigh
as an opportunity to massage my neck.

"Nigel, quit it," I said, slapping his hand away.

"You look tired. I can take care of that, you know." He
slipped into sexual healing, moving his hips around in little
circles.

"Keep dreaming, Nigel. Aren't you in enough trouble
at the office already? You don't want to be messing around
with me, because I'll go to Lily in a second. And child,
please, you couldn't handle me."

"Do you really believe that? I think, secretly, you'd love
to know what it was like to be with someone who's bisexual."

"What! You're crazy if not confused, deluded, and ready for the psycho ward. If I wanted to have that experience, wouldn't I be with a woman and not a man?"

"But I'm androgynous—effeminate, if you will. It would be like being with a woman. Look at my body." He extended his leg. His body stretched long, as if split at the seams.

"Can we stay focused here? Look there's a stuffed dog. Want do you think of that?"

FAO Schwarz on Fifth Avenue brimmed with holiday shoppers. *Hannah Montana* music blared from the speakers. It was a kids' disco in there. The decoration celebrated every candy color known to man. This place was the exact opposite of toy stores in my neighborhood. Not much was priced for an average worker as I checked out shelves packed with toys, but I wasn't there for my holiday shopping. The channel was participating in a corporate toy drive, and psycho bunny and I were shopping for a toy that would best represent the gays. Lily had made it clear to me that the Wow Factor, meaning size, was what she had in mind. The package had to be an eye-catcher under the tree in the lobby. Having grown up in the projects, the idea of a giant panda bear or a six-foot giraffe hogging up an underprivileged child's room struck me sideways, as completely out of touch with what struggling families needed. But I was armed with a corporate credit card. I had been told there was no cap on cost.

"Oh, it's so cute and cuddly," Nigel said, dragging Clifford the Big Red dog off its perch. It was over three feet high. "Don't you think it sends a message if the stuffed animal is beyond grand?"

"I guess. Is there something bigger?" I asked, looking around. There was a giant gorilla, but I didn't think that was appropriate because I assumed the kids receiving free toys were probably already traumatized enough.

"Like that," Nigel said hopping over to a life-size pony. "Little Johnny will feel like he can escape his dire circumstances, just leave it all behind! Throw off the rags and come out of his sad life!" He mounted the toy.

"Nigel, get off the pony before we get kicked out of here. Why does everything turn into sex for you? Pull it together. This is a family store."

"You're such a prude," he said dabbing his overactive t-zone. "Just remember that we're here to bring happiness into kids' lives."

"I remember why we're here. You're the one who seems to be off his medication."

"Can we get the pony? Please?"

The toy was huge, and it certainly would make a "gay" channel impression under the corporate tree. "I think you're right about this one," I said.

We hailed a taxi. The pony, a giant red bow around its neck, went in the trunk. I had also purchased Jumbo Gordy Bear and stocking-stuffer gifts. JGB settled into the back-seat between Nigel and me. Lily and Sharon met us in the lobby. Lily clapped as we entered.

"Wow, good job, good *job*, kids!" she exclaimed. Today she had worn an A-line pleated wool skirt. It was weird. I liked the pantsuits better.

"They seem like boy toys," Sharon said under her breath. "Girls like dolls, not horses and bears."

"It's a pony," Nigel said. "And every girl wants a pony."

A pony had been the farthest thing from my mind in Newark, New Jersey, but I kept my mouth shut. Let the white people argue over nonsense. Sharon helped me with the smaller packages.

"I did get some dolls. They're wrapped up inside these bags."

"I may be gay, but I loved dolls growing up. Especially the ones with beautiful blond hair," she said. "Didn't you?"

"I loved the Jackson Five," I said.

"I loved Marcia on *The Brady Bunch*. I wanted to make out with her," she said, not acknowledging my J5 comment.

"I wanted Michael to come and save me. Every time he sang, 'Look over your shoulder, and I'll be there,' I thought for sure he would be standing in the door of the living room with that frayed suede vest on and funky patchwork hat. I loved me some Michael Jackson."

Lily came over after directing Nigel where to place the pony. The stuffed animal's delighted face and round happy eyes peered out from the front of the tree. Lily patted me on the back as Sharon closed in so that Nigel was stranded outside the circle.

"Charlene, you are too good!" Lily said. "The stuffed animals make the right impression. Malcolm's going to love them. And getting smaller gifts was very smart."

"I'll put the other ones under the tree, too," Nigel said, bopping up and down behind Sharon. It would take more than someone's backside to freeze Nigel out. The lesbians left us in the lobby.

"Why do you have to act so stupid, Nigel?" I asked.

"Fuck those dykes," he said—one snap up, one snap down. "I know everyone in this city. I could have another job like that. Roger," he sneered with deep disdain, "he'll ruin this channel. People are quitting because of him. He's so fucking straight-laced. He should just go work for IBM."

"You better put that forked tongue back in your mouth," I said.

He picked up Jumbo Gordy Bear and aggressively

shoved it under the Christmas tree. "I think the bear should be riding the pony," Nigel said.

"That's not appropriate for the lobby," I said, rolling my eyes. "I'm going upstairs. You're getting on my nerves."

"Appropriate. That's a stupid word when it comes to us. What's appropriate about being gay?" he said, following me to the elevators.

Upstairs, I got away from Nigel as soon as we walked through reception. He was still babbling, but I had tuned him out. A welcome sight was Clayton coming around the corner. His electric smile lit up every pulse in my body. We walked to my cubicle together.

"You know, I'm still hoping to spend the holidays with you."

"Let's wait, Clayton. The kids know something's up with their daddy. I mean, I do have to give him some gratitude. He has had the good grace not to introduce them to his new wife. I don't know how they'll take it. The divorce was really hard on them. As a husband, he was no-good, but he's their father and they love him."

"I'm from a divorced family. Kids get over it," he said.

"Why are you rushing me, Clayton?"

"Come on, girl, you know I like you. It's been almost six months. I just want to make you happy, and I know part of that will be making your kids happy."

"You cannot be this good. There's got to be something wrong with you," I laughed, taking off my coat and hanging it on the hook by the window. Lily was on the phone. Her door was closed. I was glad, because she didn't approve of my relationship with the head of security, but she also didn't get to choose my life partners.

He gave me a knowing look and whispered, "You know my one flaw."

"Honey, you better get away from my desk before I start protesting or laughing out loud. Go on, get!"

"I ain't done with you, Ms. Thomas," he said, strolling off. "Not done at all."

Nigel came out of nowhere. "So. . ."

"So what?" I set hard eyes on him. He was under my skin now. "Why're you sneaking around over here?"

"So that's who you're messing around with—the security guard? He's caught my eye before. I wish I was there to watch."

Just as he said those last words Lily's door opened.

"Watch what?" she said.

With two hands on my hips, I waited for Nigel to squirm his way out of that one. A glossy layer of fresh sweat broke out of his clogged oily pores. Lily was no fool. She knew he was harassing me.

"Watch *what?*" she repeated as Malcolm appeared in the doorway. Oh, so Lily hadn't been on the phone but in a meeting with the president. He checked out Nigel with sly eyes.

Malcolm said, "Come up to sixty later. We'll finish up there." He ignored me on the way out.

The three of us were silent until he was out of listening range. I rested an elbow on the ledge of my cubicle, finally using it for my own boo-hoo. Nigel seemed to have shrunk a few inches. He was suddenly struck dumb. Then the worst thing happened—Clayton returned. His blackness tipped the dynamic on its head. Nigel shrank into the carpet from overexposure, and Lily became a bundle a nerves—too much maleness, too much testosterone.

"Checking in," he said to Lily. "Making sure everything is fine."

"Yes," Lily said.

"Thank you, Mr. Hicks," I said.

I didn't care what these people thought about him. He was my man, my rich and chocolaty man. Nigel slunk off, slithering down the hall like a garden snake. Clayton's hand-held radio crackled, calling him to another floor. He coolly begged our pardon and left without giving me a private signal. Good thing, too, because Lily was searching the radar for any unusual signs. She wasn't done yet.

"What was going on out here?" she said.

Truth be told, I didn't want to tell her what Nigel had said. I didn't want the Gay Channel nor my boss up in my business. It was lucky for Nigel because he had crossed the line with me, and I promised myself to burn his sassy ass.

"Nigel was being a little, well, like Nigel," I said.

"Did he say something to you?" she asked protectively.

"Yes, but I can handle it."

"You sure?"

"Yes."

"I've heard about him," she said, glazing over with some closed-door gossip about Nigel. Snapping out of it, she handed me a manila folder with a report in it to type up. "Bring this up to Malcolm's office when you're done."

As soon as Lily was back in her office, I called Nigel. He didn't pick up, and I didn't leave a message. But I knew he was at his cubicle, staring at the phone, scared as shit. I put him on my get-back list, too. He had messed with the wrong black woman this time. I was done playing.

MIMI SABLE SAT AT HER DESK in a Santa Claus-red Chanel business suit. She had had a fresh weave installed recently. Black silky hair cascaded to her shoulder in a soft flip. Her light brown skin was without a blemish or a pore. Accenting the suit was a red headband and red lipstick. She looked like a million dollars. I wasn't to be outdone, though. Mimi's conservative attire was head-to-toe tasteful, but my outfit was form fitting, sexy, and trendy-chic. I crossed the marble floor in black spandex leggings, black leather spike-heel boots, and a wool merino white-on-white sweater. A long silver chain swung from side-to-side. I matched her smile tooth for tooth, giving her the typed report Lily had asked me to deliver.

"How you doing, Ms. Sable?" I asked.

"Oh, just fine, Charlene. Ready for the holidays?" she said nicely.

"I am. Are you celebrating at home?"

"Not this year. I'll be taking my baby girl to London to do some shopping. Have you ever been? It's the most brilliant city."

"I hope one day soon," I said.

"One day soon," she said, already disengaging from our conversation.

"Well, have a good one," I said.

"Hmm."

It was awkward waiting for the elevator. The silence on the floor was made colder by the sanitized walls and floors. A welcome distraction were footsteps somewhere down the hallway, I had never seen any of the other executives on that floor. I wondered who it might be.

"Hold that," someone said as the elevators doors opened. I turned to see Nigel flapping his arms, coming from Malcolm Drake's office. He had to be the dumbest person in the world. I held the doors as he jumped inside the elevator car.

"So we meet again," he said, obviously in a jolly mood as the doors slid together.

I didn't even waste time as I slapped him twice with an

open palm across his face. "You listen to me, motherfucker. If you *ever* fuck with me again, I will have your ass."

Stunned for just a second, Nigel shook the stars from his eyes, then pushed me back. "You don't know who you're talking to!"

"You think I don't know what you were doing up in Malcolm's office? Let's just call it job security and not the other phrase with the word 'job' in it," I said. "I know! Believe me I know." I pushed him as hard as I could. He slammed into the opposite wall, the wind knocked out of him. I came down on him like a boulder, grabbing his shoulders and standing him up for another slap in the face. "I will kick your ass from here to Wall Street. I don't care what *security* you think you have at the channel!"

Nigel turned into a devil child. He growled. His face mashed up into a Halloween mask. When he spoke, his voice was octaves lower as if a possessed man.

"I'll tell Malcolm!"

Oh please, I thought to myself. That's not a good enough power move. I had the upper hand, and I knew it when I said calmly, "I'll pull the race card on you, hustler."

The look on his face was priceless. Whatever was fueling him left his body. He couldn't find the words for a comeback. I had him pinned.

"And don't think I won't," I added just in case he'd misunderstood me.

The elevator doors opened on the seventeenth floor. Barry and Derrick were waiting to take it down. I smoothed my hair and straightened my sweater. Nigel waved a little hello to the boys.

"What's wrong with you two?" Barry said, fluttering his ladylike hands.

Derrick sniffed the elevator cab and pulled at his collar.

"It's hot in here. What were you two doing?"

"Yeah, what?" Barry added as he took a good look at Nigel, "You're as red and sweaty as a dewy-fresh tomato."

Nigel tried to appear nonchalant but only succeeded in frowning. His face was melting, sort of sliding off the bone. I shrugged mysteriously. The elevator doors closed with Derrick and Barry inspecting it for clues. Nigel and I went in opposite directions. Things were getting malicious up in there. Either he was going to back down, or I was going to show these people what kind of neighborhood I really came from.

16

Don't Mess

ERRICK, THIS IS FABULOUS, HONEY! I can't believe the turnout. You've outdone yourself. Everybody is here!" I said as we entered Bryant Park. Final week of the year, the weather was ice-cold and every gay man within fifty miles was decked out in soft wools and flowing cashmeres. Arm-in-arm, Derrick and I headed toward the ice-skating rink.

"It's the best publicity stunt ever, don't you think? I mean, what a perfect way for the channel to end the year—hosting a free day of ice skating in the middle of New York City! Everybody in the world will be here or will regret not being here once they've heard about it on the news." He opened his arms wide and twirled around. "I fucking rock the house, sister!"

"Go on with your bad self, you crazy man. You really have put the 'G' in Gay today. Ain't nobody got nothing on you. Can't nobody say a thing to you, Your Majesty of Gay Media." I bowed low like a courtier.

"I'm hot," he said touching his chest with his index finger. "Ssss-sizzle and sassy."

"Omigod, omigod," Troy said, running up to us, squealing and pointing at one of the Jumbo Trons. "This is beyond, beyond fabulous. I love the huge screens, Derrick. Jerome is giving an interview underneath his, and he's mobbed with fans. This is the best day of our lives. A dream come true for me and my husband!"

"Well, you can kiss my ass later, when all the bills come in for payment," Derrick said, hugging Troy and me.

Bryant Park was packed—hordes of people from all walks of life had descended upon the event. Tourists had flooded the area. The Jumbo Trons, erected at corner entrances to the park, were showing our top rated shows—*Sex and the Pretty Black Boys, My Big Fat Fabulous Fantastic Gay Wedding, Out of the Closet and into Life,* and *World Gay Travel.* I couldn't believe all the publicity—local media reported from the scene, and the mayor had given a short speech that morning. DJ Tootie Toots spun hip-hop, house, techno, and upbeat country tunes that blasted from giant speakers as skaters circled the rink. The channel had a few closeted Scott Hamilton types as well. Barry ruled center rink with dazzling figure eights, and Nigel leapt into the air like Dorothy Hamill. Derrick, Troy, and I put on our skates and glided around the parameter of the rink.

"Look at that prick," Derrick said about Nigel. "You heard about what he told Malcolm, right? Trying to get in on planning this event with me. I wish Nigel would just drop dead. He's such a skank. He's still using my name to get into parties around town. Can you believe that?"

"Unfortunately, I can," I said. "I'm sick of him, too."

"Really?" said Troy. "I like him. He's funny. He ain't got no sense, but he's hilarious. He could use a good facial cleanser, though, and an astringent would help. The oil slick T-zone is not attractive. He should stop drinking that English tea."

"You won't think he's so funny when you find out he's jerking Jerome off," Derrick said knowingly.

"*What?*" Troy said, skating to a stop. A spray of shaved ice wet a woman's face. She laughed at the frolic and clung to her girlfriend for support.

"I'm fucking with you," Derrick laughed. "But you never know. He's a clever, sneaky person. Keep an eye on him."

Nigel did a split-leap on the other side of the rink and stuck the landing perfectly. Troy's mouth hung open as if the wind had been knocked out of his lungs. I was bent over cracking up.

"He got you, he got you good," I said to Troy. "You don't know what to believe right now."

"Is it true or not?" Troy said, ashen, although worry did nothing to alter the cuteness of his sweetheart lips. Troy's honey-brown skin was accented by a pumpkin orange scarf knotted just so and a short-waisted camel pea coat. His soft wavy brown hair framed his adorable face, and his large brown eyes made a person want to squeeze him with loving, reassuring hugs.

"I don't know," Derrick said. "Maybe. Maybe not."

Troy skated off toward the *Sex and the Pretty Boys* Jumbo Tron to either confront Jerome or cock block any potential interaction between his man and Nigel.

"You're bad," I said.

"Am I?" Derrick said wickedly. "These bitches think monogamy is a possibility between gay men. I think not!" he said, sailing away on his blades. "I think not!" he yelled to the blue sky.

I skated behind him, but he was too fast, and I quickly lost sight of him. On the platform where the announcements would take place, I saw a bunch of co-workers setting up. I glided off the rink and sat on a bench to remove my skates so that I could join them.

Someone sat very close to me as I was untying my laces. I slipped my skate off and sat up to meet Clayton's twin brother, Steven a.k.a. Stefan.

"Oh, hey, Stefan. How are you?"

"Charlene, right?" he said, sounding just like his brother.

"Yes, that's right. How're you?" I said, smiling, glad to be gazing into his Clayton eyes. He smelled good, too. Not like his brother, but like a man who knows his body chemistry and exactly what cologne to wear.

"Good! This is amazing," he said. "I love the channel. It's profound seeing images on the big screen reflecting who I am. I love it."

"Thanks. There're a lot of dedicated people working at the channel to make it a success."

Clayton's brother put his possessions in a locker. A blond man with an equally exercised body slipped an arm around Steven's waist and handed over a pair of skates. This was the guy I had seen dancing with him at the launch party. They pecked a hello kiss.

"Charlene, this is my boyfriend William. William, this is Charlene."

"I date his twin brother," I blurted out.

"So this must be odd," William said, teasingly palming Steven's hard butt cheek.

"I can't tell you how much," I laughed. "But I love seeing you both here. I'll have to let Clay know. He'll be sorry to have missed you."

Steven slipped into thought, gazing at the ground. "He's a good man."

Yes, he is, I thought, but nodded instead of saying it.

"We've been talking on the phone," he said.

"Maybe we can all get together sometime," I said, more out of politeness because I could tell this was very painful for Steven.

To my surprise he agreed as he tied up his skates. William winked at me, the signal that we should help the brothers reunite. Felt like a plan.

"Well, guys, I've got to do a little work," I said, indicating the stage on the other side of the park. I hugged Steven and William. Just as I was walking away from them, Nigel appeared magically. Typical.

"Your man is on my team now!" he said gleefully, beaming a predatory smirk at Clayton's brother, completely clueless to our past encounter in the elevator.

"Yeah, that's it. Go get him, tiger," I said in a bored voice. "I'm sure he can't wait to talk to you."

"Seriously!" he said.

I grimaced.

Nigel duck-walked on his blades a few steps and studied Steven a bit closer.

"He's got a twin?" he said.

"First astute observation you've had the entire time I've known you."

"Wow, that's hot!" he said, returning to the ice, no doubt to follow Steven and William around.

Staff from the channel gathered on the large platform overlooking the rink. Malcolm was at the mike, thanking the crowd for coming down and celebrating the channel. Lily stood by his side, gazing out into the crowd. She was easy to dismiss as some kind of faithful pet to Malcolm's master-of-his-domain persona, but I knew better. A few employees had tears in their eyes as the unbelievable reality of what the channel had achieved dawned on us. I could feel

the electricity in the air. Taking the job at the Gay Channel
had been one of the best decisions I'd ever made in my life.
A wave of unencumbered freedom overcame me. Gone was
the worrying about Warren and the custody battle and the
depression I had felt a year before about the divorce and job-
hunting. A spirited inspiration took hold of the celebration
as we all belted out in unison the Diana Ross classic:

"*I'm coming out. I want the world to know. Got to let it
show. There's a new me coming. And I just had to live. And
I wanna give. I'm completely positive. I think this time
around. I am gonna do it. Like you never do it. Like you
never knew it. Ooh, I'll make it through.*"

A 6'5" Diana Ross drag queen emerged from offstage.
Giant wind machines fanned her Seabiscuit weave and
fluffed the layers of her red chiffon evening gown in a
makeshift breeze. She drifted dreamily a few inches off the
stage floor like a jellyfish in shallow water. A roar went up
from the audience, and waving arms reached for the fabu-
lousness happening on stage. The show kicked into gear as
the sky fell dark in the late afternoon and a countdown clock
was unveiled revealing 188 days until Gay Pride on June 26,
the following year. I had heard about the countdown clock
from Derrick. He had coordinated arrangements for it to
be erected in Times Square for the next six months. The
channel was negotiating with the mayor's office a total
takeover of Broadway and Seventh Avenue on Gay Pride
Day and if discussions succeeded then it promised to be the
gayest day ever!

"Come on! Get to partying, people!" Kathleen Pendle
had taken took over the microphone; her full-bodied delivery
blanketed the audience. "It's time to show some love! No
one is allowed to leave until they've skated around at least
one time! Don't forget, there's free hot chocolate for the

kids, and hot toddies for you alcoholics!" She pumped a plump fist in the air as her Nordic wife stepped side to side at half beats behind her. Staffers danced around the drag queen; Malcolm and Lily gazed upon us like proud parents. Sharon and Roger surveyed personnel like the thought police, but no one cared about protocol that day. Even Jem was in on the action up on the platform. He/she/it/ they/both/neutral operated the giant fan, aiming the air currents at Diana Ross with a steady hand so that the hair and dress were always in motion.

It was getting time for me to leave. Leticia hadn't been able to watch the kids that night, so I couldn't stay and hang out with my co-workers while they got drunk out of their minds. But I was okay with that. The release from personal dramas and some professional ones in the last year stayed with me as I rode the train back to Brooklyn.

I came up from the subway into the crisp winter air. It was good to be home. I loved Brooklyn and its multitude of brown and black faces. Along Flatbush Avenue, a Christmas tree vendor was doing a brisk business, and there were holiday decorations inside of every storefront. I turned down my street and admired neighbors who had strung lights in the windows and had nativity scenes in their small front yards. I knew the kids were home decorating our tree, and I wanted to join them and help out.

Then I saw them: Warren *and* his new wife. Were my good intentions always going to be tested? Perhaps fate had other plans? Maybe my newfound freedom from anxiety was a hoax and could be knocked right out of my system at anytime? His wife was wearing a garish ankle-length fur coat, probably raccoon or subway rat. For a split second I thought about ducking behind a bush, but this was *my* home, *my* street, and *my* life. I wasn't going to let Warren and his brand-new hussy ruin my glorious day. He had stolen enough time from me for one life. Victim-hood was a thing of the past, so I stuck my chin way out and held my head high while walking straight at them. When he saw me coming up like that, it was obvious my inner strength intimidated him. The wife, on the other hand, thought it a good idea to cast me a nasty look. I had yet to be formally introduced to her and already she was throwing stones? *Oh. No. She. Didn't. How tired*, I thought. That bitch could have Warren, no-good lazy man. She could be my guest and work double-time for his sloth. I was the reinvented black single mother who had no idea what was going to come out of my mouth. Would I be graceful? A lady? Dignified? Respectful of Christ and this holy time of year? Hell no.

"And just what may I ask are you doing on my block?"

"Don't you be talking to my husband like that, bitch! I'll kick your black ass. You think you're so cute in your long coat. Trying to be elegant, acting like a white lady on the Upper East Side. Please. I mean who do you think you are?" Warren's hussy rotated her wigged-out head around on her globular shoulders. She was a mighty big girl, well over six feet, with gold rings on her manly hands, fake eyelashes, and a husky voice. Jem immediately came to mind. Was Warren's wife a transgender?

"In that raggedy coat? You're going to talk to me like that in that Salvation Army getup? I don't think so, 'ho trash man-stealer. What you need to do is throw that thing in the incinerator where it belongs."

"You shut up, Charlene," Warren said, not too convincingly, his youthful body now suffering beneath a beer belly and the ubiquitous tracksuit.

"She can have you, Warren. You soul-sucker. I gave you too many years of my life, and for what? Nothing! You amounted to nothing but a lump on the couch. The best thing you ever did for me was to walk out the door and into the arms of this, this, this. . ."

"This what?" the woman said, head thrust forward like a wrecking ball.

"This dragged-out, over-the-hill, done-been-through-every man-at-the-bar *whore!*"

"Will y'all take it somewhere else?" a neighbor yelled out the window. "We're trying to eat dinner."

"You're lucky there're witnesses," the woman said contemptuously. "Otherwise, I'd take you down to the ground."

"Oh, please. Warren, I can't believe you're going to present this woman as the future stepmother of our children. You have surely and completely lost the plot. I'm beyond disappointed in you."

"They're my kids, too!" he wailed, a helpless shriek that caught me up short.

I shook my head. "You are one sorry person. What did I ever see in you?"

"What did he ever see in *you?*" the hussy said. "He must have been blind."

"Maybe so, Mrs. Second-in-line Thomas, but one thing is for sure: He's certainly blind now. Get out of my way."

I pushed past them with all my might, expecting his wife to pull my hair or shove me from behind, but nothing happened. They muttered obscenities under their breath, but that was the end of it. By time I got to my building, I had regained most of my composure, but I had a pool of sweat under my arms and in the small of my back. Opening the door, I saw Tinecia, Martel, and Tonya working together to string lights around a barely decorated Christmas tree.

"Mommy!" Martel said, running over and slamming into

my body for hug. "I missed you today. How are you? Hi, Momma. Hi!"

I pressed my face into his sweet-smelling skin and held back tears. "I'm fine, baby boy. Momma is doing just fine."

"Daddy came by. He gave us gifts from Santa Claus," Tinecia said, trying to sound grown up, but I could tell she was upset. So Warren had already introduced the children to his new wife. He was the most selfish parent ever.

"Did he introduce you to his friend?" I said, facing my little girl.

She searched the floor, a bit thrown off. "Yes. She's ugly, mom. And her breath stinks."

"And mean," Tonya said in a rare moment of speaking up. "She said our tree was scrawny."

"God can't help how he makes people," I said, completely contradicting my behavior of ten minutes before. "Everyone has to move on, including us."

Leticia came out of the back room, twisting her bushy hair into a makeshift bun. "Hey, girl," she said, glancing at the kids.

"They told me Warren was here. I ran into him on the street," I said.

"He just dropped by. I didn't know what to do," she said, her face screwed up.

"It's not your problem. Don't worry about it. Thanks for watching them. How are you?"

"My Christmas gift to you is, I've been smoke-free for two days!" Leticia said with a wide smile.

I hugged her tightly. "Good for you, girl. I'm so glad for you! And us!" I winked at the kids. "Let's live a long life, everybody!"

"Here's to a long life!" Leticia said, wrapping a scarf around her head.

"You got that straight," I said, plugging in the lights, and staring at our tree.

"It's pretty," Martel said, delighted.

"I'll make everybody hot chocolate, okay?"

The kids jumped up and down. Leticia put on her coat to leave for work. I walked her to the door.

"You did right letting their father in."

"I felt so bad, but he was right on the stoop. Martel was so excited at the sight of him," she said.

I kissed my best friend on both cheeks. "The right thing will happen. It always does."

17

Hands Down

YES, YOUR HONOR." I was standing before Judge Tilton, answering basic questions about my lifestyle, income, and childcare.

"And there's someone there when the children get home from school?"

"My neighbor Leticia Smith and I share parenting. She works nights. I take care of her child, Tonya, and she cares for my two kids until I get home from work."

"What about after-work functions? What happens then? The plaintiff has raised a very good question."

My lawyer had warned me Warren would bring this up, but I was ready with the truth. "Leticia makes herself available."

"She doesn't go to her job, so she can watch your kids?" the judge asked accusingly. How could I explain the thousands of dollars Otis had gotten from the down-low interview? "Her job is more flexible than mine is. I pay her for babysitting when that happens," I lied.

"What about when she wants a day off from watching your children? Do you take the day off?"

"She's never asked me to," I said.

Judge Tilton shuffled papers around. She took her glasses off and stared at me for several long seconds. I held my breath and dug my toes into the floor.

"What kind of work do you do?"

"I'm an executive assistant and project manager at a television channel. It's a cable network, actually."

"Where?"

"The Gay Channel."

She didn't react. I felt the air leave the courtroom. People's reactions and judgments were so unpredictable. Could this really be a strike against me? It wasn't as if I hadn't lived with discrimination my whole life, it's just that oppression was oppression. I lived in New York City, for goodness sake! If there was ever a liberal and open-minded place, this was it, unless I wanted to leave the country. I couldn't think of anyplace else in the world that was more fabulous than Manhattan or Planet Brooklyn. The judge reordered some more papers and called the bailiff over. She whispered something to him and then returned her judicial gaze to me.

"I see you provide for the children—a good salary, and health care and basic needs. A single mother raised me, and I know it can be hard, but it appears you have worked out a system with your neighbor, Ms. Smith. But that's not what the petition is about. Your former husband believes he and his second wife can provide a more stable environment for Tinecia and Martel even though their financials are not as solid as yours. Their concern is your place of work, the influence it might have on the children. Mr. Thomas here believes it poses a negative effect on them. How do you respond to that?"

"Well, your honor, because you're asking, I'll tell you honestly—I haven't told my children where I work. They don't much care what I do so long as there's food on the table, clothes on their back, Nintendo games for Martel, *Teen Nick* for Tinecia, and Leticia on the couch when they get home. They each get five dollars a week for helping to wash the dishes, take out the trash, clean their rooms, and polish the furniture on the weekends. They're well-behaved, good kids who are disciplined and cared for by me."

"It's true. Children require full attention from adults and guardians," she said. "But in light of the petition, I do want to know what you're going to tell your children about what you do for work."

"I'll tell them the truth," I said, swallowing. Why was this tripping me up? "That I'm an executive assistant and project manager at a television channel."

"But not the nature of your work?"

"The nature of my work is television, ma'am."

"Do you believe in gay rights?" she said.

I did. I had to. How could I not? It wasn't a matter of sexual orientation, it was a matter of humanity. I had been called the N-word. I had been denied opportunities because of my dark skin and nappy hair. I had been subject to disparaging glances from blonds and thin-lipped men. I couldn't shop at the Gap or Banana Republic because of my brick-house behind. Who was I to deny someone his or her or *They* rights to choose love?

"I believe people should have the right to live the kind of lifestyle they want to, so long it's not hurting anyone."

"So you'll tell your children it's alright to be gay," she said.

"I'll discuss it with them," I said. Now she was getting too personal, and I didn't like it. "Some subjects aren't black and white, cut and dry. But if I have to answer yes or no, then I'll have to answer yes."

"Fair enough," she said. "You can sit down. Now I'd like to ask Mr. Thomas a few questions."

I didn't make eye contact with Warren as he replaced me in front of the judge. His second wife, dressed in lilac velour stretch pants with matching hoodie jacket, rolled her eyes at me. Luckily Judge Tilton saw her do it and gave the second Mrs. Thomas a look that only a black woman could give when she doesn't like someone's attitude.

"You were good," my lawyer said, pleased.

"I'm gonna try not to cry, but I'm a nervous wreck. What if she gives my kids to that woman?"

My lawyer placed her hand on my mine and squeezed. My mind suddenly went blank with panic. I thought I would pass out right there, but I forced myself to focus.

"Mr. Thomas, I see here you pay child support, but sometimes you're late with payments. Nonetheless, you are consistent."

"That's right," he said with hands clasped behind his back. He seemed like a stranger to me. I knew every inch of his body, every intonation of his voice, his snore, the way his short Afro was lopsided in the morning, and how long it took him to eat breakfast, yet he had nothing to do with my life today except he was my babies' daddy. I had spent years with this man, but that time in my life seemed like another time in space. I quieted my thinking.

"You filed this petition just before marrying the former Miss Pam Corbin, feeling the new union would provide a more stable home for the children in question?"

"Yes. We got to talking about the children."

The judge picked up a piece of paper and read it with her glasses at arms' length. I gripped the seat, because I knew what was coming, but I didn't know if it was enough to stop this nonsense. I heard Pam shift her weight on the wooden bench.

"Sir, is this correct? You're on public assistance, and so is your wife?"

"I'm going to find out about a new job later this week," he said. I had heard that one a thousand times. Warren didn't like to work. If there was anything I was sure of, it was that—the man's ambition had gone by the wayside too long ago to be recaptured. He hadn't cashed a year's worth of paychecks in a long time.

"Do you think honestly that being on welfare is more stable than what your ex-wife, Charlene Thomas, can provide as a single parent?"

"Yes, ma'am, I do. I don't want her bringing no faggots up in the apartment to meet my kids. The best thing is to take them out of that environment. It's unsafe!"

"Hmm-mmm," I heard Pam say. "Okay? It's a den of sin. Even Judge Judy would agree with us."

"Sir, please don't use derogatory language in my courtroom, and Mrs. Thomas, please, no outburst from the floor, or I'll have you removed from court. Now, sir, you did hear Charlene Thomas say she hasn't told the kids where she works?"

"I did. But that don't mean eventually those people won't be coming over."

"Careful," she said to him. "We will keep this clean, sir."

"Sorry. Maybe I don't know how to explain myself, and that's alright. My point is, I want a home for my children without all that." Warren waved his arms around like he was clearing out skunk smells.

"Point made and taken," the judge said, already looking down at her desk. "I'll have a ruling in about an hour. I'll see the attorneys in my chambers. That's all for now." She banged the gavel and left by a side door. The attorneys followed.

I sat alone. Warren did his pimp walk back to the bench and put an arm around Pam. He grumbled. I felt him looking over at me. I ignored the urge to see if that was true. Behind me, the courtroom door opened. I heard familiar voices. When I turned around, I saw Leticia, Tinecia, Martel, and Tonya shuffle in. My heart swelled, and a fresh tear rolled down my cheek.

"What are y'all doing here?" Warren barked, standing up abruptly.

Tinecia said evenly, "Hi, Daddy." Teachers said she was such a hard child to read, so composed and sure of herself, but I knew she was just putting on a show, wanting to make sure I was okay. Martel was engrossed in a portable video game. A bomb could go off, and he wouldn't hear it. He sat close to his sister and didn't acknowledge his father or me. Tonya, precious thing, sat with her hands in her lap, waiting to be told what to do next.

"You're trying to manipulate the proceedings, Charlene!" Warren shouted. "Leticia, did she tell you to come here?"

The bailiff swung through the wooden gate that separated the judge's bench from the courtroom floor. "I'm going to have to ask you to lower your voice or take it outside."

Warren backed down. Leticia sat next to me and ignored him altogether. Pam tried to get the kids' attention by smiling and making clucking sounds but neither one of them paid her any mind. I didn't think it was a good idea that they were there, but I was so happy to see them.

"The kids wanted to come down, so I thought I'd let the judge see how much they *don't* want to go live with their father," she whispered. "They were worried. Well, Tinecia was worried. As you can see Martel is playing one of his games."

"They shouldn't be here, but I'm glad you came. I'll give them a hug, but can you take them into the hallway until this is done? The judge said it'd take about an hour."

Tinecia came over, rustling in her new goose-down winter coat. She had on her navy blue mittens. I gathered her up in my arms.

"It's okay, Tinecia. The judge will do the right thing. Leticia is going to take you and your brother outside. I'll join you shortly, okay?"

"I don't want to live with Daddy and his new wife, Momma. Don't make me," she said in a baby's voice.

"Go on, now," I said. "Take care of your brother."

Leticia took the kids out. Tinecia hung a pitiful look over her shoulder as the door closed. Warren leaned over his wife and shook his index finger at me. I cut my eyes at him, enjoying his frustration and grateful for the kids' support.

"You're going to lose, girl. The judge knows what kind of people you hang out with. Children shouldn't be around that kind of trash," Warren said, pissed.

"You should talk, Warren. Tracksuits in court? Honestly, take a good look at your life."

He rose slightly from his seat, he was so mad. "You're so uppity. That's what I don't like about you and never did like about you. Uppity. Always thinking you're better than everybody else."

"Uppity to you is *taking responsibility* to me!" I said. "At least I know how to take care of business. What do you take care of, Warren? Other people's paychecks?"

"I'm trying, Charlene! You never did believe in me. I need a woman who believes in me," he said pointing at his chest. "My woman needs to support the dreams of her man."

"Good luck with that," I said to Pam. "What goes around comes around."

"What's that supposed to mean?" Pam said, rotating her neck around like Linda Blair in *The Exorcist*. She was good at the neck movements. This was the second time I had noticed how much practice she had declaring her point by dislocating a vertebra or two from the top of her spinal column.

I laughed. "Oh, honey, you'll see. That dent on the couch—I know it too well—will only get deeper over time."

"I will come over there and turn you out," Pam said, rising heavily from the wooden bench, the lavender valor hoodie bunching up over her stomach fat.

"Do that! Yes, do that, because the judge would really appreciate what kind of stability you're offering *my* children. Please. Educate the court on the virtues of your parenting skills. Have you ever raised children, Pam? It's not a part-time job. Oh, but you wouldn't know that, because you don't have any kind of job."

Pam was up and almost to my side of the courtroom when the attorneys entered from the judge's chambers. Warren's lawyer took her by the arm and led her back.

"The Honorable Judge Donna Tilton," the bailiff announced.

Judge Tilton followed Pam with her eyes until Warren's wife was safely seated. The judge was carrying a sheaf of papers under one arm. Her mouth was set in a grimace, but she appeared to be "judging," so I couldn't really tell what her verdict was. I had a good feeling, although I was scared. I just knew the right thing would happen, that the outcome would favor the best for the children. I believed in the system. Judge Tilton banged her gavel and set her gaze upon us.

"I have reached a decision in this case," she said. "Mr. Thomas, I believe that you have the best of intentions for your children. Filing the petition to overturn full custody by your former wife has been reviewed and taken into serious consideration." She switched her dark eyes to mine. "Ms. Thomas, you have substantially proven that you're a responsible and fit parent who provides for her children by working hard and covering all the basics needed for proper childcare. Therefore, it is my decision—" I held my breath— "to honor the original judgment in this case. The children shall stay with Ms. Charlene Thomas, with continued visitation rights for their father. I urge you both to discuss and come to an agreement about the nature of Ms. Thomas' work and how to communicate this to the children. Court adjourned." The gavel banged once, loudly.

I hugged my lawyer.

"All rise," the bailiff said as Judge Tilton left through the side door.

"*What?*" I heard Warren say. "Is that bitch serious? I can't have my kids? This is outrageous. Charlene works with the devil's children, doesn't she understand that?"

"Baby, don't you lose sleep," Pam said. "We'll fight. Let's get ourselves together, and then we'll come back here and take what's ours."

There wasn't a chance in hell of that, I thought. Out in the hallway Leticia was waiting anxiously. When Tinecia saw the smile on my face, she ran into my arms. Emotions overtook me, and I sobbed while pulling her in closer. Martel hopped down from his chair and came over.

"It's okay, Mommy," he said, patting my head.

Warren and Pam emerged from the courtroom. I didn't want to fight in front of the kids, but I was ready to if they said anything to me. Warren looked disgusted. He couldn't

even bring himself to come over to the children—selfish as
ever, today, and always. Pam thought it wise to say out
loud, "Don't worry, Tinecia and Martel, your new mommy
and your daddy will get you some day."

Tinecia started, trembling in my arms before composing
herself like the little lady that she was. "I don't think so,"
she said. "We're staying with our mother."

"See how she teaches them?" Warren said, stomping off,
playing the mobile victim that he was. "Uppity. Just like I
said before."

My lawyer slipped on her coat. "Congratulations, Charlene. The judge weighed all the options, but I think she was
always on your side."

"Honey, you never know, though. Do you? These things
can go either way. Thank you so much."

"We'll be in touch," she said, checking her watch. "I
have another case in two hours. See you, kids."

Leticia held Tonya's hand. The proceedings had kicked
up reflections of her marital woes. Otis had vowed to get
help for his down-low problems, but she had just found out
he was still addicted to sex with other straight men. I put
an arm around her and thanked her for being a good friend.
The five of us—two single mothers, and three kids—walked
out into the winter sunshine. As we descended the steps of
the courthouse, Kathleen Pendle and her wife were getting
out of a black sedan. She spotted me right away.

"Charlene! Was the court date today? Are those your
children? Hey, kids! My God, they're beautiful. Hey, little
man, what's that you got there? A video game? Who's
this?" she asked, glancing at Leticia.

"My neighbor, my best friend, and sometimes my rock,"
I joked.

"You're the cartoon lady," Tinecia said with stars in her

eyes. She recognized Kathleen from a children's movie. Martel jumped up and down, excited, because he had recognized the star from the DVD we owned at home.

"That's right!" Kathleen boomed at Tinecia. "I am the stone-age lady. You saw my movie?"

Tinecia nodded, barely able to get another word out of her mouth because she was vibrating with delight.

"You've got good taste, kid," Kathleen said, cupping Tinecia's chin.

"Mommy," Tinecia said, hugging my waist and burying her head into my side.

"She loves that movie," I said to Kathleen. "I think she's watched it about forty-five times."

"Good! I have a bunch of toys and stuff in storage. I'll have some sent to the office for them, okay?" Kathleen hollered. "And for you, too," she said to shy Tonya whose head had shrunk into her coat like a turtle's into its shell.

"What are you doing here?" I said.

"Adoption crap. Have to finish up some paperwork." She elbowed me and laughed loudly. "Remember the foster kid thing, huh? What was I thinking?"

"The judge ruled in my favor," I said, relieved.

"Of course she did," Kathleen said. "You're responsible, and you kick ass." Her wife smiled at me and tugged at Kathleen's coat sleeve. "We've gotta go."

"Well, if you get Judge Tilton, she's pretty fair."

"Donna? Oh, yeah, of course, we girls go way back." Kathleen winked at me and slapped my back as she continued up the stairs. "See you at the office!"

I put two and two together: Donna Tilton was gay. Oh, my God. What goes around certainly does come around. Just as I thought.

18

Next Steps

"HEY, CHARLENE—" CLAYTON'S BARITONE voice was full of anxiety— "one of your co-workers just asked me when I was going to make a proper woman out of you." He approached my cubicle in long, even strides. "Has that guy told the whole damn floor?"

"You're talking about Nigel. Oh, yes, honey, I'm sure he has. He was the worst person to figure out we were involved. I'm sorry, baby, but people were bound to find out one way or another. We're too sweet on each other."

"But this is my job," he said, bugging out.

"Mine too, Clayton. Don't pay attention to Nigel. I don't like people up in my business no more than you do."

"Agreed, but it's a little different with me, because I work for the corporate office. You work for one of the channels. I could get into a lot of trouble. Corporate is stricter about these things."

"What thing or things are you referring to? Two people met and decided to take it a step further. What's the big deal? I like being with you."

"I don't know about this. Us. I don't want to lose my

job. I can't lose my job. I've been here a long time. I'm
fully vested in my pension and 401K. There's no way I'd
make the same kind of money here as I would somewhere
else."

"Hold up, hold up! Is there something you want to say,
because you're acting kind of funny to me," I said.

"I don't keep secrets, if that's what you mean."

"What the hell are you talking about? Secrets! You
think I'm keeping secrets?"

"Okay. Let me just tell you the truth. I've met someone
else, Charlene. That's what I'm talking about. I don't have
to sneak around or wait to meet her kids. She wants me now,
not in a few months when she thinks I'm worthy to be introduced to folks in her life."

"You need a reality check, Clayton, because I didn't pur-
sue you. You were the one giving me the happy-as-hell-to-
see-you glad-eye. Not the other way around, okay? You
need to learn one more thing about me, too, mister. I'm not
desperate for a man up in my life. I can take care of myself.
And you're right, I will take my time before you or anyone
else meets my children. Nobody is going to force me to live
by his clock."

I was sweating bullets. My mind was a cluttered mess.
I felt like I had scored a goal for the sisters, too. Single
mothers, unite! You can live a full and abundant life without some man dictating what you're supposed to do and how
you're to do it. My grandmother married three times, but
in the end it was her pension she lived off in old age. My
mother was a reluctant single mother after my father was
killed. She held down several jobs to support her baby girl
and three boys, and she managed without public assistance,
determined to teach us that hard work pays off. I am my
mother's daughter! I thrust my head forward and glared at

Clayton with all the strength my female heritage allowed. He bared his white teeth into a beautiful smile, threw his head back, and laughed.

"You are my woman. Yes, you are! Indeed it's the truth. Ms. Charlene Thomas. Mine. All mine. I wouldn't have it any other way."

Placing both hands on my hips, he knew straight up I wanted an explanation.

"Don't you know?" he said, wiping a tear from his eye. "April Fool's Day!"

Oh, my God. Months before, Jesse had hung a silver-mirrored disco ball over my cubicle. I jumped up on my desktop, yanked it down, and threw it at Clayton. He ducked, still laughing. The nerve! Mirrored pieces showered to the floor. Thank God Lily was traveling with Malcolm on the West Coast. I was relieved, but at the same time I wanted to kick his black ass for scaring the crap out of me.

"Got you good, baby, now didn't I?" he said, coming around the desk to scoop me up in his muscular arms. "You should've seen the look on your face, girl! It was priceless!"

"Get off me! How're you going to do something so mean to me?" I struggled to break free but his laughter was infectious, and before I knew it I was laughing, too. "So there's no other woman?"

"Come on? Are you kidding? I've got the best woman right here in my arms," he said, nibbling at my neck. He made me feel so good. I knew it was wrong to be so demonstrative in the office. Up until now I'd been the prize example of a good employee. But that day, I didn't care. The joke made me feel closer to him.

"Oh, what's this?" Nigel asked, coming around the corner, inquisitive as a weasel. "Busted right in the act of sexual harassment. Mr. Hicks, does your superior know about this behavior of yours? I'm sure he'd be interested in your actions here on the seventeenth floor. Aren't you supposed to be protecting us? Isn't that the job of the security detail?" Nigel pursed his lips and pushed a lick of hair off his forehead. He had a fresh outbreak of skin irritations; pink nubs dotted his face.

"Dude, didn't I tell you to stay out of my business," Clayton said, releasing me. "Now get."

"Get? Isn't that what you say to a dog? Get. Get out of here. Go get that. Here, girl, come and get it." Nigel posed. He wasn't going to be told what to do by a security guard. Even though Clayton was the head of the department, I could see that Nigel had no respect.

"Don't play." Clayton was rounding the desk like a locomotive.

"Clayton, you know Nigel's special, right? He doesn't know any other way to be," I said, hoping my man would give Nigel the butt-whipping he had coming.

"Just saying, just checking." Nigel shrugged. "I'll motor along so you two can get back to hetero lovemaking. Such a unique state of being around these parts." He slithered off down the hall.

"There's always one, isn't there?" Clayton said, shaking his head. "Always that one person in the office who everyone hates but who never gets fired."

"Oh, I hear you," I said. "I just don't think he cares. But forget about him. What are you doing coming over here and scaring me like that? Clayton Hicks, you missed out on an acting career. Your delivery, honey, you looked as serious as a heart attack."

"I should have been an actor. I would've given Denzel

a run for his big money," he said leaning on the Boo-Hoo counter. His brown eyes wanted to eat me up. I wanted to be eaten up. I could have made love to him right there on the carpet.

"Baby, when are we getting together again?" I said.

"Tonight, right? You still on for that?" he said.

"I'll be on you, if that's what you mean."

"That's what I mean. You can be on top. Then I can be on top. We'll be democratic about it, because you are your own woman. Is that fine with you? I'm all yours, baby—just tell me what you want."

"I want *you*."

"That's all I needed to hear. About six o'clock? I'll come by then, okay?"

"You don't want to meet outside like always?" I said.

"Only if you want to."

"Not anymore," I said. "Let's take it to another level. You want to take me home?"

"That's what I'm talking about," he said, playfully pulling an imaginary trigger with his forefinger. "I gotta go. See you later today."

"Bye, baby."

I watched him stroll away from my desk. I just wanted him in my bed. Those strong fingers would be digging into my waist, holding me in place while he took possession of every part of my body. His lips would be on my nipples, aggressive and greedy. Whispering in my ear. I checked the clock: only seven more hours.

"Charlene! I'm back! Let's have lunch today!" It was Dee Dee. She looked as rested as any new mother could be. She waved a handful of photographs over her head before spreading them out on the Boo-Hoo counter. "Look, it's Jethro! He's so friggin' cute, isn't he?"

Jethro was cute. He resembled a baby Elmer Fudd giggling in the picture with a white-and-blue onesie on. I flipped through the images, remembering Tinecia and Martel as newborns. The happiness and helplessness in their faces—their tiny hands and feet and the adoring delight from having their stomachs rubbed. I loved babies.

"Dee Dee, he's beautiful! You and Sandy must be so happy."

"We are!" Dee Dee said possessed by maternal instincts. "We are the happiest we've ever been."

"Well, girl, I sure have to give it to you—getting married, having a baby, helping to launch the Gay Channel. That's a lot in one year."

"Right? I feel like I haven't stopped. That's why I took two extra months off. There was no way I was leaving this little sugar plum at home in the middle of winter. Forget that."

"You did the right thing."

"How are things here? I can't believe what I heard about Jesse."

"I know, right? He turned out to be deranged. He was such a sweetie pie. I miss him sometimes, but I don't miss the phone calls. That was straight-up crazy shit."

"I wanna see the countdown clock. Come with?"

"Fabulous, let's go."

Outside in the cool spring morning, Dee Dee and I crossed the concrete triangle separating Broadway and Seventh Avenue. Beyond the statue of Father Duffy at West Forty-sixth Street, the famous Coca-Cola sign topped a column of neon signs at the north end of Times Square. At the very bottom, atop the doorway of Olive Garden, hung the countdown clock for Gay Pride Day. The mayor's office had consented and plans were under way for the Gay

Channel to take over Times Square for a citywide LGBT celebration.

"Eighty-six more days. I can't believe it. The channel has been on the air for almost a year, too." Dee Dee shook her head in disbelief. "It's a miracle."

"I know. And everybody talks about the channel all the time. It's always in the news. We had no idea how it was going to be received," I said.

"I know. Remember Roger and Sharon blowing Malcolm's horn and freaking everybody out? Saying the Christian Right was going to protest in front of the building?"

"I know. And who was there the day of launch?"

"Nobody," Dee Dee cracked up. "Just those two fretting and freaking."

"Say no more."

Dee Dee was quiet for a minute, deep in thought. A light breeze circulated through Times Square. Tourists lined up for discounted Broadway show tickets at the TXTS booth. Lunchtime traffic was noisy, and the air was thick with exhaust fumes. My thoughts returned to Clayton and the anticipation of his touch. I couldn't wait for that man to turn me out that night.

"I have a mommy question," Dee Dee said, searching the ground. "I'm a little confused, and because you're the only mother I know at the office I thought I'd ask you."

"Go on, girl. I'm sure whatever's on your mind is something all mothers have come across at one time or another."

"How do you do it? How do you leave the kids at home or in the care of strangers like at a daycare facility? Eventually, Sandy will have to go back to work. I took maternity leave and now she's on maternity leave but after that we'll have to put our little boy in a daycare. I miss Jethro. I can't imagine him holed up with a bunch of kids somewhere strange. Charlene, I've been here for one morning, and I've already called home four times."

"I understand, girl, I do. But you'll get used to it. The feeling of being away from them doesn't leave you, ever. We do what we have to do. At least Sandy is at home with him now."

Dee Dee continued to search the ground. This wasn't the answer she had hoped for. I think she wanted me to give her permission to go home right at that moment.

"I'm thinking of giving notice," she said.

"Girl, don't do that. Think it through. Staying home all day with newborn babies is one thing. Staying home all day with toddlers is another. You'll get into a rhythm. You'll see."

"I sure hope so," she said. Her expression was pained. "I miss him."

"You'll be alright," I said, putting an arm around her shoulders. "You're going through what every working mother goes through. We can lean on each other, okay?"

She nodded, and then had a little cry on my shoulder. Wiping her nose, she sat up, sniffling once. "I guess so." Dee Dee thought for a second. "Maybe one day you'll come over and meet him. He's so adorable." A fresh pool of tears welled up.

"Girl, I'm telling you, it's not the end of the world. Everything will work out okay."

"I hope so."

We were quiet for a moment. The swirl of Times Square orbited around our resting spot. Dee Dee peered up at me, her face a hopeful mishmash of blotchy skin, red runny nose, and expectant blue eyes. She was as plain as day, but her aggressive nature gave Dee Dee animated features. The child had spunk for ages.

"I heard you're going out with that security guard," she said conspiratorially.

I sighed. "He's the head of security, and he supervises a team of twenty."

"You like him?"

"Yes, I do. He's a good man."

"Just now I'm thinking this," Dee Dee said, her face bright with possibility. "You, him, and your kids should come over and visit me, Sandy, and Jethro. The kids must like babies. Everyone likes babies!"

I put an arm around her shoulders. "Dee Dee, you have the most creative ideas."

"I'm serious," she said, loud enough for a couple of tourists to turn their heads.

"I know you are. I'll think about it. The kids haven't met Clayton yet."

"Geez, really? Haven't you been seeing him for like eight months?"

"Yes."

"And he hasn't met the *kids* yet?"

I felt a ping of shame but then regained my senses. "It's not something I want to get into. I'm just being cautious."

"You think?" she laughed. "Very!"

"Are you done?" I said, standing up, holding out my hand.

Dee Dee couldn't stop chuckling about my molasses nature. She took my hand, stood up, and embraced me.

"Well, when you get around to it. Bring everyone over— we'd be glad to have you."

I had a little laugh myself. If it'd been eight months of dating and the man I'd been sleeping with hadn't met the kids, I couldn't imagine how long it'd take me to bring them over to Dee Dee and Sandy's apartment. But I appreciated Dee Dee's openness. Regardless of hard lines drawn in the sand, we were mothers, and that was a reality that we shared.

19

Lovers Unite

THINK WE NEED TO GET one thing straight before we go inside," I said to Clayton as we stood in front of my apartment building. "My kids mean the world to me, and I don't want to disrupt their world any more than it has been in the last year and a half. So I want to be really sure you're in this for real. Know what I mean?"

"You cast those worries right out of your pretty little head, okay? I'm yours, baby, if that's what you want to hear."

Clayton held me by the shoulders. His sincerity calmed me. I blushed. It was what I wanted to hear, but I hadn't thought he'd say it out loud to me without a little more prompting. The thing about Clayton was, his actions and his words had the same meaning, and it was a priceless quality that always surprised me. There were no games with him. He was almost too good to be true, like a fantasy hero saving the life of a battered wife on the Lifetime Channel. Compared to Warren, who had one scheme after the next, Clayton appeared saint-like.

"You can believe in me, Charlene. I can see those doubts

bumping around in your head like a pinball machine. You don't have to worry about me. I'm serious. I want you to relax."

"I'm trying. I really am. I just don't take it lightly when it comes to Martel and Tinecia."

"Let me help you." He kissed me gently and then really pulled me in for a passionate and loving kiss right there on the street for all of Prospect Place to see. We were acting like teenagers in love. I was in love. I was afraid to admit it to him, but I was.

"I want you to know I feel like the luckiest man alive."

"Clayton, please be true. I can't take another heartbreak. The divorce from Warren tripped me up so bad, even though the marriage had died years before. When you get married, you still want to believe it'll work out no matter how far down the tubes a life together has tumbled."

"You know that's the first time you've said his name to me. I'm going to take that as a baby step in the right direction. Time to let that brother go. Warren may have been the right man when you were a younger woman, but I'm the right man for you right now."

I held him tightly. "I'm starting to believe you."

"Then do that. Give me the support to do that."

"Come inside? The kids won't be home for about an hour. I had my neighbor Leticia take them to the park."

"What sounds real nice? We should go meet them," he said, looking up the street.

"Serious?" I hesitated. "I thought we could, you know what I'm trying to say, baby, before everyone gets back." I had finally purchased new sheets: a fresh start with a new lover.

"Oh, baby, I know what you're saying, really I do, and I want to too, but what's more important and what's more everlasting? A little booty, or my meeting Tinecia and Martel?"

I liked the way he said their names, it warmed my insides and made me feel more peaceful than I had in a long time. He gazed into my eyes as if he was searching my soul.

It was at that moment that our relationship turned from sexual to emotional, a very hard place because I hadn't let myself believe in a man in a long time. In a couple of weeks I was going to turn thirty years old, and for a split second I let myself believe Clayton was my dream gift. I was bursting with excitement. I thought of every strong woman in my family—what would they have done at this moment? Be scared and run? Or jump into the abyss and trust God?

"Let's go find the children," I said. "You're absolutely right."

We entered the park at twilight. There were a lot of people there—joggers, dog walkers, police on horseback, guys hanging around on park benches, and Leticia on the other side of a small playing field throwing a ball to Martel while Tinecia jumped squares in a game of hopscotch with Tonya. I was anxious. Every nerve was lit up like a firecracker. Clayton held my hand tightly as if letting me walk freely was dangerous, as if I would roam away. He was right, because my resolve kept switching from how this was a good idea to how it was a bad one with every step I took closer to Leticia and the kids.

Martel saw me first. He tore across the field yelling, "Mommy, Mommy!" He collided into my legs and buried his face in my sweater. "Hi, Mommy!"

"Hi, baby. How you doing? School was okay?"

"Yes, Mommy. It was good. I drew on the chalkboard!" He noticed Clayton and stepped back from us. "Hello," he said tentatively.

"Hello, young man. My name is Clayton Hicks."

"Hello, Mr. Hicks."

"This is my new friend," I said steadily. "Do you mind if he visits with us today? Maybe stay for some dinner?"

"Are we having spaghetti and meatballs?" Martel asked with an explosion of energy. He clopped away like a toy soldier, circled round, and then came back over to us. "Okay, I guess so."

"You guess what?" I said.

"Mr. Hicks, are you hungry?" Martel asked.

"Yes, young man, I am. Mind if I join y'all?"

"I guess not." Martel ran away. "I guess not!" he yelled playfully.

I let out a long sigh. "I'm so nervous."

Martel's yelling snapped Tinecia to attention. She stopped hopping and watched carefully as we came toward her along the pathway. She made no move to greet me; instead she dropped a rock on a square and finished up her turn. Tonya—dear child—waved. She was sitting crossed-legged on the grass, obviously being beaten at the game by Tinecia but patiently waiting her turn. Leticia scooped up a giggling Martel and approached us while she balanced him on her hip.

"Come over here and meet your momma's friend," Leticia said to Tinecia.

My little girl set a polite expression on her face. She came over calmly and shook Clayton's hand.

"Hello. My name is Tinecia Thomas."

"I'm Clayton Hicks."

"Do you play?" She took his hand and led him over to the hopscotch game. Martel wiggled free from Leticia's embrace and ran circles around the sedentary Tonya, who cupped her chin in anticipation. Leticia obviously approved,

I could tell, from the way she followed Clayton's stride over to the hopscotch game.

"Honey child," she said, making smacking sounds with her lips, "you sure his brother wouldn't want to swim in my pond?"

I rolled my laughing eyes at the darkening sky. "Believe me, I'm sure."

"Sure about what, Mommy?" Martel asked out of nowhere, hanging on my hip.

"Never mind, Martel. Go play with your sister and Tonya."

Clayton tossed a rock and jumped on one foot. He was a giant compared to the kids. Tinecia directed him to pick up the rock and be careful with his balance. Tonya clapped her hands when Clayton succeeded in finishing his turn. Martel threw his ball up into the trees, ignoring the girls.

"What're you thinking?" Leticia said.

"I have no idea. My mind is blasted free of thought right now. I feel like I've been knocked out and I'm waking up out of some kind of dream, wondering what happened."

"So this is serious?"

"Very."

"Girl, that's fabulous. Embrace it, okay? And while you're at it, don't forget your single friends. You hear me? We could all use a man—" she paused dramatically— "who likes women."

"I'll keep an eye out for you. I promise, girl. As soon as I figure out what's going on here with him."

"He's fine as shit. Thick legs. Nice."

"Played football in high school."

"Well, you had better keep an eye on him, because these sisters around here will snatch him up in two seconds flat. Or in my case, down-low men."

"You'll find someone, Leticia. Clayton just dropped out of the sky, and in the most unlikely place."

"The Gay Channel. Who'd have guessed that? A straight, fine brother."

"God moves in a mysterious way His wonders to perform. Everyone deserves love and a second chance. Open your heart. You'll find someone, and he'll love you back. God does not play, girl, okay? You've got to believe. You just have to put yourself out there. Be available for loving, if you know what I mean." I winked.

"Ain't that the truth! Preach, sister woman," Leticia said. "Girl, I've gotta go get ready for work."

"Are you okay with Tonya having dinner with Clayton and the kids?"

"From what you said, he's a very positive influence. It'll be good for her to see that."

"Martel. Tinecia. Come on now, let's go," I said.

"Ah, Mom," Tinecia said, clearly enjoying Clayton's oversized self hopping up and down the chalk grid. "We're almost done. Can't we stay a few minutes more?"

"Next time. Leticia's gotta go to work. So let's go, okay? Time for dinner."

Tinecia stomped in protest, but Clayton leaned down and said something funny to her. She laughed and skipped ahead. Clayton scooped up Martel and traveled the boy's small body across his wide shoulders and back to the ground. Tonya brought up the rear. As Martel ran to catch up with me, Tonya took Clayton's hand.

"I think everyone is accounted for," Clayton said, a little out of breath from jumping around. The girls bounced up and down all around him.

As we left the park, two white men holding hands passed us on the sidewalk. They were engrossed in conversation, their obvious closeness uninterrupted by our makeshift family group. Tinecia stopped in her tracks.

"Mommy, look," Tinecia said, baffled. "Why are they holding hands?"

"They're in love," I said. "That's all. It's just love."

"But they're *boys!* They aren't supposed to be doing that!"

"Yes, you're right, they're boys. Some people would say that boys aren't supposed to be holding hands. That's very true. But those boys are special friends, and some things can't be explained. You'll understand better when you get older. And you can make up your own mind then."

Tinecia frowned. She stared after the gay couple, unsure of what was going on. Leticia pulled Tonya into her, so the child couldn't see the two men. Martel was oblivious as usual, humming a little tune and playing with the crosswalk signal button. I got down on one knee, so I could be face-to-face with my little girl.

"You know what?" I caressed her small hands. "Until we know a person's story, we try not to judge. We don't know their story, those two people, so we don't judge. Judge not, my darling, because you wouldn't want someone to judge you. Understand?"

"I think so. Still, I think it's wrong," she said, trying to make sense of it all.

"That's okay. Can I ask you a question? Do you know their names? Where they live? Where they come from? Anything?"

"No."

"Then you don't have all the facts yet. Just try to dig a little deeper before you form an opinion. It's real grown-up stuff. We'll keep talking about it. Sound fair?"

"I guess so," she said, perplexed but wanting to seem

mature. "I'll try."

"Good girl," I said as the light turned green, and we crossed the street.

Clayton held Tinecia's right hand, and I held the left. I could tell he was thinking about Steven and William. He wanted to understand, too, but Steven was his brother and that suppressed all other so-called facts. Leticia had picked up Tonya and was walking ahead, having her own private conversation, about what I did not know.

I had nothing to lose with Clayton. He was solid. Honest. Gracious. And hot as hell, despite the premature ejaculations. Every time we had sex, it happened within minutes of entering me, as he had the first time. We tended to laugh about it now, and I took it as a compliment I had that effect on him. The man just couldn't keep his passion in check! But like clockwork, it would take a few minutes for him to resume lovemaking all night long. And this man sure did know how to handle this woman.

Gaining the relationship another notch was how he acted with the children that night. I was beginning to chill until I saw Warren just ahead. "Daddy! Hi, Daddy! Hi! Hi! Hi!"

"How's my main man?" Warren said, holding his palm open for a slap-five from his son. "Hey, girl."

Tinecia didn't let go of Clayton's hand.

"Visitation is tomorrow afternoon, Warren. What are you doing here?"

"Hey, Charlene. You're looking mighty fine on this spring evening. I ain't doing nothing. Just taking a shortcut from Flatbush over to Grand Army Plaza. Don't get yourself worked up about nothing."

"Leticia, do you mind taking the kids inside?"

"Warren," Leticia said as she led Tinecia, Tonya, and

Martel away.

"Bye, Daddy," Martel said. "See you soon!"

Tinecia remained quiet. She hadn't spoken to her father since the child-custody court appearance. The moment was beyond awkward. Clayton hung back in a loose neutral state—he thrust both hands in his pants pockets and waited to see where this was going.

"You don't need no protection against me, Charlene," Warren said, palming his heart. "We should forget about that mess a few months ago. For the children's sake."

"Seriously? You mean to tell me that you want to forget how you were manipulated by Pam to upset the children and me? You ain't got no sense, Warren."

"I want to make it up. I do, really," he said.

"How about starting with paying off the attorney fees? That would help." Of course he balked by stammering and clearing his throat. "Just like I thought. I heard about Pam, you know."

"What'd you hear? You ain't heard nothing." Warren noticed Clayton shifting his weight from foot to foot. "How you doing, man? You with her?" He had the balls to shake his head disapprovingly, trying to connect to Clayton man to man.

"Man, don't do that," Clayton said.

"I heard she left you for the superintendent of the building you live in," I went on, "so she could reside rent free. That's what I heard."

"Oh, that ain't important. Obviously, she wasn't good for me because she had me involved in legal things I ain't had no business being involved in. I told Martel and Tinecia I was sorry. Pam was no good. I'm sorry to you, too."

"But she was good enough for a custody petition?" I said, not accepting his lame apology.

"I didn't mean to keep going with it. I only wanted to make sure the children weren't being exposed to any, what do they call it? Alternate lifestyles."

Clayton firmly took hold of my arm. We walked past Warren, who rustled in his tracksuit.

"Bye, Warren," I said, my back to him now.

"Woman, you're lucky you got company, because. . ." He fell silent.

"More empty promises," I mumbled. Clayton and I reached my apartment building. The anger I had shown on the street turned into embarrassment. Clayton lifted my chin and kissed my lips.

"I'm sorry you had to see that," I said, not able to look him in the eye.

"It's just the end of something that didn't work out. Happens all the time. Everybody comes with a little baggage."

"You didn't think I was some crazy banshee?"

"No, just mad at an old situation. I meant what I said earlier. I know I'm with a woman who has had a lot going on in the last couple of years. I'm not baggage free, either."

"You seem like you are."

"I'm not."

"Tell me something about yourself I don't know," I said, desperate to even the score.

He tilted his head at the ground and had a faraway look in his eye as he searched his thoughts for what to expose to me. I needed him to be vulnerable because I felt like my life was an open book. But I didn't believe he had anything as messy as being a divorced woman with two kids to feed, yelling at her ex-husband on public sidewalks.

"Mostly regrets. My friend Tommy Ross and me burned down an abandoned building that was full of crack addicts.

No one was hurt, and I wasn't ever found out, but Tommy was. He was sent to juvenile hall and never came back. I never saw him again, and I never found out what happened."

"Did you ever try?"

"Yes, but the records are sealed. Stuff like that from my past, from my youth."

I put my arm through his as we went up the stairs to my place. A car whooshed by and a siren wailed in the distance. The children laughed inside.

20

This Land Is Your Land

MIMI ESCORTED LILY AND ME into Malcolm's office. Girl was on it today. She had to have met a new man, because she was wearing about five thousand dollars' worth of clothing on her back: suede Gucci thigh-high boots, midnight black mini-skirt suit, and an eye-popping yellow diamond ring. As she departed, I saw that the crown of her head had sprouted a few new horsetails of implanted hair. The weave cascaded to the deep curve of her back and lightly brushed the crest of her high rear end. I appreciated her hustle, very different from mine, but Mimi did work it for points. My future and my assets were what? I had a stable home, healthy happy kids, and a modest but safe life in Brooklyn. Love on a budget. Mimi's future? Cat-walking the streets of Manhattan, cutting a grove in a Monaco nightclub, and flying naked in a private jet with a rap superstar. Smoke and mirrors? I had no idea. I was fine with the differences. I knew what I looked like—wide backside, thick arms and legs, full lips, dark brown eyes, and short, coarse hair. I had little time to "work it," because I was "working." She wasn't much more for this place, if she could pull off this latest romantic investment.

"Thanks for coming on short notice," Malcolm said, making notes at his desk. "Sit down. I'll be right there."

There was new artwork on the wall, a huge portrait of a gorgeous black man. Malcolm had commissioned a photograph of Djimon Hounsou with an octopus on his head to be reproduced as a painting. The piece was magnificent, because the profile of the West African actor drew a viewer right into the middle of it. I couldn't stop looking at how amazing it was. Must be a Herb Ritts image, it had to be, because Ritts had directed Djimon in Janet Jackson's video "Love Will Never Do Without You." It had been my wedding song, and the black-and-white image reminded me of it.

Malcolm sat underneath the painting like milord. Of course, I thought of Jerome toe-fucking the president of the company at that same desk last fall. My gaze went from Malcolm to the painting and back. The painting seemed to want to testify: Here was the kind of man Malcolm could snag with his millions (but if landing a handsome black man was based solely on his weird, washed-out looks, it would never happen). Every time I was invited into this office, Malcolm was less and less attractive, regardless of his expensive Italian suits and handmade shoes. His corporate ambitions and successes had long ago diminished whatever quality made a person authentic. Mimi caught me staring at the stark contrast between desiccated Malcolm and the painting of captured youth that hung over his desk.

"You might want to stop that," she said under her breath as she passed with bottles of water and fresh cut lemons. "Your expression is quite telling, Ms. Thomas."

Malcolm finished what he was doing and joined us on the couch. Mimi left the office, leaving the door slightly ajar.

I was glad we didn't have to sit in front of the desk. The memory of Malcolm giving Jerome head was still too vivid in my mind. I blocked it out by squeezing a lemon wedge and taking a long drink of water. Lily was already into the presentation for the June 26 Gay Pride Celebration by the time I put my glass down.

"Who will manage it?" Malcolm said. He was impatiently flipping through the PowerPoint slides.

"Charlene will," Lily said, pushing back a handful of light brown hair.

"Good. Everyone trusts you," he said to me, drilling those reptile eyes into mine. I smiled back. I liked being entrusted to handle big projects for the channel. My goal was to find Lily another assistant so I could become a project manager full time. For now, I would play along.

"The only problem I have are the drag queens," Malcolm said to the room in general, jabbing a finger at a slide in front of him. The pictures were of two female impersonators: Carmen Miranda and Wonder Woman. "I just don't want the celebration to become a freak show. The channel will be out there for the world to see on the largest scale yet, and Corporate and I feel there needs to be a balance between out and outrageous."

"I agree," Lily said readily. Who knows if my boss really agreed or not? Whatever the corporate juice, Lily sipped it without hesitation. She was going to take the corporate line every time. I kind of found it hypocritical that drag queens would be segregated within the LGBT community. This was another lesson in gay subculture etiquette.

"What do you think, Charlene?" Malcolm asked me. "You look like you have an opinion."

"Who, me? Oh. I don't know. I think drag queens certainly light up the office when they're around."

Lily nodded but never looked away from Malcolm. "That's true." Her demeanor was as neutral as Switzerland. "But whatever you think the direction should be is how we'll go with it."

"A few drag queens, but not a whole parade of them," Malcolm said, slightly disgusted. "I think that's a fair compromise." He leaned back expansively although he was a petite man. "I'm seeing the mayor tonight. He's invited media executives to a dinner at the Waldorf. I know we've already obtained approval to cordon off Times Square, but I think it'd be a coup if he came and spoke on our behalf. Don't you?"

"Yes, I do. Maybe Kathleen Pendle can help?" Lily offered.

Malcolm pursed his lips and hardened. Oh, the tide had changed. It was easy to guess he didn't want Kathleen involved in his idea. To the public, Kathleen Pendle was the face of the channel, and I had the feeling the original ad campaign would soon be coming to an end, gauging by Malcolm's reaction. Lily caught the change in vibe, too. She waited respectfully for Malcolm to think things over, as if she were a waitress taking a lunch order.

"I think we can handle it from my office," he said politely. A little too politely. The response had the swift bite of a cobra.

But cool-as-a-cucumber Lily hadn't gotten to where she was by fighting battles face to face. She uncrossed her legs and leaned forward. "Yes, of course, that would be the best way to do it. Let me know if my office can be of any assistance."

"Charlene, you'll have everything sewn up by the end of the day?" Malcolm asked, moving on.

"Yes. I'll coordinate with Mimi." I picked up the presentation. He had made a few indecipherable chicken scratches on several pages.

"Perfect," Malcolm said, leaving the couch. He peered out the window down into the heart of Times Square. The channel's countdown clock could barely be seen from that height. "Only forty-five days left."

We shuffled toward the door.

"Oh," Malcolm said, causing us to turn around. "Happy Birthday, Charlene. Thirty is the new twenty, so you don't have anything to worry about."

"Thank you, Malcolm," I said. What an odd thing to say, I thought.

Lily and I rode the elevator in silence to our floor. She was pissed, but it was a low simmer compared to the heat of other explosive types at the channel. Lily told me to hold all calls, including any from Malcolm Drake. She went into her office and shut the door. It was battle of the sexes, *gay and lesbian á la mode.*

BARRY HAD SWITCHED HIS STYLE because he wasn't going to be outdone by Nigel, who had stolen the bodysuit look. The previous winter, Barry had retired his spandex one-pieces and, over the spring, adopted the wardrobe of a circus barker. I followed him down the aisle of the auditorium as he marched to his own tune, holding my hand, occasionally flirting with me over his shoulder. He pumped his walking stick and bowed deeply when we reached the correct row. Anyone's first impression would have been of a nut-bag, a loud and crazy hag in a top hat, vest, bowtie, and tuxedo jacket with tails. He pointed to my seat with the tip of his walking stick and kissed me on each cheek before palming my ass. Nigel was in the seat next to mine. He snickered and meanly cut his eyes at Barry, who sneered and bared his teeth before parading back up the aisle to show employees to their assigned seats.

Corporate had arranged the internal event. Each channel was to present its programming lineup and ratings to the whole company. It was a veiled way of forcing channels to defend their corporate budgets. Whichever channel rated highest and had strong word-of-mouth usually received more money and support from the board of directors. As soon as a channel failed to meet its numbers, Corporate tended to yank money and support. Luckily the Gay Channel was first up. Our launch had been the most successful in cable history, and it was #1 in ratings and word-of-mouth. We had little to worry about, being the clear winners. Malcolm operated to our advantage in this company arena. His competitiveness aimed to cut anyone down at the knees trying to second-best him. I certainly wouldn't have expected anything else.

Behind me I heard Jerome coming down the aisle, bitching and moaning to a mute Troy. Jerome had been complaining for weeks about Malcolm's intention to introduce *Sex and the Pretty Black Boys* without inviting him, the creator and director, up on stage to say a few words. This was just another obvious shift in the wind of changing tides at the channel. Gone were the days of a Kumbaya LGBT vibe within the office. Executive politics, land grabbing, promotions, salary increases, and gay men versus lesbians had begun boiling over and tipping people into paranoia and closed-door plots. Everyone had a label or an agenda: can't-be-trusted, kiss-ass, out-for-himself, not-qualified-for-that-position, over-her-head, exploits-favoritism, has-Malcolm's-ear-but-doesn't-know-what's up, etc. It wasn't all poison; it just wasn't the communal feeling we had experienced the previous year. Some of us missed the old days; some, like

me, had adapted. I was a survivor with a keen eye on opportunities. I had enough sense to dig in my heels for the
long haul. I thanked God on my knees and noted the gifts
the job at the Gay Channel had bestowed upon me: a big
bonus the past year, paid-off debts, a nice man, and happy
children. I wasn't about to jack up my life over pissing
matches in the office.

"That jerk-off," Jerome said, stretching his long legs
into the aisle. "This is the kind of shit I hate about white
people—always taking credit, always taking our stuff and
making it their own. As if he could create the kind of show
that I do." He crossed his arms over his chest and scowled
at Troy, who had tuned out his husband days before. "I
want to talk about my show, my baby. I don't want him up
there representing. He obviously wasn't the motherfucker
who wrote the show. Men like him don't know nothing
about our world—the black gay man. It's different, you
know? Why doesn't he see my point, Troy? I mean, it ain't
hard to guess that I'd want to stand up in front of the company, in front of my peers, and be seen."

Troy took a deep breath and kept his mouth shut. I felt
sorry for him. Must be hard to be the doormat for a diva
and at the same time want to keep your job safe and secured.
Jerome towered in the second row, and his voice carried far
enough for all of us to hear him rant. If it had been my
show, I'd have felt the same, but the trick was to get renewed
for another season and not get canceled. Complaining about
the guy who would make that decision probably wasn't a
good idea, but every man and woman for themselves in this
situation. That's why I kept my eye on the prize: a prof-
itable future.

"He's so stupid," Nigel said under his breath, sinking
down and propping his knees against the seat in front.

"Might as well give Jerome a shovel so he can dig his own grave. I can't believe he has the nerve to be so loud in front of the whole company."

I wasn't about to engage in gossip with Nigel. He was at the top of the heap of those who couldn't be trusted. He had finally stopped flirting with me after I slapped him silly in the elevator, but I wouldn't put it past Nigel to whisper in enough ears to get Jerome's show snatched off the air. He was a sneaky person and loved instigating chaos. As long as he had ceased messing with me, I felt it wasn't any of my business, but I kept tabs on him just in case.

Barry appeared at the end of the aisle and presented Derrick as if introducing a judge at a beauty pageant. I felt as if I hadn't seen the head of publicity in weeks. Derrick made his way to the empty seat next to me; the closer his good looks came, the more I felt blessed to be in that row. He bestowed that charming smile at me. Derrick had inarguable star power, and I loved it. Work had been slammed, so most people had retreated into their offices or traveled a lot. Derrick had stopped playing music after Jesse was fired. But he wasn't the only one. Lily's attitude had downshifted into a dark place after Malcolm's reaction to Kathleen Pendle. What a difference a year made.

"What's up?" Derrick said, pecking me on the forehead like a father kissing his daughter. "I've missed you, darling Charlene. Pretty soon we'll have to schedule lunch to stay in touch. Actually we do have to meet soon. I heard through the grapevine you're heading up the Times Square thing."

"Hah!" Nigel said, unable to contain his jealousy. "This fucking channel is so backwards. A straight woman organizing Gay Pride, that's ridiculous."

"You better take your own advice about Jerome and

shut up, Nigel," I said.

"Maybe if you didn't look like Olivia Newton John in that stupid spandex suit, you'd be taken more seriously." Derrick reached over and slapped Nigel's knees down.

Nigel straightened up, grumbled attitude, and turned his back to us. Two rows ahead, Roger had witnessed Derrick slapping Nigel's knees. He said something to Sharon, who whipped around as if checking out a skidding car to see if it would slam into the rails. Both execs kept an eye on us for a few long moments just in case something else happened that could help build a future case.

"I look hot," Nigel said. "At least I go to the gym. Look at you. Nice belly."

Derrick paid him no mind. "Just a few more weeks until we blow this town to pieces." He adjusted his tie and crossed his legs. Cary Grant had nothing on that man.

"We've come a long way, haven't we, baby?" I said.

Derrick faked-smoked a cigarette. "You got that right, sweet pea."

The house lights blinked on and off. People lingering in the aisles and talking to each other near the stage returned to their seats. The company auditorium was packed. Dee Dee had been working for weeks assembling snippets of programming and organizing footage to present. The reel would be shown in a few minutes. She was somewhere backstage, no doubt bossing everyone around. Motherhood had done nothing to tone down her barks. I loved her for it, though. Working mother. Working girl.

In the first row, the CEO of the company (and Malcolm's boss), an ancient man with thin white hair, sat like an erect statue in a town square. His sagging face seemed permanently set in stone. His mouth, void of lips, appeared to have been sucked in from his insides. Men cut from the same cloth, and who looked exactly like the CEO, flanked him. The only difference between the owner and his cronies was they gleamed with hero worship and he didn't. How do people make it to that level? No doubt there were a few bodies flung in back alleys and across dirt roads. Malcolm had that quality. Mimi did too, and Lily, on alternating days, possessed a sharklike quality not to be messed with.

I shut off my mind as the lights went down. Relaxing into my seat, I watched as the company logo, our mothership, flashed on a giant screen, and I felt as if I were part of something big. The image dimmed as graphics for over a hundred channels materialized over the company's logo. Different sections of the audience cheered when their channel's logo faded in. Last but not least was the Gay Channel. We jumped out of our seats and screamed like lunatics until Malcolm appeared stage right at the podium, clasping his hands over his head like a champion, and slightly bowing in our direction. The screen went black.

In the darkness, strobe lights flashed throughout the audience as house music thumped from speakers in the theater. As the house lights came back up, Barry marched out from stage left, leading a brass band of scantily clad, buffed gay men adorned with large red dots on their cheeks and Clara Bow-painted lips. They circled around the stage, stomping in black cowboy boots, before coming to a stop in geometric formation. Behind them on a giant screen, Dee Dee's reel began. The footage of a young white woman with cropped black hair and black-rimmed Poindexter glasses was intercut within digital images from our hit shows. It was the first public viewing of a re-branded Gay Channel as Malcolm assumed all credit for our successes. In the blink of an eye, he had pulled every billboard, commercial, and print ad with Kathleen Pendle's face on it, and, to completely banish her image, he had appeared on all the morning shows. Rumor had it that Jay Leno would book him if Letterman didn't do it first.

"Welcome to the Gay Channel," Malcolm began, speaking authoritatively into the mike. Lily was nowhere in sight. "I'm lucky to be a part of such an amazing lineup of programming. We have broken the mold!"

From the mezzanine, several water balloons hit the stage. The disruption didn't throw Malcolm off. He continued on as if the puddles of water weren't ten feet from the podium. The CEO stood up from first row center, shielded his old eyes, and gazed up at the balcony. Off to the side, I saw Clayton radio his guys to check out what was going on. A few black-suited security guards fanned out into the aisles.

"Payback is a mean bitch," Jerome clucked.

There were popping sounds, like firecrackers or gunfire, coming from the back of the auditorium. The CEO ducked as the whole audience looked over their shoulders in unison to see what was going on. The house lights went up full power, and the images for the Gay Channel were turned off. Jerome started to laugh hysterically. Nigel stood on his chair and covered his mouth, feigning shock.

"Oh, my God," he said.

People rushed into the aisle. I saw Jem leading a handful of drag queens and gender-queers into the theater. They waved protest banners and blew whistles. *We Will Not Be Ignored* placards bobbed up and down on long wooden sticks. Drag queens in six-inch heels shot popguns and then reloaded by inserting the cork back into the nozzle. Roger jumped over several rows and ran toward his assistant.

"No!" he yelled at the top of his lungs. Having Jem ruin the channel's presentation wasn't going to win Roger any popularity awards. He was going to have to fight real hard not to be blamed for what was happening. But Jem had a strategy up his/her/its/their/both/neutral's sleeve. Seeing Roger barreling up the aisle, Jem readied for the attack by crouching. The head of programming flew over Jem's hunched body, headlong into the audience.

"We will not be stopped," the protesters chanted. "Times Square now. Times Square now." They broke out into a rendition of "This Land is Your Land," replacing the lyrics with "This Channel is Our Channel."

I wondered who had blabbed about drag queens being kept under wraps at the Gay Pride celebration? I didn't have to look too far as I watched Nigel tiptoe out of the auditorium. But then I suspected Lily, too, as she was conspicuously missing from the day's events.

21

Countdown

I COULDN'T BELIEVE MY EYES. Far and wide, Times Square was a sea of people. Clayton's department had worked closely with the NYPD and traffic control on a plan to contain the area and control the crowds. He had done an excellent job. I loved that my man had our backs.

The Gay Channel had blown the lid off gay culture, and its devoted audience had shown up in droves to take over the most popular destination in the world. Seeing the spectrum of humanity hanging around the fifty-foot stage erected for the ceremony gave me a deep sense of pride—gay, black, and otherwise. This was a cultural and universal phenomenon, no matter what anybody had to say, and I was sure, as sure as sugar was sweet, there would be no turning back after this throwdown. My gay brothers and sisters were going to be heard, and they were never going to stop shouting out.

The weather couldn't have been more perfect, a kiss from Mother Nature. The sun suffused Times Square, and a light breeze cooled the canyons of midtown Manhattan. NYPD continued to steer the last of traffic away. Security details blocked off side streets. Rainbow-colored banners hung from office windows. Balloons and silver streamers had been suspended between street lamps. Our logo graced T-shirts, headbands, book-bags, and beach balls tossed high into the air. Dykes on bikes had parked their Harleys—a good two hundred of them—along Broadway, manning their motorcycles with motherly care. Militant black women straight out of the Civil Rights Movement mingled with lithe gay men speckled with glitter, shaking their teeny bubble butts in shiny boxers to Justin Timberlake's "Sexyback."

Derrick had his arm around my shoulders, moving to the beat, swishing his hips side to side. I was dancing, too. The sun inched higher in the sky and unleashed a surge of energy throughout the crowds and up onstage.

"Honey, you look fabulous today. I could eat you up!" he said to me. "I love the miniskirt, and you are giving the boys some cleavage today. I don't think you've given that much cleavage since I've known you. All I can say, Ms. Charlene, is hot, hot, hot. You are a morsel to be consumed by any straight man—if you can find one in this crowd!" Derrick cracked himself up.

"I don't think there's a straight man within a hundred miles of this gathering except security from the office."

I winked in Clayton's direction. He was stationed by the rear stairs that led into the V.I.P. section, where Malcolm was conducting press interviews in a roped-off area underneath the countdown clock. Two hours to go. What was happening behind the stage contrasted greatly with what was happening out in the streets. It was whites behind the stage (like wizards pulling levers), and a cross-section of humanity out in the streets, representing the common idea. The Gay Channel was the best job I'd ever had in my lifetime, but I wasn't delusional. The channel was a business,

and the people who made that business possible counted on
the masses to fuel the image of a cohesive LGBT community. The only executive in the press area was Malcolm
(being catered to by his elegant, top drawer, B.A.P. royalty,
Mimi Sable). No Lily. No Jerome. And definitely no Kathleen. Malcolm owned his moment. Picking up the pastel
blue in the channel's logo, he was wearing a robin's-egg-blue
linen suit. The summer color complemented his pale skin.
He actually seemed to have some blush in his cheeks that
day. I wasn't sure if it was a natural God-given blush or an
expensive powder purchased at Henri Bendel. Nonetheless,
he exuded power and success, and for followers the image
worked perfectly. Of course, he was smart not to have worn
a tie. Accurate and on point as a prima ballerina, Malcolm
knew this wasn't an occasion for corporate demonstrations.
After the fiasco at the company presentation, his life was
probably in danger of being stomped to death by drag
queens in high-heels if he came out clad in business attire.
Jem's little sideshow the other day had convinced Malcolm
to change his mind about controlling the number of drag
queens in the Gay Pride parade sponsored by our channel.
He/she/it/they/both/neutral had balls after all. Jem had
slipped the noose because he/she/it/they/both/neutral was
the only transgender at the channel, and the company didn't
want to be sued for discrimination. Roger, on the other
hand, had been demoted: a comeuppance for those of us
who hated his guts and had been a victim of his backstabbing manipulations.

"*Look* at this. Can you believe it?" Derrick asked.

We danced toward the edge of the stage.

"Child, this is the bomb," I said. "Look at all these people!"

The place was lit up like New Year's Eve. Neon signs

displayed a medley of our logo animating on and off like a spray of digital fireworks, intercut with segments from our best programming. We had taken over the area, a first for the city and a milestone for gays and lesbians everywhere. It was a long way from the Stonewall riots in Greenwich Village over thirty-five years before, the confrontation that kicked off gay rights in New York City. It was a milestone for me, too. Although Warren had outright challenged me in court, none of that had stopped me from spreading my wings and feeling the freedoms of success in money, love, family, and self-respect. I gazed out into the faces of people who had experienced or were experiencing acceptance from the city that loved them for exactly who they were. This was indeed a time to shine.

When the clock struck midday, I thought the roar was heard around the world. Huge speakers set up on each corner blasted Kool & the Gang's "Celebration." Singing voices nearly drowned out the song. I thought I would burst out crying, I couldn't believe the unity connecting us.

The mayor took the stage next to Malcolm. He grinned at the gathering and seemed genuinely pleased with the turnout.

"Today is the day we say goodbye to old ideas and old ways of judging people who are gay, lesbian, bisexual, and transgender residents of New York City. Our Gay Pride March was the first in the country and has been supporting gay rights since 1970. I'm truly amazed and awed by the numbers, the strength, the bravery, and the confidence of marchers who believed, and still believe, change is possible. Taking its battle cry from the Civil Rights Movement, the Gay Rights Movement organized at grass roots levels, inspiring cities across the nation to follow suit. I see a lot of couples here today. So I feel I have to say to you, I will fight and walk side by side with you to end discrimination against gay marriages! We will win this fight!" He pumped a fist.

The crowd crushed the stage in a flail of outstretched arms, yelling, and pumping fists. Grown men cried. Women hugged their partners. Young people danced and climbed up on each other's shoulders. People hung from poles and had overrun Father Duffy's bronze memorial. An outpouring of emotion besieged us on the stage. I was overwhelmed. Derrick and I clasped hands tightly.

"Let's get this party started!" the mayor said into the microphone.

From either side of the stage, flatbeds that were part of the platform disconnected and slowly inched away. Drag queens trussed up like Marilyn Monroe, Billie Holiday, Jean Harlow, and Dorothy Dandridge threw carnations and small fruit baskets into the audience. I had heard from Derrick earlier in the day that the CEO had come down on Malcolm like a ton of bricks about the downsizing of drag queens at the Gay Pride March. Revenue was revenue, and if a gay, a straight, or a drag queen had a dollar in his/her/its/both/ their/neutral's pocket, then the company wanted to extend a friendly hand to dig it out. Money was green no matter who was clutching the cash.

"Get the fruitcakes on board!" the CEO had advised Malcolm.

Two more parts of the stage broke away and bucked south on Seventh Avenue. I tossed candy, t-shirts, and DVDs into the crowd. We held hands, sang, and shook our moneymakers. Mimi crouched under the disc jockey's table in the middle of the platform. Her face had the look of someone locked inside a vault of stinky cheese. She squirmed from embarrassment in her yellow Nicole Miller sundress and Audrey Hepburn up-do. I wondered what her

rapper millionaire thought of her today. I had heard she
had pocketed nearly half a million dollars for getting pregnant again. I could see the little bump as she put on dark
sunglasses and covered her ears against the deafening thump
of music and happy squealing. I'm sure any day now she
was going to give notice and quit.

At Forty-second Street, the floats headed east toward
Fifth Avenue, the traditional route for the march. Crowds
twenty people deep stretched several avenues in opposite directions. The passion, the praise, and the cheers shocked us,
because the turnout was beyond our wildest dreams. I
thought the whole world must have driven, flown, or bicy-
cled across both rivers. I knew for sure there weren't that
many gays and lesbians living in New York City. I understood completely what African-Americans marchers had
done for my generation back in the sixties. I raised a fist of
solidarity, and hundreds of people returned the salute.

I wanted to float all the way down Fifth Avenue to the
gayborhood of Greenwich Village, but I had some unfin-
ished business back at the office. At Union Square, I took
the subway uptown. Coming out of the station, I saw that
city workers were already cleaning up the debris in Times
Square and traffic had been restored to normal. The countdown clock was in the throes of being dismounted, and neon
signs had resumed normal activity advertising Broadway
shows, perfumes, sodas, news crawls, and financial market
updates.

"Woo-hoo!" hollered Security manning the front lobby
as I slipped through the turnstiles toward the elevator bank.

"What's up, y'all," I called back, vibrating with the energy from the parade. I wanted to finish up and get back
down to the action. There was a party on Jane Street, and
a couple of clubs I wanted to hit with Barry and Derrick

before going home to Brooklyn, my children, and Clayton.

The hallways of the office were half-lit. Desks had been left in various states of work mode. The place was empty except for a murmur of conversation coming from Lily's office. Regardless of what was going on downtown, she was the reason I had come back up. If she hadn't hired me—a single mother with long gaps of unemployment on her résumé—I wouldn't be enjoying the emotional gratitude bubbling inside of me.

I lightly rapped on the door to let her know I was standing in the doorway. Lily was having an intense conversation with a black woman with severely pressed hair. The woman smiled knowingly at me. I had that familiar pang of wanting to declare my sexuality ("Hold up there! I'm a straight girl!"), but I knew from past experiences at the channel that things didn't always seem like they were.

"Charlene," Lily said, happy to see me. She sprang from the couch with an extended hand and led me over to sit down. The black woman was dressed as conservatively as Lily. I shook her hand. I noticed business contracts on the coffee table.

"Nice to meet you, Charlene. I'm Nina Hughes. Lily has told me about you and what a successful transition you've made from assistant to handling high-profile projects. Celebrities can be quite the handful."

"Thank you," I said, a bit confused as to what was happening. "I like being in charge and having responsibility."

Lily sipped water. "Thanks for agreeing to come here. I wasn't sure you got my e-mail with all the commotion that was going on outside. How was the parade down Fifth? I heard the noise and music from here! Sounded like a lot of fun. Was it?" she asked, steady as ever, as she made eye contact with me.

"Yes, the best event for the channel ever. Everyone was there," I said, meaning everyone but her. "The crowds were rowdier than any I've ever seen. If you can believe that," I added, folding my hands in my lap as I caught the vibe in the office. "Folks everywhere." Looking around, I saw several taped boxes and books stacked on the credenza and table near the window. Lily's computer had been dismantled. "Hey," I said as the realization of what was going on escaped my lips. "Are you leaving?"

"I am," Lily said without a trace of regret. "A new opportunity." Her steel resolve was as fortified as ever. She didn't flinch; not a muscle moved, nor an eye twitched. Even if I wanted to find out the reason(s) why she was leaving, there was never ever going to be a snowball's chance in hell that she'd tell me. "It's an offer I couldn't pass up." She paused and sized me up. "I want you to come along."

I nearly passed out. My heart hammered. But I had learned a thing or two from Lily about maintaining a straight face.

"I'll be heading up a new venture," Lily said.

"You'll be promoted with a lot more accountability," Nina Hughes added. "Also, you'll have a couple of people to manage. But from what Lily has told me, I think you'll fit in flawlessly."

Quickly now, I said to myself. Say the right thing. I nodded instead.

Ms. Hughes continued, "It's a women's channel, a start-up just like the Gay Channel. If you accept, you'll be working with Lily as head of multi-cultural integration. It's a marketing job, very international, but I think from what Lily says about your skills, you'll do fine."

Cotton balls stuffed my mouth. I couldn't find the words to say anything. I made myself think logically. What was the salary at the new job? Would it be more than what I was making now? Would I have my own office? Where was the office, in Times Square or another part of the city? If I said no, what about my job here if Lily left?

"What do you think, Charlene?" Lily asked, easily reading my thoughts but wanting to move on with negotiations.

"I'd like to get more details, of course, but it sounds like a great chance to move up. I just want to make sure the benefits I have here will be the same or better at the new job."

"You won't be sorry," Lily said. "This is an excellent chance. It's what I like so much about you—seeing the lighted path, and jumping in with two feet."

Nina Hughes said. "Welcome to the team."

"You'll have to pack up today, though, because the position starts in less than a week, and Malcolm won't want you here if you're coming with me."

"What happened?" I said, not able to help myself.

"Another door opened," Lily said before pausing for a second. "Don't be concerned about salary, you'll be compensated fairly. Your first project will be with Kathleen. She requested you personally."

"Oh," I said, flattered. "What's the project?"

Nina flipped through papers spread out on the coffee table. She pulled out several sheets with the heading: *Our Voices, Women's Rights at Home & Abroad.* "Ms. Pendle will host our first documentary."

My heart sank. I pictured Mimi hiding underneath the disc jockey table as the flatbed was besieged with gay people. Would that be me ducking behind a tent in the Congo while Kathleen attempted to get into the hearts and minds of suffering African women, urging them in that husky Broadway delivery to rise up against their oppressor? What

about Cambodians? South Americans? I surprised myself
and the two women in the room by seizing upon an idea so
crazy, it nearly slapped me down on the couch.

"What about me, instead?"

"As the spokesperson?" Lily said, catching on before
Nina did. "I don't know about that. No one knows who you
are, Charlene."

"That's the point," I said, gaining strength in my belief.
"Exactly why I should be the spokesperson. Not only will
I represent the women's channel, I'll be a blank canvas.
Kathleen comes with a lot attached to her image, don't you
think?"

"Yes, that's true," Nina agreed without hesitation,
jumping on board. "You might be onto something here."

"I feel I am," I said enthusiastically. "Think about it,
Lily, will you? I believe I can make a bigger impact."

"Where is this coming from, Charlene?" Lily said. I had
completely caught her off guard.

"I have no idea. But I know I can do this," I said.

Lily studied me. I remained as composed as ever. I had
no clue where the desire had come from, but I knew that following Kathleen around to third-world countries didn't sit
well with me. I had something to say, I realized. I had
something to say!

"We'll start at home," Lily said. "Harlem will be the
first stop. Then let's see from there, okay?"

I clenched my fists in triumph. "You won't be sorry,
Lily. Nina. Thank you."

My sisters, my sisters! I thought. You won't be sorry at
all. I was going to do this and never look back.

INSTEAD OF TAKING THE SUBWAY back downtown to party
with the Gay Channel peeps, I went home, because I

couldn't think of better people to celebrate my leg up in the world than with Tinecia and Martel. I inserted the key into the lock and, before I turned the handle, heard Martel's pitter-patter across the living room floor.

"Momma, we saw you on television!" he said.

"Girl, you looked wild up there dancing with that boy. He was all over you." Leticia was gathering up her belongings into a plastic bag.

"Ha! That's Derrick. He's crazy, but I love him."

"Ms. Charlene, since you're back, I'm going into work early and get some overtime. You don't mind, right?"

"Nah, go on. I'll take the kids out for ice cream." I hugged Leticia goodnight. "And tomorrow, when Warren is with the kids, I'm taking you out for a much-deserved dinner. I have news for you, but later, okay?"

"I'll be there," Leticia said. "Is that what your job is like, dancing in the streets on a sunny day?" she added as she opened the door to leave. "I am working at the wrong place, okay?" She blew a kiss at Tonya. "Bye, honey. Be a good girl."

"She's always good," I said, kissing Tonya's cheek as she played a noisy computer game at the kitchen table.

"Bye, Mommy," Tonya said.

Tinecia hadn't said hello. She was sitting on the couch, studying one of her picture books, one of the ones from when she was a baby. I knew she was still not satisfied with my explanation of gay men and women. She took after her daddy, if I ever had to confess the truth about her nature, but she was my baby, and I had to let her know that not everything in this world was going to go her way. I was so glad to be home and alone with the children, I thought that, after ice cream, I'd take everybody to the movies over on Atlantic Avenue. Tinecia sighed and snapped her book closed.

I sat next to her as she put the book on the side table.

"What's wrong, Tinecia?"

"Nothing," she said, crossing her arms. "I don't want ice cream."

"You don't have to have any if you don't want to. Nobody's forcing ice cream down your throat."

She sighed heavily through her nostrils. I had to keep it together, because the frown on her face was so cute I almost burst out laughing. She was trying to formulate what she wanted to say, so I waited.

"Were you embarrassed by Mommy?" I asked.

She didn't want to admit it. She clamped her jaw tighter. I massaged her shoulders and pulled her in for a long hug.

"Let me just tell you something, Tinecia, that you might not understand until you're older. What you saw on television today is part of the future, baby girl. It's an important part of our culture. I don't know, I probably don't have all the answers, but. . ."

She looked up at me. "What, Momma?" she asked in her little girl's voice.

"I do know one thing though."

"What?" she said.

"We have a future to live right now."

Acknowledgments

Baugh Family, Boo, Brett Vinovich, Brian Tolleson, Chris Wagley, Dan Shaner, Deborah Bart, Deborah Reichman, Eileen Cabiling, Ellen Markham, Elizabeth Trundle and Pete Stein, Janet King, Johnson Family, Jon Sechrist! Logo peeps 2004–2007—Monsieur Parmentier and Señor Parent, Lisa Cortes, Lori Johnson, Marianne Jean-Baptiste, Mr. Daniels, Nicholas Roman Lewis, Petina Cole, Rebel Steiner, Rochelle Joseph, Steven Corbin, *cheetahrama.com*, and the pumpkins.

About the Author

Darlyne Baugh's film and television credits include *In Dreams, All Over Me, Caught, Oz,* and *Showtime at the Apollo*. During her cable network years she worked at Nickelodeon, Fuse TV, and the LGBT channel, Logo. In her debut novel, *Black Girl @ the Gay Channel*, she has given up a little dirt but has saved most of it for her next project. She attended Emerson College back in the day. Currently she lives in New Jersey. Visit the author's website: *www.darlynebaugh.com*, or follow on Twitter @Johannesgirl.

Breinigsville, PA USA
30 March 2011
258762BV00003B/2/P